Treacherous Hack

A Mike Stoneman Thriller

Treacherous Hack

A Mike Stoneman Thriller

Kevin G. Chapman

Other novels and stories by Kevin G. Chapman

The Mike Stoneman Thriller Series

Righteous Assassin (Mike Stoneman #1)
Deadly Enterprise (Mike Stoneman #2)
Lethal Voyage (Mike Stoneman #3)
Fatal Infraction (Mike Stoneman #4)
Perilous Gambit (Mike Stoneman #5)
Double Takedown (Mike Stoneman #6)
Fool Me Twice (A Mike Stoneman Short Story)

Stand-alone Novels

The Other Murder
Dead Winner
A Legacy of One
Identity Crisis: A Rick LaBlonde Mystery

Short Stories & Novellas

The Car, the Dog & the Girl
Ghost Creek (a romantic mystery novella)

Visit me at www.KevinGChapman.com

Chapter 1
Pawn in Play

New York, New York

SUNDAY

L OU PALAZZO's HAND TREMBLED when he answered the phone in his Lower East Side electronics store and pawn shop. He leaned against the counter to steady himself. There was a time, not so long ago, when Lou's hands were rock steady. He silently cursed both the aging process and his current project, which was so important it made him nervous.

"Lou's," he snapped into his mobile. When he heard the voice on the other side, the nervous tremble returned. "Oh, hey, Cannon . . .Yeah, I'm still workin' on it . . .I dunno how long, but I'm close. It's a bitch of an encryption. It's taking some time . . .I'll probably have it by Tuesday. Maybe by tomorrow."

Lou rolled a kink out of his tired neck and gazed out the window at the falling snow. It was only mid-December, but already bitterly cold. The snow had started right after lunch and had cut the neighborhood foot traffic down to near zero.

That was bad for his business but good for giving him time to work on the dingus. From above the door frame, the sad brown eyes of Humphrey Bogart and the steely blues of Katharine Hepburn stared down at him from the deck of the *African Queen*. "We've been in tougher spots than this, Bogie," Lou mumbled.

Lou was a whiz at most computer hacks and could crack a password in a few minutes. He had developed the algorithm during his years as a foot soldier in the Gallata crime organization. He told new acquaintances the Gallatas were a bunch of guys whom he considered his friends, but whom the police considered criminals. Lloyd Cannon and Lou did time together in an upstate prison ten years earlier, after each of them had been nabbed while engaged in separate business dealings on behalf of the old man, Mickey "Slick Mick" Gallata. Neither of them squealed on their boss. They did their time and kept quiet, which was why they were both still alive. The Cannon, as he was known, returned to the family business, while Lou opened his shop and began squeaking out a living among the law-abiding and tax-paying citizens of New York. Mostly.

The Cannon's angry voice snapped Lou back into the present. "Yeah, I'm listening," Lou muttered. "You think I don't remember? . . .No, it's not necessary to come down here . . .Hey, you owe me some consideration. I done right by you more times than you can count . . .Yeah, I got it. I'll get you the unencrypted file by Tuesday or I'll pay back the five grand advance and we can forget about the rest of the hundred . . .Yeah, fuck-face, with interest."

Lou wasn't worried about Cannon. He knew there was somebody else with him, listening in on the conversation. Cannon needed to play the tough guy. It was all a show. He held the phone away from his ear while Cannon yelled some more about how Lou had promised that the hacked data file was a gold mine, when in fact he hadn't gotten past the encryption yet. He assumed it was a gold mine. Why else would the hackers have used such a bitch of an encryption?

When there was a pause in the diatribe, Lou shouted back, "You wanna let me get back to work, or are you gonna keep tellin' me shit I already know? . . .OK. Thanks for calling."

Lou slammed the phone down on his glass countertop, hoping the noise would annoy Cannon. He punched the red END button. He had not eaten lunch and needed a break. The AMC channel was running a Bogart marathon and he wanted to catch the end of *Casablanca* and the beginning of *The Maltese Falcon*. He lamented that Ryan had to go back to campus, but at least it allowed him to continue work on the dingus.

He regretted making the deal with The Cannon before he cracked the encryption on the data file. If it contained what Lou expected, it could be worth ten times more than the hundred-thousand-dollar finder's fee he had negotiated. Maybe a lot more. But he wanted a sure thing, just in case the file turned out to be garbage. He was sure The Cannon would carve him a new asshole if he couldn't get the damned thing open. He was less sure that The Cannon's boss would come through with the hundred grand if the file was unlocked, but still not worth a million.

In the old days, he would not have been worried. Slick Mick Gallata never welched on a deal. But since the old man's murder, the family's integrity had slipped. Slick Mick allowed Lou to retire, in appreciation for him doing his three quiet years in Sing Sing. But now, Mickey's son, Albert, was running the show, and "Fat Albert" didn't owe Lou any favors.

But the risk was worth it to Lou. The hundred grand would nearly pay for the rest of Ryan's tuition. His nephew was the only person in the world Lou cared about.

Two hours later, Lou turned off the work light behind his shop counter with a satisfied snap. The file was open, but his eyes were bleary from staring at code. There had been few customers, which gave him the time he needed. Tomorrow, he would start inspecting the contents and copying anything he could use to his own advantage.

Lou stared at his phone's screen. Cannon had sent a text message an hour earlier, asking if Lou was planning to be at his store all day. The question made sense only if Cannon planned to come by for an in-person visit. "I told him by tomorrow," Lou said while looking up at the *African Queen* poster and fingering the fuzzy rabbit's foot fob on his key chain. "You don't suppose my old friend would play me for a sap?"

He transferred the now unencrypted file to a thumb drive and walked down the narrow corridor in the back of the shop to his office. Once the precious data was safely stored in a secure location, he reformatted the thumb drive, then deleted the file on which he had been working all afternoon from his laptop. Then he purged the deleted file, using a data security program called "the muncher." It sliced the file into a million-piece jigsaw puzzle. Normally, he would back up an important file in multiple places, but he didn't trust Cannon – or Fat Albert – to pay up if they thought they could steal it. That was why he had devised the contingency plan. He needed a safety net for Ryan.

Lou consulted his watch, sighed, and pulled out his keys and phone. If The Cannon had not arrived yet, he could wait until Monday. The snow was still falling. He reached under the cash register, its brown paint peeling like a molting snake, and retrieved a blue goose-down parka. It was only a few steps to reach the door leading up to the building's residential floors, but the frosty wind outside warranted the extra time to bundle up. The way his miserly landlord kept the heat down during the day, he might need the coat even inside his second-floor apartment. Finally prepared for the elements, Lou shuffled toward the front door.

When he turned the hanging cardboard sign behind the beveled glass from OPEN to CLOSED, he spotted two tall men wearing dark pea coats approaching the shop's entrance. It was late in the day for unfamiliar customers, but he recalled Cannon's text message. Lou stepped back. He sloughed off his coat, tossed it on top of a display rack filled with used video games, and retreated behind the counter. He always kept the forty-inch-high barricade between himself and any strange faces.

A tinkling bell chimed when his two new patrons stepped through the door. A third man entered behind the pair. He was shorter than his companions. The buttons on his extra-large overcoat strained to contain his bulk. A roll of flesh around The Cannon's pale neck spilled over a dress shirt collar. A black wool hat covered his bald head. Lou could not read any expression on his old colleague's face, but he didn't have much time to look since the two tall Asian men held most of his attention. Neither man spoke. They stayed several feet back from the counter and fixed their unnerving blank stares on Lou.

"These guys don't look like your usual associates," Lou observed, looking at Cannon. He placed his left hand on the countertop while carefully reaching underneath with his right, feeling for the butt of a sawed-off shotgun mounted on plastic clips. He might not need it, but something about these two silent statues had the hair on the back of his neck standing on end.

"That's very observant, Lou," Cannon said. The man had put on fifty pounds since their prison days, but the voice still reminded Lou of Groucho Marx.

"What brings you and these two bridesmaids here, Lloyd?" Lou knew that The Cannon hated being called Lloyd, but couldn't help himself.

Cannon scowled. "These two gentlemen are here to listen while I ask you some questions."

Lou's fight-or-flight sense was immediately on full alert. If The Cannon wanted to nag Lou about the promised data file, he could have called – which he already did. Coming in person and bringing along two pieces of Asian muscle was way outside the Gallata playbook. You didn't absolutely have to be Italian to work for the family, but these two were definitely not on the same team. Unfortunately, there was nowhere for Lou to run.

The two Asians advanced a step and reached into their pea coats. They both pulled out handguns. But they made the mistake of thinking they had the element of surprise and didn't rush the process. By the time the man on the right looked up, he was staring down the short muzzle of Lou's shotgun.

An explosion reverberated around the cramped space after the Remington's flash. The impact of a few dozen size 00 buckshot balls blasting bridesmaid number one in the torso blew him backward. The heavy coat might have saved his life, except that he had opened it to reach for his gun.

Lou deftly swiveled the shotgun to the left, toward the second pistol-toting man. The other bridesmaid was skilled enough to get off a shot at the same moment Lou fired. The bullet caught Lou in the right shoulder, knocking the shotgun from his grasp. The tall man crumpled to the ground. The majority of the shot had found his neck and face, splattering blood, flesh, and bone fragments against the shop windows. If anyone had been walking by, they might have thought a horror movie was being filmed inside.

The Cannon moved carefully toward the counter, pulling out a silver Colt .44 with a black handle. He peered over the edge and locked eyes with Lou, first to determine if his old friend was alive, but also to make sure he hadn't pulled out another weapon. Lou lay against a wooden cabinet that lined the wall behind the counter. Above it, an eight-foot mirror reflected the scene. The Cannon crept behind the partition and kicked the now-spent shotgun farther away, not that Lou was in any condition to fire it again even if he had another shell. Blood gushed from both the entry and exit wounds as Lou futilely held his left hand against the front hole in his powder-blue work shirt.

"Why'd ya hafta go and make such a mess, Palazzo? Now you've put me in an awful spot."

Cannon stood over Lou, who had pushed himself into a sitting position. The exit wound throbbed as he pressed his back painfully against the cabinet containing used cell phones. "They drew first," Lou grunted through the pain.

Cannon smiled and leaned on the counter, his pistol held casually. Lou clearly was no longer a threat. "I would've been happy to do business without anybody getting killed. You didn't need to shoot those guys. Now you've created a scene, which is unfortunate. And I have to explain to the Chinese boss how these two morons got ambushed by an old fart like you."

"Yeah, 'bout that." Lou looked his tormenter in the eye. He was panting from shock and blood loss. "I don't suppose you could call me an ambulance, huh?"

"Oh, I will. But first, you're gonna tell me where the data file is. These idiots' boss thinks it belongs to him."

Lou winced. "That's crazy."

"Yeah? Why don't you tell me where you got that file?"

"What difference does it—"

Cannon stepped forward with surprising quickness, planting a sharp kick into the prone man's kidney, which caused him to topple. Lou moaned and clenched his teeth when his head hit the linoleum floor.

"Palazzo, you can't bullshit me. These Chinese fuckers need that file."

Lou was perplexed, in addition to being in agony. What did the Chinese guys have to do with Ryan's file? He couldn't figure it, but it was clear that his deal for the hundred grand was blown. Lou's eyes were inches off the floor. He spied the Louisville slugger he kept under the register for times when the shotgun was overkill. "I couldn't crack it, so I trashed it."

"Oh, now, Lou. I know very well that you are not the type of man to give up so quickly on a project. Not with so much money involved. And I remember how good you used to be. Don't play me for a fool. I know it's here. You may as well tell me now and save yourself some suffering."

Lou slid a few inches on his left shoulder, grimacing. Through the pain, he knew that The Cannon couldn't let him be a witness to this massacre. His voice was faint. "I'll tell you what. I can get it for you, but you gotta . , ."

The Cannon inched closer and bent down to hear Lou's words. Lou reached out, grabbed the bat with his left hand, slippery with blood, and swung as hard as he could manage backhanded. A crack accompanied the contact between the Louisville Slugger and the big man's wrist. The Colt flew across the counter, landing on the far side next to the shoe of dead bridesmaid number one. Cannon slumped forward, grabbing the counter's edge with his left hand and groaning as pain shot up to his elbow.

Lou swung the bat again, this time making contact with Cannon's knee. His adversary flopped to the floor, smearing some of Lou's blood while shouting obscenities through pain-clenched teeth. Lou used the bat as a crutch, pushing himself up to unsteady feet. Blood dripped down his limp right arm.

Lou gingerly lurched around the register side of the counter, heading for the door. His left hand pressed against the throbbing hole above his right clavicle, which oozed blood with each heartbeat. He shoved past the door into the still-falling snow. Winter wind cut through his light shirt, but flight instinct and adrenaline pushed him forward without a coat. Lightheaded, he stumbled forward into the slush-covered street, swiveling his head in search of someone who could call 9-1-1. He would be happy to explain his situation to a cop, for a change. His phone was in his coat pocket, back inside the shop.

Stumbling forward in the middle of the dark, empty street, Lou hoped for a passing cab or bus to see him in distress. He glanced back and saw The Cannon limping from the shop door. His right arm hung slack; the silver Colt was in his left hand. When he saw Lou, The Cannon pushed forward, slowed by a painful kneecap and the slippery conditions.

Lou kept moving, but descended further into shock from the pain and blood loss. The Cannon would not start shooting wildly. The shots would attract unwanted attention and Lou assumed his old friend's shooting hand was hurting. Lou's breath came in shallow gasps. He needed someone to help him. The street lights blurred – whether from snow in his eyes or something worse, he couldn't say. Why wasn't there any traffic? He tried to call out, but the effort only made him cough. Looking back, The Cannon was gaining on him.

Lou reached the intersection of 12th Street and Avenue C. He fell to his knees in the center, but no traffic came to his aid. The Cannon pushed forward, sweating and panting in the bone-chilling wind. Lou could not get up. He retched into the slush.

The Cannon approached, gun in hand. When he reached Lou, he kicked him again, sending the bleeding man sprawling. "Now you've pissed me off, Palazzo! Tell me where the file is!"

At that moment, a pair of headlights three blocks south caught The Cannon's attention. Blue and red lights flashed above the vehicle's two white eyes. Lou also saw them.

"Shit!" The Cannon leaned down, pushing the barrel of his Colt against Lou's temple. Even left-handed, he could make that shot. "Last chance, asshole."

Lou had sufficient recognition in his blurry brain to realize that he wasn't leaving the intersection alive, even if he gave Cannon what he wanted. "Go fuck yourself." He flailed his left arm toward his attacker's head, hooking a finger into The Cannon's black winter hat. When the bullet pierced his skull, Lou's arm dropped, pulling the hat down with it.

The Cannon's bald head reflected the street lights as he turned and hobbled away as fast as his injured knee would move, in the direction of the pawn shop. From above and to his left, he heard a dog's high-pitched barking. He looked up toward the sound. A small white fluff-ball poked its head between the iron bars of a balcony. A man in a baseball cap stood there, watching the scene below.

The Cannon limped to the sidewalk next to the apartment building. Flipping his collar up against the elements, he hugged the buildings along 12th Street, trying to appear casual while returning the Colt to his London Fog overcoat's interior pocket. A police siren whined to a stop in the intersection, where Lou's limp body leaked a scarlet pool onto the accumulating snow. At the corner of Avenue B, The Cannon ducked back inside Lou's blood-soaked shop and closed the door.

Chapter 2
Weekend Coverage

NYPD HOMICIDE DETECTIVE JASON DICKSON bounced his three-year-old son, JJ, on his lap. The living room sofa faced an ancient cabinet-style television, muted and tuned to the Jets game. The Brooklyn house experienced a rare moment of quiet, save for JJ's happy squeals each time his bottom rose into the air above Jason's knee. Triangles of white gathered in the corners of the window panes as a soft snow settled over New York City.

JJ's mother, Rachel Robinson Dickson, put the last dinner plates into the dishwasher, then peeked around the corner at her husband and son. She smiled and unconsciously placed her left hand under the subtle bulge at her waistline. In the privacy of their home, she didn't try to hide her pregnancy. Rachel appreciated the pleasant change from her daily search for what she called "obfuscation wear" for her job. At the American Cable News network, a noticeably enlarged tummy would undoubtedly draw glares from her managing editor. Rachel's mother, Olivia, said Rachel should be proud of her motherhood. But Olivia didn't understand television, or her asshole of a boss.

The idyllic scene was shattered by the introductory chords of "Takin' Care of Business" from Jason's mobile phone. Rachel rounded the corner to take JJ. Jason and Mike

Stoneman, his partner, were the on-call homicide team for the weekend. At 6:30 on Sunday, Jason had hoped to complete the football game without a fresh stiff. The ringtone, however, was linked to the department's dispatch number. He didn't need to answer to know his quiet evening was shot to hell.

After listening for forty-five seconds and writing down an address on a notepad, Jason said, "Yeah. I have it," and hung up. He gave Rachel a what-can-I-do? shrug. "Sorry, honey. We've got a stiff at 12th Street and Avenue C."

"Oh, dear." Rachel squeezed JJ. "It's going to be nasty out there tonight. You be sure to wear your good coat. And take a warm scarf!"

"I know." Jason walked to the hall closet. "Snow, slush, cold, and an outdoor crime scene. These are a few of my least-favorite things."

"Wear your boots, too. You'll need to stay warm."

Jason carefully wrapped a knitted scarf around his neck and pulled on his full-length wool overcoat. He was searching the pockets for his black gloves when Rachel's phone rang on the kitchen table. She balanced JJ in one arm and punched the ANSWER button and the speaker icon so she didn't have to hold both the phone and JJ. Jason, waiting for his good-bye kiss, listened.

"Robinson!" a brusque male voice shouted through the tinny speaker. Rachel shot a panicked glance at her husband. Jason also recognized the voice.

"Yes, Mr. Butler." Rachel struggled to keep her voice calm. It was unprecedented for Dave Butler to call Rachel at home.

"You're up, Robinson. You wanted to work breaking news, right?"

"Um, yes, Sir."

"Good. We have a probable murder at 12th and Avenue C. The cops are on the scene. Terry is on his way in the van. You need to be there for a stand-up on the ten o'clock show. You're the producer and reporter. Can you handle it?"

"Um, absolutely, Sir. You bet. I'll be right there."

Butler did not say another word before ending the call.

Rachel settled JJ into his high chair, then turned to Jason. "I'm sorry. I know you're on call this weekend. It's just – I mean, you know how much I've been wanting to get a chance at a real assignment. I'm sure Momma will be fine taking JJ. Can you wait five minutes? We can go together." She flashed an excited smile that melted Jason's stern countenance.

"We talked about this," he said, removing his gloves. "I'm glad you're getting a shot at a breaking news story. But I didn't want it to be my case. It puts me in a conflicted position. You know I can't give you any information."

"I don't need you to." Rachel reached down to soothe JJ, who had startled at her raised voice. She composed herself while gently stroking her son's back. "You'll treat me the same as any other member of the press. I won't share anything with you, and you and Mike don't share with me. That's fine. I can handle it. And so can you."

Seven minutes later, Olivia waved them both goodbye, as did JJ. Shallow tracks in the new snow marked their progress toward the number 4 subway train. After a mostly silent ride into Manhattan, Jason and Rachel trudged up the sloppy station steps and made their way to 12th Street. Flashing blue and red lights identified the position of police vehicles. Rachel scanned the scene for the white ACN news van. Not immediately seeing it, she pulled out her phone to send a text to Terry, her cameraman and van driver.

"I'm going in," Jason said, flakes of snow sticking to his shoulders. "Be careful out here in the snow." He pressed his lips gently on hers. "Go be terrific."

"Thanks," Rachel said, already working the keypad on her phone. When she glanced up, Jason's tall form was silhouetted against the police lights.

* * *

TWENTY MINUTES LATER, Rachel stood at the edge of a yellow crime scene tape streamer, looking in at the unhurried activity in the middle of what was normally a bustling Manhattan intersection. The snowfall would have diminished the traffic anyway, but the active crime scene left the space empty save for the cops and emergency services personnel. One block away in each direction, squad cars blocked the streets, detouring the traffic to the honking objections of the intrepid Manhattan motorists who had braved the December snow. Rachel's feet were already cold inside over-the-calf leather boots that were supposed to have been waterproof. She could have worn better winter footwear, but wanted to be slightly more stylish for her on-air appearance. She had picked out a purple overcoat and a matching knit hat, which were both warm and photogenic.

Terry hefted his HD video camera onto his right shoulder, attempting to get a usable image of the body on the ground under a white sheet, or at least the police activity. An ambulance idled nearby, waiting for the corpse to be released.

"Should I do a stand-up from here?" Rachel asked. Terry was an experienced cameraman and had covered dozens of crime scenes, so she knew she could trust his advice. "There's no producer out here to give me a script, huh?"

"You'll be fine," Terry encouraged his neophyte reporter. "I've seen your studio pieces and you're great on camera. What we need is some useful information, like the dead guy's name. Don't you have inside contacts with the police?"

"Not tonight," Rachel said. "You stay here and get pictures if anything happens. I'll see what I can find."

She walked down the block to the west, toward Avenue B. After being so excited about getting the call to cover hard news that she had wanted so desperately, the reality of covering the story and having something meaningful to share with viewers was sinking in. She had not studied journalism and her limited experience hosting studio pieces did not prepare her for a nighttime crime scene. The reality of the situation hit her harder than the icy wind.

The sidewalk was deserted until she reached the corner of Avenue B, where a black-and-white cruiser with its lights on blocked the street. On the southeast corner, two uniformed officers stood on either side of the door leading into a shop. A small swath of yellow tape covered the lock and knob. The sign over the door read *Lou's Electronics & Pawn*. While she walked back toward Terry and the crowd around the corpse, she searched on her phone. The shop had a website listing the owner, Lou Palazzo, along with an email address and phone number. Wondering if maybe Palazzo was their corpse, she called the number, which rang a dozen times before disconnecting. She also sent an email, just in case.

The north side of the street was lined with apartment buildings, some with ground-level retail space. Rachel crunched past under windows where curious residents peered out. On the New York sidewalk, falling snow disintegrated into thick slush on contact. A white crust formed on parked cars and trash cans. Reaching the curb, where the yellow tape encircled a light pole, Rachel caught the eye of a young, Black uniformed officer assigned to keep the public and the press from crossing the barrier.

"Nasty night for this duty," she commented sweetly.

"It's never easy," the officer replied without making eye contact.

"The dead guy is Lou Palazzo, right?" she guessed.

Now he looked at Rachel, who smiled and held his gaze. "I'm sorry, Miss. I can't say anything about that."

"I understand. My husband is a detective." She paused to see whether the officer would recognize her, but he showed no sign. "I don't see anybody talking to witnesses. I guess nobody was out in the snow to see, huh?"

"I guess not," came the mumbled reply.

Rachel looked up, scanning the closest apartment building. Despite the softly falling snow and freezing temperature, residents stood gawking on many of the small balconies overlooking the street. Most were wearing heavy coats and hats. On a third-floor terrace on the southeast corner, a man with white hair around his ears stood in short sleeves. The snowflakes accumulated on the bill of his cap suggested a lengthy vigil. Apparently, he hadn't gone inside for warmer clothing, probably not wanting to miss something interesting.

"I'm meeting my grandmother in this building," Rachel said, stepping closer to the officer. "I know it's behind the line and all, but may I please go through to the door?"

The officer stood aside, inviting Rachel under the yellow tape line. She walked confidently through the building's outer door into a ten-foot-square vestibule. There, an inner door with a black key-card scanner next to the handle blocked her access. Above the card reader, an LED screen bearing the title *Resident List* stood at attention. She tapped the digital menu, chose someone named *Anderson,* and pressed the call button.

After a short wait, a tinny female voice hesitantly said, "Yes?"

"Hello. I'm Rachel Robinson from the American Cable News network. I'd like to talk to you about what happened outside tonight if you can spare me a few minutes."

"I'm not interested," came the terse reply. Then silence.

"Hello?" Rachel called out, to no response. She tried again with a *Johnson*, but got no answer to the initial call. Then, she tried *Robinson*. When the resident answered, she tried the same honest pitch.

"What channel?" came the response.

"ACN cable news," Rachel repeated. "I have ID if you have video down to the door." She pulled out her press badge, hanging from a lanyard around her neck under her coat. She held it up to the circular camera eye above the LED screen.

"It's 10-F," the voice said. The door buzzed, prompting Rachel to grab the handle and pull.

Once inside, Rachel intended to make a beeline for the third floor, but she had a momentary qualm about leaving her fellow Robinson hanging. She rode the elevator to the tenth floor and knocked on 10-F. Mrs. Eloise Robinson was excited about answering questions, but had not seen anything and did not know the identity of the dead man. Rachel thanked her and left after four minutes. She rode the elevator to the third floor and exited into a long corridor. She found the door to apartment 3-R, the one at the extreme eastern end of the building facing the street.

A sharp yip from a dog greeted her knock, followed by a torrent of intense barking. Pressing her ear against the thick wooden door, she heard a man's voice say, "Sergeant! Stop!" The dog quieted and Rachel heard footsteps coming in her direction. The door opened a crack, then caught on the end of a security chain. A wrinkled male face peered through. "Who are you?" A flash of white fur across the opening and a low growl told Rachel that the dog was still in play.

Rachel held her ID card up to the crack at the man's eye level. "Hello. I'm Rachel Robinson. I'm a reporter with American Cable News. I saw you out on your balcony. Did you see anything tonight?"

It was a question the man couldn't ignore. "What channel did you say you're with?" His scratchy voice sounded interested rather than skeptical.

"I'm with ACN news. It's on channel 72 on Spectrum or 148 on Verizon." Rachel flashed her white teeth in her most welcoming smile.

The door shut, then opened again after the elderly resident removed the chain. Joseph Aaronson introduced himself, welcomed her inside, and led the way to the balcony, where the sliding door was half open. The little white dog continued a suspicious growl and circled around Rachel's legs.

Joe was not bothered by the cold or the still-falling snow. He resumed his posture at the railing, ramrod straight, feet shoulder-width apart. His skin was leathery and wrinkled, suggesting a lifetime spent working outside. His hands were similarly weathered, but had smooth nails. Rachel quietly engaged the audio recording function on her phone. "Did you see or hear anything?"

"I heard a gunshot," Joe said without hesitation. He did not make eye contact with Rachel. "I came out right away because, with the snow and all, it was unusual to hear something like that. When I got here, I seen Lou on his back on the street in the snow. Not wearin' no coat or nothin'. I spent four years in Vietnam, and I know what gunfire sounds like. There was blood all around his head, so he was shot there for sure. There was another guy. Big guy. Bald head, wearin' a long tan coat."

"Did you say Lou? You recognized the victim?"

"Yea, Lou Palazzo. Sure of it."

"Did you get a look at the bald man?"

"Sergeant barked, and the guy turned his head and looked up. I saw him for a flash, but didn't get a good look. He was a white guy, for sure. Saw the light shine off his head. After that, he went over to the sidewalk and I lost sight of him. But Lou was down and out in the middle of the street. A minute later, the cop car arrived."

When Joe paused his narrative, Rachel asked, "How can you be sure it was Lou Palazzo?"

Joe didn't hesitate. He turned toward Rachel. "Lou owns the shop on the corner down at Avenue B. Nice guy. Younger than me, but he's been around some. We sometimes talk, when I get down there and he's not too busy. He wasn't that far away down there in the muck. I recognized him well enough."

"You ever see the bald guy in the coat before?"

"Can't say. Didn't get a good look at him." Joe was a man of few extraneous words. Sergeant filled the silence, barking several times in his high-pitched excitement. "Sergent! Stop!" Joe scolded. The dog whimpered, but ceased barking.

"Do you know of any reason why someone would want to murder Lou?"

Joe was silent, returning his eyes to the still-active crime scene below. After a minute, he said, "I can't say anything for sure. Lou was no angel. He done some time and he did some things a man might regret, that might get a man killed. It don't mean that's what happened. I can't say. But it don't surprise me that somethin' like that might happen to Lou. But he's a – he *was* a good man. I'll tell you for sure. He had integrity. He ran a clean shop. He wasn't doin' nothin' illegal down there. He did his time and was legit. That's what I think."

Rachel thanked Joe for the information. When she asked him to spell his name so she could get it right for her report, his eyes flashed angrily. "No. Don't say my name. I'm bein' nice to you because old Lou deserves to get a shout out. But I don't want you usin' my name. I don't need no trouble. I do not give you permission to use my name. Is that clear?"

"Absolutely, Mr. Aaronson. No names. I'll describe you as an eyewitness who lives in a nearby building. How's that?"

"That's fine."

Within a few minutes, Rachel was back on the sidewalk. The snow had stopped, but the temperature had fallen perceptibly. The slush was already turning to ice. She needed to be careful walking in her fashion boots. When she reached the spot where she last saw her cameraman, Terry was gone, meaning he had returned to the van. Rachel found it parked two blocks away. Terry was inside, keeping warm and editing video on his laptop.

"You get anything?" Terry asked without looking up.

"Yeah. I got an eyewitness. He doesn't want to be identified, but it's good stuff. I know who the dead guy is. He owns the electronics store and pawn shop on the corner. The cops have it sealed up, so we should go over there to do the live shot. I'll let Dave know."

Before leaving the van, Rachel sent a text to Jason:

I have a witness who has ID'd the victim as Lou Palazzo, who owns the store on the corner of 12th & B. I'll give you his information, but don't tell him I told you. He didn't get a good look at the killer. Can you confirm the ID?

When she and Terry reached the storefront and were setting up their shot, Rachel got a return text from Jason:

Cannot confirm any information. Should not ask me that. Call me to give info on the witness.

Rachel kicked herself mentally for creating an electronic record of her request. Then she thought twice. It was not out of line for a reporter to ask a cop for the information, even if it was confidential. The cop wasn't likely to give it up, but asking wasn't a crime. Of course, most reporters didn't have such close personal relationships with cops. On the other hand, most other reporters wouldn't give the cops a tip about a witness. Rachel wondered whether she should have mentioned that she had a witness, but she had already done it.

Rachel called Jason and relayed the information about Joe Aaronson. Jason said he would send a couple of officers to canvas all the apartments on the lower floors to ask if anyone saw or heard anything, but would make sure they got to apartment 3-R. He thanked her for the tip.

Rachel settled herself in front of Terry's camera, now mounted on a tripod. Her earpiece gave her a feed from the producer in the studio handling the ten o'clock news broadcast. When she heard the countdown to her live shot, she smoothed her hair and took a deep breath. When the red light went on, she smiled.

"Tonight, here in Lower Manhattan, a shop owner named Lou Palazzo was brutally gunned down in the middle of an intersection in what can only be described as an execution-style killing."

Chapter 3
On the Scene

DETECTIVE MIKE STONEMAN CALLED OUT to his partner as soon as Jason ducked under the crime scene tape stretched across the sidewalk.

"Jason! Over here." Mike waved his arm, beckoning Jason toward the center of the intersection. Since Mike lived in Manhattan, he had arrived fifteen minutes before his partner. A clot of officers and emergency services personnel milled about without much urgency.

"Nice night," Jason said sarcastically.

Mike, dressed in a down parka and a blue-and-orange knit hat pulled down over his ears, grunted his agreement. Mike was a full five inches shorter than Jason and twenty years older. Even in their winter clothes, Jason's style showed through, with his tailored wool overcoat, gloves, scarf, and LL Bean duck boots. Mike had long since stopped worrying about the fact that his partner was taller, better looking, in better shape, and a better dresser. Mike possessed wisdom that came from experience, which was the one thing Jason could not have. At least not until he had twenty-five years on the force like Mike. They had been partners for five years.

A uniformed officer with a plastic cover over his hat approached Mike as Jason arrived. "Detective Stoneman, the medical examiner is finished. Can we remove the body now?"

"Not yet," Mike responded. "I want Detective Dickson to get a look at the scene first."

The officer left to give his fellow officers the bad news – they all had to stay outside their warm squad cars.

As they walked around the intersection, Mike gave Jason the rundown. "The stiff's name is Lou Palazzo. His wallet was in his pants pocket with a driver's license, so the ID was pretty easy. He's got a record from years back. Did three years in Sing Sing in the twenty-teens for conspiracy to commit murder. He was connected to the Gallata family. Since he got out, he's had no arrests. He ran an electronics store and pawn shop over on the corner of Avenue B, a block away." Mike pointed to the far end of the block. "He had a little cash and some credit cards in his wallet."

Jason looked down at the remainder of the dead man's head. "So, not a robbery, then?"

Mike didn't laugh. "The snow and slush on the street mangled any physical evidence here, but there is blood in the snow outside his shop. It looks like he was shot inside the shop in the shoulder, tried to escape in this direction, then got caught here in the intersection and plugged once in the head. No cell phone on him. He wasn't wearing a coat, so he left in a hurry. When we finish here, there are two more stiffs in the shop."

"So, there's more to see?" Jason asked.

"Oh, yeah. Plenty. We'll get over there in a minute. The officer in the first squad car saw two figures in the middle of the street from a few blocks away and hit his lights. By the time he got here, Lou was dead on the ground and the other person had fled the scene on foot."

Jason squatted to get a look at the body without dipping his knees into the slush. The kill shot entered the man's head above his left ear and exited through his neck – a clean kill, likely fired by a person standing over the victim.

"Seen enough?" Mike asked.

"Sure. Thanks for doing the reconnaissance."

"Let's go see the shop. That's where the action was." Mike turned to the west. "Oh, and by the way, was that Rachel I saw over there with a cameraman?"

"Yeah," Jason said without stopping. "She got a call from her network to come work this scene. She's been bugging them for weeks about getting a chance to cover breaking news instead of the fluffy studio stuff. You know, the healthcare pieces and emergency services and such. She's been on the on-call list every weekend since Halloween, hoping to get a call. Unfortunately, tonight was the night."

"You need to be careful, Jason. You can't spill any information to her. I know we talked about this possibly happening someday. Well, shit just got real. Sully will have your hide if he thinks you're feeding her inside dirt on the investigation."

"I know. I'm not telling her anything. But I can't stop her from working. This is a big deal for her."

"Sure. I get it," Mike said. "But be careful."

"You don't need to tell me."

Several slushy minutes later, Mike and Jason stomped the winter precipitation off their shoes outside Lou's Electronics & Pawn. After donning plastic crime-scene booties and gloves, Mike motioned for the officer guarding the door to remove the seal so they could enter.

Jason had seen bloodier crime scenes, but not many. The glass-topped cases around the store amplified the spatter of blood and other body fluids and remnants. Jason stood at the threshold for two full minutes, taking in the gory vista.

Inside the door was the shop's vestibule, an empty space roughly ten feet square. Directly ahead, an eight-foot-long counter stretched across the center of the room. A bulky metal cash register perched on the right corner. Under the glass-topped counter, Jason saw a potpourri of electronics, jewelry, and weapons. These, he surmised, were the biggest sellers (or at least the highest-profit items), kept under glass and behind a locked door accessible only from behind the counter. On either side of the counter, a wooden door three feet high blocked customers from intruding on the proprietor's domain. Around the rest of the store, shelves and display racks contained a variety of retail items ranging from video equipment to DVDs to mobile phone accessories.

Looking past the blood spatter, Jason noticed that the shelves and display cases had been rummaged through, and not subtly. Glass was smashed, merchandise thrown from shelves to the floor, and electronic equipment strewn about. Several knives and two handguns lay among the shards.

"Somebody left behind some attractive options," Jason observed.

Officer Ray Evans, their escort, reported that when he arrived there were puddles, probably melted snow, inside the door. There were also several sets of bloody footprints leading both in and out. The officers had done their best to avoid adding more footprints to the crime scene, but protocol required them to enter the shop in case there were victims in need of medical attention. Since then, multiple cops had trodden upon the original prints.

"The forensics team hasn't been here yet," Mike warned, "so we need to be careful. But a photographer has taken a bunch of pictures already."

Very little floor area was completely free from blood. The two detectives maneuvered carefully around the space to examine the carnage without spoiling potential evidence. On the floor between the door and the sales counter, two men wearing black pea coats lay dead, their heads facing the door. One had a large portion of his torso gutted, but his face was intact, showing Asian features and short, black hair. The other man's face was barely recognizable. Buckshot from a shotgun, presumably the one on the floor behind the counter, had eviscerated his features. Footprints smeared the floor all around the bodies. Jason wondered how many of them were from the first officers on the scene. Behind the counter, blood obscured much of the tile floor and spattered against the wall on the left end, farthest away from the register. Jason immediately saw a bullet impact hole in the big mirror behind the counter. Two sets of bloody footprints led from behind the counter toward the door from the register side.

Mike and Jason carefully searched the corpses' clothes. Jason found a wad of cash in the pants pocket of the man who still had a face, secured with a rubber band. Jason didn't count the money, but dropped the rolled bills in an evidence bag. The dead guy also had a clip for a Glock with 17 bullets in the inside pocket of his pea coat. After bagging the ammo, they turned to the man without a face, finding a similar ammo clip but no cash. That man had a container of Tic Tacs in his coat pocket, along with a paper receipt from a restaurant in Chinatown and one pack of cigarettes bearing Chinese characters. Neither had ID.

After securing the contents of the dead men's pockets, Jason stood up and scanned the bloody floor. "Where's the brass?" he asked Mike.

"Great question. The shopkeeper, Palazzo, took a slug through the shoulder. These two thugs certainly came in with guns that fit those clips. I'm guessing we'll find powder residue on their hands. So, somebody came in and removed their weapons and all the shell casings after the fact." Mike carefully walked to the relatively bloodless cash register and looked behind the counter. "We'll let the forensics team document everything, but it looks to me like Palazzo was behind the counter when these goons came in, along with whoever made the kill shot a block away. Palazzo pulled out his trusty shotgun and fired at Mutt and Jeff here." He gestured toward the dead men. "He got 'em both, but I'm guessing one of them, or the third guy, got off some shots, one of which got him in the shoulder. The guy went down, which accounts for all the blood down there behind the counter. Then, somehow, he got up and ran out the door. The third guy followed him, which accounts for the two sets of footprints heading out."

"It accounts for the trail of blood outside, too," Jason confirmed. "Palazzo ran down the street, pretty injured and bleeding. He got as far as the intersection over at Avenue C before the chaser caught up to him and shot him in the head."

"So, was it an execution from the beginning?" Mike asked.

"No," Jason responded as he carefully traversed the gory floor. "Look around. The display case is open from the back. There are empty spaces. Looks like somebody grabbed some merch on the way out. So, robbery gone bad?"

Mike didn't respond immediately. He walked behind the counter and examined the wooden credenza against the mirrored wall. Its doors were also open, with obvious signs of having been rummaged. Under the front glass counter, cabinet doors were smashed. It was difficult to tell for sure, but it seemed like more goods had been thrown to the floor than stolen.

The credenza behind the counter sported a cardboard display listing the features of an iPhone and several three-ring binders with what looked like inventory records. In the middle, a rectangular area the size of a laptop computer was empty, leaving a shadow of its former location in the light dust. A wireless mouse sat idle to the right of the blank space. The chrome plug of a power cord was jammed into the gap between the credenza and the wall, preventing the cord from disappearing behind.

Mike pointed. "Looks like somebody lifted a laptop from this counter. And not a display model for sale – looks like something that was in use."

"What are you thinking?" Jason asked. "Why does the killer take the time to come back to the shop after plugging Lou, take the guns and the brass, then rifle through the cases and lift the laptop?"

"It makes sense to clean up the scene and remove the guns and casings. And he didn't have much time," Mike said absently, still scanning around the space. "The officer driving the patrol car saw a man in the intersection. He arrived within a minute of Palazzo getting snuffed. He didn't immediately know where the shooter went and he was following active shooter protocols, so it took a while for the backup to arrive and find the shop. But our killer had to know that we would eventually trace the victim back here. And since there were shots fired, including at least two shotgun blasts, he must have figured somebody called 9-1-1. So, he hustled through what he needed to do and then got the hell out."

"It's a damned puzzle," Jason observed. He stopped and pulled out his phone, then frowned. He tapped out a text message and turned back to Mike. "Does it look to you like a robbery, or a search?"

Mike cocked his head, then scanned the room again. "You're right. It looks more like somebody looking for something. I doubt there was anything in this dump valuable enough to require an armed three-man crew. It's also hard to believe that poor Lou Palazzo would have defended any of this junk with his life."

"Was the register emptied?"

Mike walked carefully to the bulky cash register, which was closed. He could not easily figure out how to open the cash drawer without potentially sullying any evidence. "Doesn't look that way, but we'll need the tech team to open it after it's swept for prints."

"Maybe somebody pawned something that was more valuable than they thought?"

"Great," Mike sighed, "a room full of blood and questions. Let's get out of here so the forensics team can do their work. We'll come back tomorrow to put the pieces together." Then, turning to the officer still standing at the door, he said, "Officer Evans, make sure this shop is secured after the forensics team gets done. We'll be back in the morning."

"We will, Detective," came the crisp reply.

Outside, the sky had partially cleared and a waning gibbous moon peeked out from between wispy clouds. Jason stepped away ten feet and pulled out his phone. When he returned to Mike, who was chatting with a uniformed officer, he relayed Rachel's witness information. Then, Jason gave instructions to the officer to canvas the apartment building near the Avenue C intersection. "If you find anyone who saw anything helpful, make a note in the report and we'll see it in the morning. Make sure you cover the apartments with balconies near the intersection on the lower floors." Jason looked down at his older partner. "I'm going to meet up with Rachel to see if she's ready to head back to Brooklyn. Unless you think we should hang around in case the witness has something more than what he told her."

"No. I'll stay in case there are any other witnesses. You two get home to my favorite godson. And, Jason, be careful about what you tell Rachel."

"I know. It's going to be awkward, since I usually tell her everything. This time I have to clam up."

"Can't be helped. Keep *clam* and carry on." Mike smiled and waved to his partner.

He wondered what he would say to his own wife. Normally, Mike openly shared the details of cases like this with Dr. Michelle McNeill. As the county medical examiner, she would soon be performing the autopsies on Lou Palazzo and the two Asian gunmen. But Michelle and Rachel were best friends. He would need to caution Michelle about sharing confidential information. Neither he nor Michelle would want to be the source of a leak that might be blamed on Jason.

"This is going to get complicated," Mike muttered.

Chapter 4
A Polite Conversation

LOYD CANNON TENDED TO SWEAT when required to stand for long periods of time. His considerable bulk put pressure on his lower back, hips, and knees. The effort to maintain an at-attention posture produced drops of moisture on his forehead and neck within minutes. His boss, Fat Albert Gallata, had a short temper and a propensity for severe and often arbitrary punishment for underlings who disappointed him. The boss had been yelling for the past four minutes. The Cannon stood at attention, his injured knee throbbing, and absorbed the abuse.

Fat Albert inherited the family business five years earlier when his father was eaten alive by tigers at the Bronx Zoo. Everyone thought it was a hit carried out by a rival mob, but it turned out to be a serial killer later dubbed "The Righteous Assassin." Fat Albert was heavier than Cannon, but showed no signs of similar flop sweat.

"You had one simple fucking job!" the boss screamed, repeating the mantra for the fourth time. They were in the back room of Shelly's Pub on Mulberry Street. The owner had become indebted to the Gallata organization decades before and paid off his nut partly by providing meeting space, free drinks, and a well camouflaged and secure basement storage unit. The back room at Shelly's became the *de facto*

Manhattan home office for Fat Albert. He preferred his Brooklyn enclave, but sometimes business needed to be conducted in Little Italy.

"I know, Boss. The two Chinese clowns pulled their guns way too fast. We didn't know old Lou had a shotgun behind his counter."

"Why the fuck didn't you know that? You were in charge of the operation, *Lloyd*."

Cannon fumed. He had been in the organization for fifteen years and had always been called The Cannon. He was fine with simply Cannon, but calling him Lloyd would get his underlings slapped. Or worse. It was disrespectful, and something the old man never did. But since the son rose to the boss' chair, The Cannon got less respect. More and more members of the organization had been elevated above him. More recently, after Fat Albert cut a deal with the Chinese gang, even some of the foreign guys had more authority than The Cannon.

"You're right, Boss. I was in charge. I gave those Dragon idiots instructions, but I don't think they fully understood my English. I wanted to talk to Palazzo and get him to cooperate, but they pulled their pieces before I had a chance to say hello."

"So, you didn't get the fucking file?"

Cannon took a breath, calming himself and avoiding snapping back that he had already answered the question. "Like I said, the guy refused to give it up. I grabbed what I could in the short time I had. I got the laptop and phone and a bunch of other computer equipment. We'll go through it and see if we can find the file, assuming it was ever there."

"We know it was there! Your boy, Lenny, has been listening to the bug in that snot-nosed kid's room. The Chinese sure as fuck expected it to be there. You couldn't force the old guy to spill the location? You had to waste him first?" Spittle sprayed in Cannon's face from Fat Albert's rage.

"He whacked me with a baseball bat. I plugged him in the shoulder and thought he was down, but I was wrong." Cannon grabbed the opportunity to take credit for the shot that wounded Lou, although he hated having to admit he had allowed his mark to escape the shop. "He ran out into the street. I caught up with him, but the cops were coming. You think I should have left him alive?" Cannon let a bit of sarcasm seep into the response, then instantly regretted it.

"I wanted you to get the Chinese Dragons their data file so I can get my money. I know you don't like having them around, but we're working with them whether you like it or not. Your decision to snuff Palazzo made our job harder. You get that, right, *Lloyd*?"

Cannon gritted his teeth. "Yeah. I get it, Boss. I fucked it up. It was my operation and it went bad. I'll take the responsibility." Cannon had learned long ago that taking responsibility and apologizing was far better than claiming it wasn't your fault. It earned you respect. At least, it used to.

"You're goddamned right you will!" Fat Albert huffed and then turned his back. "Was there any other computer shit inside that shop when you left?"

"Probably," Cannon admitted. "I only had a few minutes before the cops were going to get there. I had to clean up the shop and make sure they couldn't trace anything back to you or the Chinese. I'm going back in with a team later tonight to make sure we got everything. We'll find that fucking file. It'll just be a little harder now."

"That's the first intelligent thing you've said. Fine. Get some guys and get it done, assuming the cops haven't already got it."

"Not much chance," Cannon replied quickly. "They don't know what they're looking for."

Chapter 5
Extra-Curricular Activity

THAT SUNDAY NIGHT at 10:05 p.m., in a dorm room at New York University, Ryan Gelb swiveled violently on his rolling desk chair. A gunmetal gray video game controller held firmly in both hands, Ryan called into the microphone curving around his cheek. "I got him! Move left!" He pumped a lanky arm into the air in celebration when the boss fell. He then reflexively attempted to brush his bushy brown hair away from his eyes, banging his fingers on the exterior of his headset. Ryan's playing partner, Will, whooped his affirmation on the other side of the headset's audio connection.

Before any new enemies appeared, Ryan's phone rang with the opening strains of Paul Russell's "Lil Boo Thang," meaning the call was from his girlfriend, Star Albertson. As much as Ryan hated to interrupt the game, a call from Star was more important. Ryan told Will to hang on.

Ryan met Star in the first-year writing class they were both required to take. Ryan had put it off until sophomore year because he hated writing. Star, who was an accomplished scribe, offered to help Ryan, the computer nerd, with an assignment. That was six weeks ago and they had been together ever since. It wasn't that Ryan never had a girlfriend, but he was hardly a ladies' man. Thin and wiry, he was decent at basketball. But standing several inches under six feet and barely a hundred fifty pounds, he was not varsity material. Besides, he enjoyed video games more than sports. Will's cousin was his senior prom date.

Star was, to Ryan, an exotic southern girl with an enchanting accent. She was by far the smartest, most popular, and prettiest girl he ever dated. He was trying his best not to blow the chance to keep her interested in a nerd. Pushing the headset off his left ear, Ryan snatched his still-singing phone.

"Ryan, are you watching the news?" came Star's excited voice.

"No. I'm playing with Will. Why?"

"You need to turn on ACN. It's on channel 72. I was watching because my Aunt Michelle's friend Rachel is a reporter there and I saw on her Instagram that she was doing a live report. But that's not the point. Ryan, she's reporting on a murder. And the victim is Lou Palazzo. Isn't that your uncle?"

"Holy shit!" Ryan exclaimed.

"What?" Will's voice came through Ryan's right ear, still connected to the game.

"I'm turning on the TV." He pulled off the headset, holding the microphone to his mouth as he fumbled for the remote. "Hey, Star says to turn on channel 72. It's something about Uncle Lou."

"Is Will there with you?" Star asked over the phone, still pressed to Ryan's other ear.

"No. He's on my headset."

Ryan pointed the remote control at the 20-inch flat screen mounted on his dorm wall, next to a poster of Bill Gates. When the screen switched inputs, he saw a Black woman wearing a purple overcoat and matching knit hat holding a microphone. Behind her, he could see a familiar storefront and the sign reading *Lou's Electronics & Pawn*. He tried to swallow, but his throat was constricted. The woman on the screen was talking.

"No, Marina, the police on the scene have not confirmed the victim's identity, but an eyewitness who knows Lou Palazzo did. We have no additional details at this time, but we will continue to report on this tragic murder. In Lower Manhattan, this is Rachel Robinson reporting."

"Holy shit!" Ryan repeated. "That's Uncle Lou's shop. Oh my God! Somebody killed Uncle Lou!"

"I'm coming over there," Star said.

"OK," he replied, then ended the call. Repositioning his headset, he said, "Did you see that, Will?"

"I didn't see it, but I heard you. Are you serious? Your uncle's dead?"

"It doesn't necessarily have anything to do with the file, right?"

Will did not respond right away, leaving only the game's sounds in Ryan's ear. "Maybe not. I mean, you said yourself that your uncle was into some shady stuff. But the timing is—"

"I know. What are we gonna do?"

"Stay cool," Will said. "Don't say anything to anyone. Not Star. Not anyone. Nobody knows we gave him the file."

"Right. It probably wasn't about that. You don't think Uncle Lou would have told somebody about it, do you?"

"I don't know. Maybe it's got nothing to do with the file. We don't know what happened. We need to stay calm. I'm on my way."

Before Ryan could mention that Star was also coming over, Will was gone. He could text his friend and tell him not to come, but he figured it was just as well to have him there. With his uncle murdered, a romantic moment with Star was not likely. He looked around the room and picked up some dirty clothes, then searched for his deodorant and a fresh shirt.

* * *

STAR ALBERTSON ARRIVED for her freshman year at NYU from Buckhead, Georgia with lofty ambitions about majoring in theater and having a career on Broadway. She was pretty, petite, an accomplished dancer and singer, and she had what every successful performer needed: supreme self-confidence. But her first personal encounter with Broadway left her scarred, emotionally and physically. In September, her uncle, homicide detective Mike Stoneman, staged a sting operation at the bar where Star worked. It was part of an investigation into the murder of a Broadway actor. The suspect had briefly used her as a human shield when the cops were closing in. It had left her shaken. A faint scar the size and shape of a pistol's muzzle remained an inch below her left ear.

It was a few weeks after her close encounter with the murderer that Star met Ryan. He was a tonic for her. Sweet, unassuming, and totally devoted to her, Ryan helped Star get past her traumatic memories and refocused on school and friends. Plus, Ryan was a movie lover, like her. Their early dates were often at the art houses in Lower Manhattan. He made her happy and he was a love-sick puppy around her. She liked the attention, but did not take undue advantage.

Between her part-time job waiting tables at a local bar called *The Scampering Squirrel,* her challenging class and study schedule, and making some time to hang out with Ryan, Star's schedule was overflowing. But she gladly put down her literature assignment when she saw Rachel's Instagram post about doing a live news report. When she realized the report was about the murder of her boyfriend's uncle, her mood changed from excited to horrified.

When Star opened the unlocked door of Ryan's dorm room, his best friend, Will Scarano, was already there. Star was never surprised to see Will hanging out with Ryan. Will was Ryan's oldest and closest friend. They were both computer science majors, talked computer-eze constantly, played video games and RPGs together, and were working on a joint project in their cybersecurity class. Will had a girlfriend named Sarrie, so Ryan having Star to hang out with balanced his social life with his friend's.

"Hi, Star," Will called out as she entered Ryan's room. Will was taller and more athletic-looking than Ryan, with sandy blond hair and blue eyes. Unlike his fellow nerd, Will did not wear glasses, opting instead for contact lenses. He was dressed in his standard *Legend of Zelda* t-shirt and cargo shorts.

"Hey, Will," she called back, then went to Ryan and planted a quick kiss on his mouth. "I'm so sorry about your uncle." Star stroked Ryan's face.

"Thanks. It doesn't seem real." Ryan grasped Star's hand and held it tight. "I'm really freaked out."

"It's awful, bro," Will said. "It doesn't make any sense."

Over the next fifteen minutes, they talked about Uncle Lou, including how Ryan and Will played as a team with Lou in their current favorite multi-player game, *Blades of Karma*. They talked about hanging out with Lou at his shop on weekends. They both considered the store to be much better than a museum. Lou knew more about computers and electronics than anyone. He was funny and didn't treat them like kids. And he insisted on indoctrinating them in what he called "the classics" of American movies. They made the twenty-minute walk to visit the shop frequently.

"He was the mellifluous maestro of contemporary celluloid." Ryan fought back a tear.

"The purveyor of paramount prestidigitation." Will locked eyes with his childhood friend and they exchanged a joint acknowledgement of their loss.

"Oh, please." Star rolled her eyes. "Not this again. I know you two consider it clever to speak in SAT vocabulary words like it's code nobody can understand. Do you really think I never met a thesaurus?"

"We know you get it," Ryan said, "but it's still fun for us. We used to play the thesaurus game when we were with Uncle Lou. He probably knew more words than he admitted to, but he let us have our fun."

"When was the last time you saw your uncle?" Star asked.

Ryan hesitated. "Um . . .I'm not sure."

"It was a week ago," Will cut in. "Remember? We wanted to talk to him about our project design."

"Right. Right. Yeah, that was it. He was super helpful."

Ryan shot a glance at Will that Star could not decipher. During the entire discussion, they both seemed upset, but also frightened. Perhaps the concept of urban crime so close to home freaked them out. Star had already been close to a murder case and talked to her Aunt Michelle all the time about bodies and autopsies. Maybe she was jaded and desensitized to it. There wasn't much she could say to make her boyfriend feel better, so she held his hand. Ryan squeezed back frequently.

After a half hour of commiserating, Star said she needed to get back to her own room. She had a hundred pages of reading due the next day. Will helpfully excused himself to use the bathroom, leaving Star and Ryan alone for their good-byes.

"I'm so, so, sorry," Star said, encircling his neck with her slender brown arms. "I've never dealt with something like this in my own family, so I can't imagine what you're going through. Just know that I'm here for you if you need me. Call me anytime you need to talk." She pulled him into a long, tender kiss, then hugged him as tightly as she could in silence until Will returned. Star gave Ryan one more quick kiss and left the room, blowing another kiss at the threshold.

With Star gone, Will said, "I've been thinking about the file and Uncle Lou."

"I know. Me, too. I can't shake the thought that his murder could be connected to the file."

"I know, bro. But Uncle Lou hadn't decrypted it, so it wasn't worth anything to anyone. If we both keep our mouths shut, we'll be fine and nobody will be able to connect it back to us. We have to forget it ever existed."

"What about our project?" Ryan asked.

"Fuck the project! That's the least of our worries. We have to let it go."

"Fine. I won't tell anyone, not even Star. And you can't tell Sarrie, either, right?"

"Right," Will agreed. "Total silence. That's our best strategy. Agree?"

"Agree."

Will stalked out without another word, leaving Ryan alone with his thoughts and his grief. Ryan picked up his video game controller and put it away in a shoebox, which he shoved under his bed.

Chapter 6
The Scene of the Crime

THAT SUNDAY NIGHT – actually 2:19 a.m. Monday morning – the clearing skies over Manhattan dropped the temperature into the high teens, turning the accumulated slush on the streets and sidewalks to thick ice. The Cannon sat impatiently in the front passenger seat of a black Ford Explorer parked on the north side of 12th Street, near the corner of Avenue B. Cannon and his three companions could clearly see the yellow crime scene tape stretched across the doorway of the storefront once owned by Lou Palazzo. The silent foursome watched a police cruiser crunch up the icy street. The same car, with ID number 5524, drove past the storefront at 1:20, a few minutes after Cannon's crew arrived at their surveillance position.

"OK. We wait ten minutes, then we move," Cannon said without looking at his posse.

The forensics team and the last officers had packed up at 11:45, not bothering to leave a live guard at the crime scene. Once the bodies were removed and the tech teams finished taking photos and sweeping the interior for prints and fibers, there was little to protect. The last officers on the scene used Lou's keys to lock the front door, then pulled down the metal mesh security screen to cover the shop's windows. They didn't have the combination for the lock on the gate, so they left it loose. The storefront appeared secure.

Cannon figured the police cruiser would swing by every hour or so to make sure the scene remained undisturbed. It was possible the cops wouldn't even bother with the hourly checks after the 2 a.m. drive-by, but he wasn't taking any chances.

The Explorer's passenger compartment was freezing. A half hour earlier, one of the men recruited for the excursion, Hunter Lebowsky, asked if they could run the heater for a few minutes. Hunter was new and didn't know any better. Starting the engine to run the heater would identify the car as occupied. Even engaging the electrical system without running the motor would activate the running lights and mark them as a stake-out. They could all live with the cold rather than getting chased away and missing their chance to complete their assignment. Cannon emphasized his point with several colorful expletives and a smack across Hunter's face with the back of his hand. The move was particularly impressive since Hunter was in the back seat. Hunter promptly stopped complaining.

Mo, a burly Black man whose chest was barely contained by his leather jacket, laughed at Hunter from the front passenger seat. "Boss, if we're goin' in there soon, maybe you should tell us what we're lookin' for. It'll keep Hunter's mind off his frozen nuts."

After another good round of laughs at Hunter's expense, Cannon sighed and rubbed his gloved hands together. He had been a soldier, then a leader, then a lieutenant in the Gallata organization for fifteen years. Slick Mick had recruited him after his brother, Marco, proved his loyalty by taking a beating at the hands of the police rather than flip on the family. When Marco was unfortunately killed while in state prison, Slick Mick took care of Lloyd's mother and her surviving kids.

When Lloyd finished his tour of duty in the Marines, "Uncle" Mick made sure he had a job.

At this point in his career, The Cannon figured he was due for another promotion. Handling this transaction with the Chinese was an opportunity for him, but he had messed it up. But maybe it wasn't fully botched, yet. That was why he was freezing his ass off at two in the morning instead of being snug in his king-sized bed next to his hot Italian wife. Nobody had explained to Cannon what exactly was in the hacked file their Chinese colleagues wanted so badly, but it was clearly valuable to them – and to Fat Albert. That was enough.

Cannon did not like the Chinese agents, who had shown up a few years earlier after the boss made a deal for an exchange of information and resources. The Chinese showed up only when they needed help from the New Yorkers. He assumed the arrangement went both ways, but he didn't know what operations Fat Albert was running in Shanghai. Cannon was aware of six Chinese agents who were permanently located in The Big Apple. There could have been more that he didn't know about. They acted like they were in charge – and never said thank you. In the past week, several new Chinese had arrived. Most of the new guys didn't speak much English, like the two gunmen the Chinese boss sent with Cannon to Lou Palazzo's store. He could do without all of them, but he wanted to make his boss happy. That was how you got ahead in the organization. At least, it used to be.

"Alright, listen up, you morons. The boss made a deal with the boss from Shanghai. I hate calling their syndicate the Corporate Dragons, which is a horseshit name, but it's easier than pronouncing the Chinese words. Apparently, our Chinese friends ran a computer hacking scam and tricked a dipshit college student into letting them download data from NYU's system onto the kid's computer. The Chinese want that data. They want it a fuckload. They needed some help, so they offered the boss a bundle. Which means *he* wants that data. Which means *I* want that fucking data. Which means that you morons want that fucking data. If we do this right, we'll all get a bonus. Even Hunter-the-Idiot."

"Why are we here if this college kid has the data?" Charlie asked from behind Cannon. Charlie was five years on the Gallata team, the last three working under Cannon. He had earned enough respect from his boss that he was allowed to ask questions.

"The Dragoons figured out who the kid was." Cannon used the derisive parody of the Chinese mob's name. "The big boss in China wanted us to find him and lift his computer. It was supposed to be an easy gig."

"So?" Charlie asked, "Why didn't we grab the kid, squeeze him a little, and take his computer?"

"That was the plan," Cannon said, "but the Dragoons didn't know for sure what computer the data file was on and didn't want to lose it by tipping the kid off or having to kill him. So, The Dog broke into the kid's dorm, figuring to nab his laptop. But it wasn't there and neither was the kid. The backup plan was to put a bug in his room. So, now we have the new guy, Lenny, listening to him. Lenny figured out the kid didn't have the file. He gave it to his uncle because he couldn't figure out how to get past the Chinese encryption or some shit. Turns out the uncle was Lou Palazzo. He used to work for the family and I knew him from years ago. He's a computer specialist."

"OK, so," Charlie cut in, "if this Lou guy had connections, he should have made a deal."

"No shit," Cannon lashed back. "He tried. Like I said, Lou knew me from the old days. We did some time together. He called me and said he had a hacked file of data and said it could be worth a bundle. He was working on breaking the encryption. I sent him five grand as a holding fee and told him I'd give him another hundred Gs once he got the file open – if it turned out to be worth anything. I don't think Palazzo knew where the file came from. He called me about the hacked file before the Chinese boss reached out to Fat Albert. Once we were clued in and Lenny heard the college kid say he gave the file to his Uncle Lou, we figured it out."

Charlie loudly cleared his throat to get his boss' attention. "I still don't get it. You already agreed to pay Lou for the file. So, why didn't you pay him and get it?"

Cannon turned his head away, not wanting Charlie to see him snarl. "The Chinese boss insisted that I take two of his helpers when I came to visit Palazzo. The plan was to convince him to give up the file for free. I was even going to pay him a little more, but the Chinese didn't want to cover the full hundred Gs and Fat Albert didn't want to take a haircut on his profit. I'm sure I could have convinced Lou to give up the file for a small additional payment, once I explained that it was our Chinese friends who hacked the data in the first place. But the stupid Dragoon dudes flashed their pieces and idiot Lou decided to pull out a shotgun and get himself killed instead of making a deal."

"I thought you got the dude's laptop after you dropped him," Charlie said.

"I did. And his phone. But I was kinda in a rush, seeing as how the cops were gonna be busting in as soon as they figured out who he was. It's a fucking electronics store. I didn't have time to grab all the computers and gadgets where old, dead Lou might have stashed the file. That's why we're here. We may already have the file, but I need to be sure. We bust in, grab every computer and phone and hard drive we can find, then get the fuck out and let the tech boys figure out where the file is. Should be a quick grab. Even you morons should be able to handle it."

At 2:25, Cannon said it was a safe bet that the cruiser wouldn't be coming by again until after 3:00 and released his cold crew from the Ford Explorer. They slipped and slid their way across the street to the doorway to Lou's Electronics & Pawn. Cannon lagged behind, still limping from getting cracked on the knee.

Cannon said, "OK, Hunter. Do it."

The main reason Hunter was along on this high-value excursion was his proficiency in lock-picking. They could bust down the door after getting the security screen up, but Cannon was keen on stealth rather than smash-and-grab for this project. Hunter was happy to find the security screen unlocked and cracked the door lock in under two minutes. The crew stepped from the cold street into the nearly-as-cold shop. At least the frozen conditions tamped down the stench of death permeating the still-bloody space. Cannon saw the keypad for an alarm system next to the door, but the cops didn't have the code needed to set it, leaving only the deadbolt to prevent their entrance.

Over the next twenty minutes, Cannon's crew filled four large canvas bags with merchandise. Anything with a hard drive was on the shopping list. They found a drawer full of thumb drives and several peripheral hard drives, three laptops, a dozen cell phones, and even an old desktop tower unit they ripped from its CAT5 cable in Lou's rear office.

Before finishing up, Mo and Hunter circled around the corner and visited the second-floor apartment above the shop where Palazzo lived. They rolled through the small unit, finding two more thumb drives and an old laptop covered in dust and buried under a stack of DVDs. They took it anyway.

As the clock approached 3:00 a.m., Cannon ordered the crew to wrap up. They returned the crime scene tape to some semblance of its former position on the way out and pulled down the metal security screen. Cannon wondered whether the cops would even notice the shop had been visited by Santa's helpers in the night. While walking carefully across the icy street to the Explorer, he was determined to come through for Fat Albert. He had botched the first visit. He wasn't going to fail again.

Chapter 7
Pawn Shop Puzzle

MONDAY MORNING, Mike arrived at the precinct house on 94th Street at his usual time of 8:45. The icy sidewalks of the Upper West Side, which building owners were supposed to shovel and salt, had been treacherous. The walk from his apartment on 68th Street left his hands cold, his socks slightly soggy, and his temperament decidedly grumpy.

As always, Jason was there first, enjoying a hot coffee and a whole wheat bagel. Mike grunted a greeting while hanging up his overcoat. "Don't you have a toddler at home to delay your arrival at work?"

"Yeah, but I also have a wife who doesn't have to be at work until noon and a mother-in-law. So, I'm a lucky man," Jason quipped back.

Before Mike got settled into his desk chair, their captain poked his head out from the corner office door and bellowed, "Stoneman! Dickson! A minute, please."

Captain Edward Sullivan was a ruddy Irishman with large hands and a perpetually red, bulbous nose. Like every other cop in history named Sullivan, he was called "Sully" by everyone in the unit. He was a bulldog in supporting his detectives, but also held them accountable when they screwed up. Sully ran a tight ship and would quickly ream out any cop who didn't toe the line, but always with the office door closed.

Mike and Jason silently filled the two guest chairs in Sully's office. They expected an interrogation about Jason's report on the prior night's events.

"Only eight total hours of overtime, huh?" Sully studied the brief summary of the triple murder. "This report doesn't make it seem like a simple case. Gimme the quick version, Stoneman."

Mike looked at Jason and shrugged. Although Jason wrote the report, Mike was the senior member of the team and Sully usually wanted to hear from him first.

"The first stiff – the one that prompted the original call – was shot in the head in an intersection downtown, a block away from his pawn shop. Name was Lou Palazzo. He did three years in the New York State men's club more than a decade ago as a Gallata soldier, but seems to have been pretty clean since then. He was shot in the shoulder before the head shot."

Mike paused to make sure Sully was following, but his head was buried in the printout of Jason's report.

Mike continued. "One witness saw a bald guy in a tan overcoat walking away from the intersection, but we got no better description. The uniforms will be out this morning, looking for any street cams that might show his face. Meanwhile, we went to the dead guy's shop and found two extremely dead Asian males with no ID and what appeared to be shotgun wounds. We also found a shotgun that we're guessing belonged to the owner. There was at least one shot fired at the shop owner, but there were no shell casings and no guns. So, it looks like the guy who executed Mr. Palazzo went back to the shop and cleaned up. There was some merchandise missing, including what we think was a laptop computer. We're going back this morning to do a closer inspection now that the bodies are gone. We'll see if the ME can get us an identification on our two dead Asians. Anything else, Jason?"

When Sully raised his head from the paperwork, Jason said, "That's about it, Cap."

"I see it got some press." Sully looked directly at Jason. "That figures, being a triple murder. You two make this a priority. I'm sure the commissioner's office will be calling. If the dead guy is an ex-con and the two others are somebody's muscle, the media wolves may not give a shit. Let's keep a lid on it. Understood?"

"Understood, Sully," Jason said softly. Nobody mentioned that Jason's wife was one of the media members who had reported on the case.

"Well, get to it!" Sully shouted loudly enough for the other cops out in the bullpen to hear.

Mike followed Jason to his desk as the other detectives either expressed their commiseration or chuckled softly. They all dreaded a weekend call turning into a time suck case on top of their regular files. As it happened, Mike and Jason were not in the middle of anything particularly hot and had some time.

"Did you and Rachel talk about how to maintain appropriate confidentiality on this?" Mike asked.

"No, Mike, we did not. She didn't talk about it, and I didn't talk about it. We're both well aware of the problem and how to handle it."

"Fair enough." Mike sat on the corner of Jason's pitted wooden desk. "When do you want to head downtown?"

"Give me ten minutes to wrap up one thing. You want to get a car? You look like you could use a heater today."

Mike laughed. "Is it that obvious?" Then he added, "Don't answer. Sure. I'll be happy to grab a ride and avoid the subway, and the sidewalk. I could have given out twenty tickets this morning for uncleared sidewalks."

* * *

BY THE TIME MIKE AND JASON PARKED the unmarked sedan in the loading zone in front of Lou's Electronics & Pawn, a cold drizzle was transforming the ice into a slippery glaze. Mike figured he would give Lou Palazzo a pass on not clearing the ice from his sidewalk.

"I'll start working on the books and records," Jason said. "See if you can figure out what the killer was looking for in the detritus. Hopefully, we'll get an ID on the two Asian stiffs after Dr. McNeill finishes the autopsies."

"Who knows," Mike said, "maybe something about their injuries will give us an angle. But I'm betting Palazzo's prints will be the only ones on that shotgun and the forensics will tell us exactly the story we expect."

A uniformed officer stood next to the shop door. Mike apologized for making Officer Evans stand out in the cold rain.

"No problem, Detective," Evans replied more jovially than Mike expected. "I got warmers in my boots." Evans pulled a key ring from his topcoat's deep pocket. From the chain dangled a furry rabbit's foot and a tiny black falcon statuette. After lifting up the metal mesh screen covering the store windows, Evans turned the key clockwise. It did not move and there was no clunk from the deadbolt.

"Problem, Evans?" Jason asked.

The officer straightened and grabbed the knob. It turned easily, allowing the door to swing inward. "Sir, this door is unlocked."

"I thought you locked it up after the ME removed the stiffs," Mike said.

"I did, Sir. We got the key from the owner's coat pocket. You left instructions to secure the scene, which I did. I checked it. Somebody unlocked this door between midnight and when I got here at seven o'clock. We had a patrol car checking on the place through the night and got no reports of any activity."

Mike's face resembled that of a man who found his new car dented in a parking lot. "We didn't leave an officer here to guard the crime scene?"

Evans swallowed hard. "No, Sir. I called in for it, but dispatch said there was no unit available because of the snow. I was instructed to lock up and that the patrols would be sufficient."

Mike and Jason made eye contact. "Weapons," Jason said calmly.

All three cops produced their service pistols. Mike and Jason assumed positions on either side of the door, then Mike signaled Evans to go inside. He pushed through the door, gun extended in front of him. The two detectives rolled in behind, forming a triangle. Within a few minutes, they cleared the interior, determining that there was no one inside. They holstered their weapons.

Regrouping at the front door, Mike instructed Evans to go outside and call for a backup unit. Mike scanned the room, noting the markers on the still-bloody floor where the two bodies had lain. The cold had frozen the blood and kept the smell manageable. Mike immediately noticed that the main retail space looked more ransacked than the night before. Glass cases that were closed and locked now hung open. Shelves had been stripped of contents. The display cases under the main counter were even more jumbled. The floor was covered with bloody footprints. Mike wasn't sure, but suspected they had multiplied since the night before.

Jason stated the obvious. "Somebody came in overnight."

"Ya think?" Mike picked up a pink cell phone cover and tossed it back inside the case from which it came. "Is there any point calling the forensics team back to dust for new prints?"

"If it was somebody unconnected to the killings, running the prints would distract us."

"That lock wasn't smashed," Mike observed. "Somebody had a key, or it was picked."

Jason agreed. "If our visitor was connected to the killer and the two dead Asians, there's not likely to be anything helpful. But I guess we should, just to follow protocol. How about after we get finished?"

"Sure." Mike pulled out latex gloves from his inner pocket. "Let's suit up and treat it as a fresh crime scene again."

Jason spun slowly, taking in the entire room. "The bald guy who took out poor Lou came back here immediately afterward. He wasn't just cleaning up the brass; he was looking for something. But he didn't have time to find it after the shooting. Makes sense. Didn't have long before the responding officers were going to show up. So he came back later to finish the search. The question is, did he find it?"

"And what was it?" Mike stepped back into the shop. "You go to the back room and work on the documents, like we planned. See if you can get into the computer back there. I'll try to make heads or tails of this pile of shit."

* * *

AN HOUR LATER, Mike joined Jason in the small office in the back of the store where Lou Palazzo kept his records. The cramped quarters were adjacent to a rear door locked with a solid deadbolt. The path of destruction inside was only slightly less noticeable than in the front of the store. It was obvious that someone had searched the office. A flat-screen computer monitor lay broken on the floor. Mike was certain it was perched on the desk the night before.

"Anything useful?"

Jason carefully arranged a stack of papers, slid them into a manila folder, and returned it to the bottom-right drawer of a metal file cabinet that looked to be government surplus. A black wire taped to the desktop snaked down to a keyboard in a slide-out tray. The gray cord of a computer mouse disappeared into the crack between desk and wall. If there had been a desktop computer tower connected to the keyboard, mouse, and broken monitor, it was missing.

"Zip." Jason rolled his neck one circle around his shoulders. "The guy kept decent records. Seems to be paying his bills but not making a ton of profit. Can't say I'm shocked about that from the looks of the place. Nothing obviously criminal or suspicious. Nothing I would want to kill him over."

Mike's phone rang with the theme song from *The Addams Family*. He placed the unit on the desk and pushed the answer and speaker buttons. "Michelle, Jason and I are alone. You're on speaker. What have we got?"

The county medical examiner, while on duty and on an official call, always kept things professional. But she appreciated her husband confirming that there were no outside ears listening. "This is only preliminary. We don't have lab work back yet. But the print reports are back and I can give you the obvious causes of death. Lou Palazzo is positively ID'd based on his prints. The shot to his right shoulder was a single slug with a clean entry and exit wound. It would have bled a ton, since it severed an artery, but it would not have been fatal for a while. In fact, it would not have killed him at all if he got proper medical attention. The kill shot to his head was another single slug. It definitely came after the first wound. The two Asian males appear to be Chinese, but we're running DNA for that. Neither of them have prints on file or any ID on them, so they are John Doe #107 and #108 for now. Both suffered multiple penetrations by buckshot, likely from the shotgun you found. That's the cause of death for both."

"Anything of note about the John Does?" Jason asked.

"Only one had gunpowder residue on his hand. Will that be all, Detective Stoneman?"

"OK. Thank you, Doctor McNeill," Mike replied stiffly. They often played this game of pretending to be detached professionals when other people were around. Mike could never be sure when there was someone listening on Michelle's end. "Let us know when the lab work comes back if there's anything significant."

Mike ended the call and furrowed his brow in Jason's direction. His partner was swiping his finger down his phone screen vigorously. "What's up there?"

"Report from forensics. The only prints on the shotgun are Palazzo's. Not that surprising. The blood on the ground outside the shop is also his type."

Mike walked to the office wall, where a framed photo showed Lou at what looked like a high school graduation. Palazzo's arm was thrown around a young man wearing a black gown with a gold mortarboard and gold tassel, holding a diploma case and smiling ear to ear. The frame bore the inscription *Class of 2022*. Next to it hung a black-and-white photo of a man Mike recognized as actor Humphrey Bogart. It was signed in blue ink. On the opposite wall, slightly askew, hung a color poster from the movie *The Treasure of the Sierra Madre*. "He doesn't look like a mobster."

"What does a mobster look like?" Jason retorted. "From what we know, the guy was connected and did a stint in prison, then stayed clean since he got out. Maybe he successfully disengaged from the family. It can happen, especially if he did his time and kept his mouth shut."

"Yeah, sure," Mike said absently, still staring at the photo. The recent shot, framed and mounted in a position of prominence, suggested that this kid was someone important to Lou. Mike knew from his bio that Lou had never married and had no kids. He plucked the photo from its hook and left the office. In the hallway, he stopped and turned to Jason. "Why did he shoot?"

"Who?"

"Palazzo." Mike wandered back toward the bloody counter at the front of the store. "If these three guys confronted him, likely all with guns, why would he pull out his shotgun and go at them one-on-three? Why fight?"

"He was protecting something he was willing to die for."

"Yeah. But what?"

Jason waved an arm around the room. "It looks like they nabbed every computer in the place. Seems likely that what they were looking for was something digital."

"Probably," Mike agreed. "So, it could be anything. A video, a document, a program, the access code to a trove of bitcoin, or a thousand other things. Maybe we should search Lou's apartment, in case the treasure of the Sierra Madre wasn't here in the store. The report on him says he lives in an apartment in this building."

"And we'll see if our mysterious searcher has been there," Jason added.

Mike inspected a wire running across the ceiling from a bulky camera mounted over the cash register. It led down the far wall behind the counter, where it ended in two bare, frayed wires instead of a recording system. "Looks like Lou was more concerned with privacy than security. OK. We've got the uniforms looking for any street video that might help us, right?"

"Yes."

"Fine. Let's wait to see if it helps. For now, I think we're about done here." Mike took one more scan around the frozen, gory scene.

Fifteen minutes later, Mike and Jason, along with two uniformed officers, opened the door of the rear apartment on the second floor above the store. The interior closely resembled the pawn shop. It was clear the place had been searched. The sofa cushions were not cut open, nor the clothing removed from the open drawers, but somebody thoroughly went through the place. Next to a flat-screen television mounted on a stand made from thick, polished hardwood, Mike noticed a full-sized black falcon statuette matching the one on Lou Palazzo's keychain. There was no sign of a computer or mobile phone. After ten minutes of looking, they abandoned the exercise. There was nothing of significance to be found.

Chapter 8
In the Game

RYAN TRUDGED THROUGH Monday's cold drizzle to meet Will for lunch at a café on 13th Street that took NYU dining credits for payment. After he enjoyed a succulent turkey, lettuce, and tomato on basil-parmesan bread and a can of Diet Coke while Will devoured a cheeseburger, they set out for Ryan's dorm.

When there was nobody nearby, Will couldn't hold back his frayed emotions. "Dude, I'm still fully freaked out about your Uncle Lou."

"I know. I feel the same way." Ryan shoved his cold hands into his pockets. "But we can't talk about it. Remember?"

They continued to walk in tense silence until they reached an intersection where they waited for a WALK signal.

"I have something I need to tell you." Will put a hand on the sleeve of his friend's polyester jacket. "I know all this has to be super-secret and all. But . . .I told Sarrie." When Ryan did not respond, the confession poured out like a spilled drink. "She came over late last night after Star texted her about what happened. She could tell I was freaked out. I told her it was nothing, but she said if I was hiding important things from her, then she couldn't trust me. Man, you know how it is. I swore her to secrecy. She won't tell anyone. But I had to. I mean, she's the only girl I ever—"

"Not here," Ryan said in a hushed whisper.

The light turned and they crossed McDougal Street, not saying another word until Ryan closed his dorm room door behind them.

"Will, this is going to get us both expelled if we get caught. But I get it. You couldn't keep it secret from Sarrie. I told Star, too."

Will's jaw dropped. He reached out and shoved Ryan, who toppled across the three feet of empty floor before landing on his tiny bed. "You asshole! You let me spill my guts and you did the same thing?"

"Yeah, well, Star called last night after you left. She could tell something was really wrong from the way we were acting. She forced it out of me."

"Over the phone?"

"Yeah. It was – you know I can't keep a secret from her. She did that 'y'all' thing and, well . , ."

The two boys shared a relieved laugh. They were computer nerds, not spies. Girls were their kryptonite.

"But, nobody else, right?" Ryan's voice displayed all the worry he felt.

"God, no! Nobody. It would be suicide. If the school finds out that we hacked their server—"

"We didn't hack the server!" Ryan shot back.

"Sure." Will folded himself onto the floor. "*They* hacked the server. We just watched. It wasn't our fault."

"It wasn't *your* fault. But it was my account. I'm the one they'll be coming after." Ryan rolled over on the New York Mets comforter covering his mattress and scooped up a black game controller from the floor under his headboard. "OK. It's you, me, Sarrie, and Star. That's it. Did you tell Sarrie everything?"

"Pretty much. I told her about the data file and how we got hacked and how we gave the file to Lou to see if he could decrypt it. I guess he didn't. You think it was the hackers who killed him?"

"I don't know, dude. I don't see how they could know that Lou had the file. Unless he told somebody. It doesn't matter now. We gotta forget about it. Pretend it never happened."

"Yeah. I know." Will sat down next to his friend, switched on the TV, and slid a thin, black, rectangular box out from under the bed. Ryan plugged into his laptop computer. Within a minute, they were playing *Blades of Karma*. "It's weird doing this without Lou, right?"

"I know. We almost never played without him. I keep expecting his avatar to come around the corner any minute. He was a fun guy."

They played in silence, except for shouts of instructions to each other. When they completed the session and returned to the menu, Ryan said, "Dude. Look!" He pointed toward the screen. "There's a message in my inbox. It's from Uncle Lou!"

"That's creepy. It's like a message from beyond the grave."

"Yeah, but you know Lou was always sending me his little notes, telling me to study harder or asking about Star. It's probably one of those."

"OK, so open it already."

Ryan hesitated. "It's totally bizarre, getting a note from him after he's dead. Maybe I should just leave it?"

"No possible way! If you don't open it, I'll do it for you."

"Fine. Fine. I'll do it." Ryan navigated to the flashing envelope on the screen. After he clicked on it, the envelope sparkled and burst open like it was revealing the winner of an Oscar. The boys read the message simultaneously:

If I'm ever gone, find the secret path. The falcon is uncaged and it's in the game.

"What the hell?" Ryan blurted out. "What's he talking about? What does he mean, 'If I'm gone?'"

"You think he's talking about the file? When did he send it?"

"It's from yesterday at 5:05 p.m. So, that was before he was murdered."

Will rolled his eyes. "*Of course* it was before he was murdered! He didn't write it from the afterlife. But what was he trying to tell you? It's like he was worried that he wouldn't be around, so he sent you a message. You think the falcon means the file? And what secret path?"

"It has to be a *Maltese Falcon* reference, and it has to be important or he wouldn't have sent it inside the game. He knew I'd see it, and he must have been worried about sending a text or email. You know how paranoid Lou was about electronic messages being intercepted."

"Dude, his message was in the Sony cloud," Will said. "It could also be hacked."

"Sure, but who would know to look for it here?" Ryan paced around the ten square feet of open space in his dorm room. "And even this message is cryptic, like Lou was worried somebody else would see it. He wants us to understand and find the file. Nobody else would be able to figure it out."

"Dude, *I* don't understand," Will threw his hands into the air. "All I know for sure is that we gotta find the file. If the guys who killed Lou get it and use it, we'll be so screwed."

* * *

IN A SPARSELY APPOINTED BASEMENT office, Lenny Martin listened to the boys' voices through a headset.

Lenny's cousin, Eddie, had promised to get him some work for the Gallata organization. Eddie was doing well working for the family. At least, that's what he claimed. After years of hounding, Eddie got Lenny a gig driving an expensive car from Boston to Brooklyn. That job became much more complicated than anyone expected when a dog and a girl got involved, but Lenny came out of it in decent shape, in the sense that he was not dead.

Eddie put Lenny in touch with a guy named The Cannon, who was supposed to be high up. It turned out to be another shit job. He was told to listen to a college kid and his friends, and tell The Cannon if anything important happened. He also was told to follow instructions from a Chinese boss named Yung Ji, a short man with black-rimmed glasses. The Cannon did not explain to Lenny how Yung Ji and his underlings were connected to his listening project. Lenny knew better than to ask questions.

There were usually two or three Chinese men in the cavernous room where The Cannon had set up the listening station. They barely spoke English, except for Yung Ji. From the looks and smell of the place, Lenny figured that the Chinese guys were living in the office building. Lenny figured their assignment was possibly even worse than his. At least Lenny got to go home at night.

Lenny knew that one of Cannon's guys, called "The Dog", planted the bug and he was listening for information about a laptop computer or a data file. If the kid said anything about having the laptop with the file on it, he was supposed to tell The Cannon immediately. Most of the time, the room where the bug was planted was vacant and silent. His headphones were hooked up to a laptop computer in front of Lenny that pinged – loudly – whenever the bug picked up conversation. Lenny got to eat or piss only when the bug was inactive. The problem was that whenever a police siren blared outside the window or the noisy guy in the next room yelled loudly enough, the damned bug activated, the system pinged, and Lenny was compelled to pay attention. It sucked, but he was determined to do the job as well as it could be done. He wanted a better assignment next time.

Lenny was pretty sharp. He put together a few snippets of conversation and figured out that Ryan and his friend, Will, had been in possession of the data file, but it was encrypted and they couldn't open it. Ryan and Will didn't mention what computer the file was on until Lenny heard them say they had copied the file to a thumb drive and taken it to Ryan's uncle, Lou. The boys did not mention Lou's last name, but The Cannon seemed to know who he was. Cannon told Lenny not to mention this information to the Chinese boss and said he was going to handle the retrieval of the data file himself. He told Lenny to take the weekend off from the listening assignment.

When Lenny arrived in the listening room Monday morning, he thought his job was done and that he'd be getting a pat on the back for solving the mystery. That was before The Cannon told him what happened Sunday night. Now, Lenny was sharing the open office space with a whole gang. There were four techs from the Gallata family and four Chinese guys spread out at a long series of portable tables erected across the room. The tables were strewn with a hodge-podge of equipment – laptops, a desktop tower, cell phones, disembodied hard drives, and small thumb drives. Each man around the table worked from his own laptop. Power cords snaked into the gap in the middle of the row of pushed-together tables and disappeared into the void where they plugged into power strips on the floor.

The Gallata techs clued in Lenny about the operation and how The Cannon and his team had cleaned out Lou Palazzo's electronics shop. And that The Cannon wasted old Lou. Lenny felt a pang of sadness about the death of the man about whom Ryan and Will spoke so fondly.

Lenny moved his work table to the far end of the space so he could hear better. He was supposed to continue listening because The Cannon wasn't sure whether the mysterious data file was on one of the drives they lifted from Lou's store. The joint Chinese/Gallata crew was looking for it. But until they found it, Lenny needed to keep up his surveillance. Lenny was not thrilled, but figured it was another chance to do something right and get some recognition from The Cannon.

Yung Ji lounged near the room's makeshift kitchen. It had a sink, a coffee maker, and a refrigerator. Ji smoked and chatted with one of his team in Chinese. The Gallata techs smoked and drank beer on their side of the long table, talking about football. They all ignored Lenny.

Lenny's stomach was rumbling when he heard Ryan say something about "the file" and a message from his uncle. He bookmarked the spot on the audio file, then sent a text to The Cannon. Lenny's instructions were to send Cannon the important parts, then wait a while before sharing with the Chinese boss.

Ten minutes later, Lenny called Ji over with a shout. Once, he made the mistake of whistling to get the man's attention. Whistling in public was rude, Ji told him after slapping him across the face. Now, Lenny gave his best attempt at a Mandarin greeting instead.

"You hear something?" Ji asked Lenny, without any preliminary pleasantries.

"Yeah. Maybe. Ryan said something about a message from his Uncle Lou, and he mentioned the file, and a falcon. I marked the spot."

"I will listen," the Chinese boss snapped, grabbing the headphones off Lenny's head. "What is falcon?"

"I have no idea," Lenny responded. It was the truth, but Lenny might not have told him even if he knew. Ji never asked politely. All the Dragons treated him like a servant, even more so than the Gallatas.

After playing back the recording twice, the boss handed back the headset. "You keep listening. Make copy of what you heard and send to me." He turned and walked to the main work table, where he entered into an animated discussion in Chinese with one of his techs.

Lenny was left to return to his surveillance, but the room was now quieter. He listened to the parts he missed while the Chinese boss was using his headset and made a mental note to get a second one. He made a second copy of the dialogue clip he had already sent to The Cannon, then attached it to a text message to Ji. He didn't send it right away.

Chapter 9
On the Story

O N MONDAY, Rachel begged Dave Butler to let her continue to follow the story she referred to as the "triple murder" that she started Sunday evening. Dave was torn between not wanting to cover the story at all and wanting to assign a more senior reporter. But Rachel was persistent, and since her husband, the homicide detective, was working the case, he assumed she would have inside information. Dave couldn't turn down the chance for a scoop. He allowed her to chase the story, but told Rachel he expected exclusive information.

While Jason and Mike were inside Lou's Electronics & Pawn reviewing the physical evidence, Rachel canvased the neighborhood, talking to locals. She wanted to put together a human interest story about the murdered shopkeeper. It was not what she promised Dave, but something she thought would resonate with viewers. She hoped to have something meatier soon, once the police investigation progressed, although she wasn't exactly sure where her exclusive material would come from. Jason told her about the two dead Chinese men inside Lou's shop, but only after the information was included in an NYPD press release about the prior night's murders.

After finding Mr. Aaronson on Sunday night, Rachel expected to meet dozens of neighborhood residents with fond memories of Lou, the local shopkeeper. To her surprise, after three hours of searching, she found none. A young mother named Claire, pushing a stroller down the chilly sidewalk, said she would never frequent a pawn shop. While patting down her baby's plush blanket, Claire said the only people she ever saw going in or out were "seedy." An elderly man exiting an apartment building refused to give his name, but said he had never been inside "that ratty place." Apparently, old Lou was not the loveable icon she hoped to portray.

Edgar Edgardo, the cameraman assigned to Rachel for the day, dutifully followed along as Rachel grew more and more frustrated. Born in the Dominican Republic, Edgar (whose given name was Quito Zacharia) had been "Edgar" since his family moved to New York when he was six.

After another failed attempt with a middle-aged Black woman, who was friendly toward Rachel but had never met Lou, Edgar made a suggestion. "You should try talking to the cops."

"I know, but I can't talk to Jason – Detective Dickson – or Detective Stoneman." Rachel pouted into her hand-held microphone.

"They're not the only cops here, you know." Edgar cocked his head in the direction of a squad car parked near the pawn shop entrance. One uniformed officer stood near the door while his companion kept warm inside the car. Rachel turned and walked toward the far side of the street, away from the officers. A confused Edgar stood on the sidewalk, watching his reporter's backside. "Where you going?"

"Stay there," she said over her shoulder. "I'll be back with some ammunition."

Five minutes later, Rachel returned to a shivering Edgar holding a cardboard tray bearing four Starbucks cups. She handed him one. "Black with three sugars." Edgar happily accepted the offering, then scuttled behind Rachel. "Hang back," she said as they approached the police cruiser.

Flashing her brightest smile, Rachel stood next to the driver's window, tantalizingly displaying the remaining three cups. The other officer hurried over as his partner lowered the glass. "The press is not permitted here." He slipped on a patch of ice when he stepped off the curb. His name plate read *RODRIGUEZ.*

"I know, but you boys look cold and I figured you could use some hot coffee." Rachel held up a distinctive holiday red cup. She knew cold cops could never resist. Donuts would have been an obvious bribe, but coffee was a kindness. "I'd bring some for the detectives, but I'm not allowed to talk to Jason. You know, he always says you are the best at maintaining a crime scene, Officer Rodriguez." Rachel was not certain that this Rodriguez was the same officer on whom Jason often bestowed compliments, but it was worth a try.

"We know," Rodriguez said, removing his black glove and reaching for a cup. "Detective Dickson warned us that you might be coming around."

The officer inside the car emerged and helped himself to one of the two remaining cups. While the cops happily sipped the steaming liquid, Rachel carefully removed the final coffee and placed the tray on the cruiser's roof. She left a stain of red lipstick on the lid. "Mmmm," she purred, "why is their coffee so much better?"

"It's got a little cocaine in it," joked Officer Callahan, whose nameplate was now visible. Rachel laughed heartily and put her hand on his coat sleeve.

"Fine with me." She raised her cup in salute to great coffee. The two officers joined her and "clinked" their paper vessels. "I've been freezing my ass off out here looking for residents who knew the dead shopkeeper, but it seems that almost nobody hung out in the electronics store. It's a shame. The one person I found who knew him said he was a nice guy. It'll probably go unsolved, huh?"

"Depends on the cam footage," Callahan said as he lowered his cup after a long sip. The comment drew a glare from Rodriguez.

"I know. It always comes down to the security cameras. So many cases turn on the video. Like that one where the big Ukrainian wrestler carted the quarterback's body out of the building on the Upper West Side? That was a bizarre one." She lifted her eyebrows above her lipstick-stained cup as she enjoyed a deep draught.

"Oh, yeah," Rodriguez agreed, confirming to Rachel that he was indeed the same officer who worked with Jason on the Jimmy Rydell murder investigation back in 2019. "Poor Meyer got stuck looking at video for two solid days."

"You got spared that duty this time?" Rachel inquired.

"Yeah. We're stuck here guarding the frozen ghosts, though. But, could be worse." He held up the coffee and smiled.

"But it was pretty dark when the killers went in yesterday, so the video may not help much."

"Even darker when they came back in the middle of the night." Callahan laughed.

Rachel froze her lips in a tight smile. This was news. "I know," she lied. "It's so weird that a killer would come back to a crime scene. Where'd you find the camera?"

Rodriguez shrugged. "Across the street. The bank branch on the corner across there has an ATM. Somebody uptown should have the file by now. I don't envy that duty, although I'm sure it's in a warm room."

"I'm sure I'll hear all the details over dinner tonight." Rachel glanced toward the pawn shop and saw a tall figure near the door. Most likely it was Jason. "Well, stay warm, Officers. I'm off to find more neighborhood folks." She gave a quick wave and carried her nearly empty cup back to Edgar.

Five minutes later, she was set up to tape a shot from in front of the Citibank branch on the far corner, trying to capture the same view as the ATM security camera. She watched as Jason and Mike left the shop, conversed briefly with officers Rodriguez and Callahan, then walked to a dark sedan parked in a no-parking zone and left the scene. As they pulled away, Rachel nodded to Edgar and waited for the little red light atop the camera.

Rachel recorded a ninety-second report revealing that Lou Palazzo's killer had returned to the pawn shop in the middle of the night. "For what purpose? The police are still investigating and reviewing security video that might include images of the culprits. This is Rachel Robinson, reporting for ACN News."

Chapter 10
Panning for Gold

LLOYD CANNON WAS ANNOYED. The Chinese Dragon techs were jabbering away in Mandarin, or maybe Cantonese. He couldn't tell the difference. There were plenty of times that Fat Albert kept him in the dark about certain operations, but when he was supposed to be running the gig, he hated not knowing what the guys he was supposedly in charge of were saying. Fat Albert sent him to the boiler room to make sure he found out whether the Dragon techs found the data file. He suspected the Chinese boss might abscond with it without paying. So far, both the Gallata and Dragon techs had come up empty, as far as Cannon could tell. Each group was slowed down by the need to watch and listen to the other team. The Dragons held the advantage of knowing much more English than the Gallata techs knew Chinese.

The dank room was in the basement of an office building Fat Albert's accountant purchased out of a bankruptcy foreclosure during the COVID-19 pandemic. It was mostly vacant until early 2023, but now boasted seventy-five percent occupancy. Half of the tenants were connected to the family's criminal operations, while the other half were unsuspecting legitimate businesses. The sprawling subterranean space had no interior walls, except for a bathroom in the corner. It previously served as a factory floor for drug packaging and as a counting room for money being laundered through the organization's twenty-two Manhattan parking garages.

Today, the portable tables were strewn with computer equipment and cell phones. Eight men hunched over keyboards and monitors, searching the hard drives. On one side were four Gallata techs drinking Coke and Budweiser. On the other side, four Dragons chugged Red Bulls and something in a green can with characters Cannon could not read. Fat Albert promised the Gallata techs a $5,000 prize if they found the data file. Cannon knew the Chinese techs were promised a similar bounty, but didn't know what a million Yuan meant.

Cannon shook his head and tapped Sean "Red" Clancy on the shoulder, motioning him to step away from his work. Red sported a mop of auburn hair, a deep voice, and a Brooklyn brogue. He was also Fat Albert's chief technology officer. He ran the operation's cybersecurity, communications, and cyber-crime initiatives. When the boss dispatched Red for this treasure hunt, Cannon knew all he needed to know about the importance of the impromptu operation. It also indicated the shit he would be in if he failed to deliver the goods after killing the one guy who knew where the file was.

"What the fuck is the problem?" Cannon whispered, not wanting the Chinese crew to overhear.

Red slumped his shoulders. "It's a single file. It could have any name and could be on any of these hard drives. The guy had a load of computers in that shithole shop, plus the smart phones. It's a needle in a fucking haystack. If it's here, we'll eventually find it. But it's like finding one particular dollar bill in a pile of a million – or a hundred million. You gotta look at each one to see if it's the one you're looking for. We don't know how big it is, but at least we can rule out anything under one megabyte. Lou had a tech background. He was smart enough to give the file a coded name and make it hard to find. At least, if he suspected how valuable it is. I'd like to know what the bejesus is in that file the Dragons want so badly. All I know is that it's encrypted, or at least it was. So, if I find it, I probably won't be able to open it, unless old dead Lou got it unencrypted before you snuffed him. Do you know what kind of information is in the file?"

Cannon shook his head. "Fuck no. Some kind of data breach shit, so I'm assuming credit card numbers or Social Security numbers and such. But who the hell knows? All I know for sure is that the boss really wants to please these Chinese bastards. They must be paying a shitload for it. Did you give their guys the less likely gadgets?"

"Yeah. I think. Who knows? We have to hack the password on the laptop that we think belonged to Palazzo. That's the most likely place, but Joey hasn't cracked it yet."

"OK. Get back to it."

While Red resumed his file hunt, Cannon crossed to the opposite end of the cavernous space where Lenny sat at his cluster of portable card tables. Lenny wore over-the-ear headphones and stared intently at his phone. A computer and two monitors filled his table. Cannon tapped Lenny's neck, causing the man to jump.

"Pisser!" he shouted, snapping off his headphones. He changed his tone upon identifying his attacker. "Oh, sorry, Boss."

"Anything more from the student?"

"There was that one reference this morning. I sent you the clip, but nothing since. Ryan's Uncle Lou sent him some kind of message. He and Will said something about *The Maltese Falcon*. So far, they don't know what it means and they don't know where the file is."

"You're on a first-name basis with these shitheads?" Cannon inquired.

"Sorry, Boss. But they're not bad kids. They have no idea what they're dealing with."

"Yeah, well, don't get too attached. We may have to kill them."

Lenny looked sad, but quickly recovered. "I know that, Boss. It's no problem."

"OK. Make sure I'm the first to know if you get anything. I want it before these Chinese fuckers and I want our boss to have it before their boss."

"You mean so your ass won't get fried," Lenny quipped. "Whatever it's worth to the boss, it's worth twice to you, huh?"

"Shut the fuck up," Cannon scolded as he walked away from the surveillance table.

In the empty space between the card tables and the tech guys, he stopped and looked around. If they didn't find the data file on one of Lou's computers, maybe the two college kids would find it. So far it was clear they didn't know shit. But if they found anything useful, Cannon wanted it. The idiot kids didn't know they were bugged. If they found something, Lenny would know and they could extract it. The thought of having a contingency plan made Cannon feel better. He needed some good news. He rubbed the bruise above his right wrist and wished like hell he hadn't killed Lou.

Chapter 11
Spilling the Hill of Beans

THAT MONDAY EVENING after dinner, Ryan and Will met up with Star in Sarrie's dorm. Like Ryan and Will, Sarrie was a sophomore, which entitled her to a single room. Sarrie's was a superior group meeting space because it was clean and had two chairs. After Ryan told the girls about the message Lou left inside *Blades of Karma*, the boys resumed their speculation about its possible meaning.

Star held up her hands. "Stop! Just wait a minute. Ryan told me about the hack and how Lou was trying to decrypt the file, but maybe it would help if you told us the whole story. We need to know everything he knew. Like, for example, how did you get the file from the hackers?"

Over the next twenty minutes, Ryan and Will both tried to tell the story, interrupting and speaking over each other multiple times. They managed to spill out the essential information with some gentle prodding and encouragement from the ladies.

For their cybersecurity class, they came up with an idea to show how a hacker on the dark web might try to infiltrate a computer for nefarious purposes. They wanted to observe phishing and hacking behavior and develop countermeasures, but the main point was to capture the behavior and show it to their professor. They knew they were not supposed to be tramping around on the dark web, but they thought they had the situation under control. Until they didn't.

They used Will's old laptop, which he wiped and reformatted back to factory specs. They set it up with a peripheral monitor so they could see what was happening and rigged a video recorder to document what they saw, in case the drive got erased. They set up a pristine Gmail account and started surfing around for a site where they could purchase a discounted debit card. This, they figured, would lead them to someone selling stolen cards. They hoped that such sites might well be phishing scams where the operators would try to get them to click on links that would trigger a hacking attack. They were entirely correct.

After making contact with a seller, they got an email offering to sell them a $1,000 debit card for $200. When they clicked, the link triggered a hidden download of a "Trojan horse" program, which started running in the background. The boys watched in fascination as the clandestine program logged into Ryan's Google account, accessed his saved passwords, and logged into his NYU student account.

"Wait," Sarrie broke into the narrative. "You said there was nothing on that laptop. So, how could the hackers log into Ryan's account?"

"Because," Will grumbled, "Ryan just *had* to swap out a player on his fantasy football team. We were working in the basement of the computer science building, where he couldn't get a cell signal, so he used the laptop and logged into the fantasy website, which is linked to his Google account." He glared at Ryan, who looked away in shame.

"Fantasy football?" Star cast an incredulous glance at her boyfriend.

"It mattered, OK? It was important." Ryan's voice trailed off, knowing Star and Sarrie would be even less persuaded than Will.

"Anyway," Will continued, "As we watched, the program logged into Ryan's bursar's office payment account and started downloading a bunch of documents. At first, we thought it was only Ryan's account information, but after a while, it was clear they were downloading more than that. Somehow, the hackers got into other accounts. That shouldn't have been possible, but it happened. The hackers must have used an algorithm that got past the university's security. Once the hacker program was inside the NYU server, it could have accessed almost anything, including peoples' payment information, bank account details, and credit card numbers. Which is why we cut it off."

"What does that mean?" Star asked.

Ryan took Star's hand. "We disconnected from the internet. We were working on a hard-wired line, so we pulled the plug before the hackers finished downloading. We later found a file hidden inside a folder deep in the user account that the Trojan Horse program set up on the machine. We probably would have never found it except that there wasn't much else on the laptop to hide it. Anyway, we found the file, but we couldn't open it. It was protected by a sophisticated encryption."

"Why in God's name would you even want to?" Sarrie asked, looking at Star for confirmation. Star nodded. "I mean, you don't know what's in that file, or whether it's dangerous or whatever. You should have destroyed it."

The boys exchanged sheepish shrugs. "You're probably right," Ryan said. "We wanted to know because if it was something really critical, we were thinking that we maybe should tell somebody about it. Remember, we were working on a project. If we could have opened the file and figured out how the hackers broke through the NYU system security, it could have been gold for us. Plus, with the machine offline, the worst-case scenario is that the file would fry the hard drive."

Sarrie was stunned. "Couldn't you get in big trouble for letting the hackers in?"

"Yeah, of course," Will acknowledged. "But we also thought that if we found some vulnerability in the NYU security system—"

"—we were going to give it back to the school and be heroes and then maybe the school would give us a reward, or waive our tuition or something," Ryan said, realizing as he saw Star's doubtful expression that it had been a pretty stupid idea. "Well, anyway, we didn't want to take the file to the school until we knew what was in it, but we couldn't figure out how to access it. We researched it for a few days, but couldn't break it. So, we told Uncle Lou about it."

"Because he was some kind of computer genius, right?" Star asked.

"Right. Nobody knew more about computers and hacking than Uncle Lou. He told me to copy it to a thumb drive and bring it to him so he could work on it with his decryption software."

Sarrie asked, "So, you still have the file on your laptop, right?"

"No," Will said. "Once we gave the file to Lou, he told us to wipe the hard drive, leaving him with the only copy."

"But Uncle Lou had as much trouble getting past the encryption as we did. He was getting close," Ryan said. "At least, that's what he said when we last visited him on Sunday."

"Sunday!" Star and Sarrie both said at once.

Star said to Ryan, "You said the last time you saw your uncle was a week ago."

Ryan blushed and dropped his head. "Well, that was before I told you the truth about the hack. We visited Lou on Sunday afternoon. He was working on the file, so we didn't get to play any *Blades of Karma*. He was hoping that the crazy-hard encryption meant the file might be valuable. That's the last thing he said to me."

"Except for the message," Sarrie pointed out.

"Yeah. True," Ryan agreed. "But we still don't know what it means."

"Unless uncaged means unencrypted!" Will shouted, then lowered his voice. "Sorry. I mean, if Lou's message means he cracked the file and put it somewhere so we could find it, maybe we still might."

The girls stared with a combination of confusion and fear. Star softly said, "Are you sure that's a good idea? I mean, your uncle got murdered. If it had anything to do with that file, it could be dangerous."

"I know," Ryan said, "but if somebody else finds it and it turns out to be a big data breach, the university is going to crucify whoever was responsible, meaning us. We need to make sure that doesn't happen. Besides, if Uncle Lou died because of us – because of me – then I owe it to him."

Nobody responded. The room was filled with vacant stares of understanding mixed with fear. After a pause, Star put her arms around Ryan, who melted into her shoulder.

Will picked up the story, unwilling to leave it unfinished and wanting to impress Sarrie with his bravery. "Lou said we needed to keep the file totally secret. He said not to write about it or text about it at all. He was pretty paranoid. We told you how Lou loved his old movies. He used to let us watch some with him in the back room after he closed for the day. His favorite was *The Maltese Falcon*. So, after he started working on the file, he started referring to it in code. He called it 'the dingus' or 'the falcon', like in the movie."

"You know you are going to be in a shit-ton of trouble if the school finds out you've had this file now for so long and haven't said anything, right?" Sarrie said, reaching out to touch Will's elbow.

"Yeah. We know. At this point, our options are to forget about it and hope nobody ever finds it, or find it and hopefully turn it in to prove that there was never any actual breach."

"I think we can do it," Ryan said. "You two don't need to be involved. We'll handle it." He looked at Will, who gave him a clenched fist of affirmation. "But you have to promise to keep this secret. You can't say anything to anyone. Agreed?" Both boys looked at their girlfriends with pleading eyes.

"Fine," Sarrie said. "You probably won't find it anyway. Whoever killed your uncle must have it now, so it's gone. You can decide to turn yourselves in or not. If it were me, I guess I'd keep quiet and hope nobody ever finds out."

Star hesitated, then said, "OK. Fine. But my uncle is a cop. If you find anything that might be related to your uncle's murder, you have to tell him."

"OK," Ryan agreed.

Sarrie took control of the situation. "We're all in the shit on this now. If anyone finds out that Star and I knew about it and didn't report it, we'll be in almost as much trouble as you. Great. We had to ask. But now it's up to all of us to keep our mouths shut."

Sarrie embraced Will. Star did the same with Ryan.

Chapter 12
Roll Camera

A S SOON AS HE LOGGED into his NYPD email Tuesday morning, Mike received a message and a summary report from Officer Cheryl Ridgeway, who spent Monday afternoon and some off-the-clock time Monday night scrutinizing video from the Citibank ATM across the intersection from their crime scene. She also reviewed video from the intersection cameras on Avenue B, Avenue C, and 12th Street. The murder of Lou Palazzo and the two additional as-yet-unknown bodies constituted a significant case. Rachel's reports on ACN news spawned follow-on reporting by other local news outlets, which made Sully nervous.

"This is better than I thought," Jason said as he and Mike read through the information at their respective desks.

"Yeah. It's amazing we ever solved a case before there was video on every street corner." Mike was halfway out of his chair before he finished his sarcastic reply. "Let's brief Sully. We're gonna need more resources."

Four minutes later, the two detectives and Cheryl were jammed into Captain Sullivan's office. Jason walked Sully through the essential facts, embellished by the information they gleaned from their crime scene review.

Because of the snow, there were not many people walking on the sidewalks that Sunday. The ATM's camera observed a total of seven people entering and exiting the shop before the events at the end of the day. None appeared to be connected to the murders. Four were single individuals who appeared to be male. Everyone was bundled against the cold weather, including hats, gloves, and heads bowed against the elements. The video was not clear enough to make any IDs, but each person went in, stayed for between four and ten minutes, then left. A fifth visitor arrived in a cab, dashed inside wearing a light tan raincoat, then dashed back out to the same waiting cab a few minutes later. The camera got a decent image of the man's face, but they had not yet matched it to a name. The other two visitors were a pair of young men wearing down parkas and boots. They stayed for a half hour, including the duration of one of the other customers' visits. They left at 2:45 p.m.

"The action started at 5:32 p.m. The two Asian goons and the bald guy, then wearing a black hat, go into the shop. We see Lou stagger out. The bald guy chases him, catches him in the intersection, and gives him the head shot. But the cams aren't clear enough to make an ID. The bald guy's hat comes off during his struggle with Lou. Then he goes back to the shop and comes out again five minutes later. He gets into a dark SUV and drives away."

"So, nothing you didn't already know, right, Dickson?" Sully's impatient voice signaled it was time to pick up the pace.

"Until this," Jason said, turning the page on his notes and handing Sully a print of a still image. "This is from 2:15 a.m. Monday morning. We have an intersection cam from Avenue B that shows their car. Looks like the same dark Explorer, but the plates were covered. Four guys got out and walked across the intersection a few minutes after a squad car swung past the site to check on it. The intersection cam shows the car parked on the street at 1:06 a.m. Looks like they were waiting for our patrol to pass. The four guys walk over to the shop and one kneels down, lifts up the security screen, and picks the lock. They all go in, spend 45 minutes searching the place, and then come out carrying bags, which were likely full of computer equipment. One was carrying a big-ass tower unit. One guy came out ten minutes before the others and walked around the side of the building, where we think he entered and searched Palazzo's apartment on the second floor."

"OK." Sully studied the image. "Any ID on these guys?"

"The bald guy is there again," Mike said. "The others we can't ID, but we're working on it. Jason, tell him the good part."

Jason smiled and motioned to Cheryl. She fumbled with her notes for a moment, but composed herself and said, "Since there were so few cars on the street because of all the snow and ice, we were able to follow theirs over the intersection cams around the city. They drove into a parking garage on 9th Street, under an office building."

"Alright. Now we're getting somewhere. So, where's the car now?"

"We don't know, Sully," Mike said calmly. "You didn't authorize any overtime for this, so we got this report from Ridgeway a few minutes ago. Our next stop is to get some research on that building where the car parked. We don't have enough for a search warrant, but we'll see what we can dig up."

Sully fumed silently. He hated it when his decisions could be questioned after the fact, but he hated blowing his overtime budget slightly more. "Fine!" he bellowed. "Get going!"

Chapter 13
A New Source

TUESDAY MORNING AT ACN, Dave gave Rachel permission to take a cameraman and chase her triple-murder story for one more day. He had not been thrilled with her lack of a scoop on Monday, but the video generated enough views on their website that he was willing to try one more time. He wanted interviews with people who knew the dead guy and who could put some context around the tragedy, or with people who would say that Lou was a scumbag criminal whose mob-style execution was what he deserved. Either story was fine with Dave as long as it caused their audience to cry or wave their fists in anger toward the television.

Dave assigned Terry to be her cameraman. Rachel was comforted to have such an experienced partner. For years, Jason had told her how tough it could be to find witnesses willing to talk to you. She always believed it was a reflection of the public's general reluctance to speak to a cop. She now knew that people simply didn't like to talk on the record. Without any way to track down Lou's clients or business associates, and with no clear leads on any additional witnesses, Rachel asked a production assistant at ACN to track down Lou's relatives in the area. Surely his family would have something to say.

While they waited for the research, Terry suggested that Rachel do a re-creation. "Show the viewers the crime scene. Let 'em know how it happened."

"But I don't know exactly how it happened, Terry."

"Yeah, sure. But they don't know that. We could give 'em a show."

Lacking any alternate suggestions, Rachel allowed Terry to direct the piece. They started outside the shop, yellow police tape still strung across the threshold. "I'm standing outside the scene of a horrific crime that happened Sunday evening. This electronics shop on the corner of Avenue B and 12th Street was as quiet at 5:30 two days ago as it is now. The shopkeeper, Lou Palazzo, was inside tending to his customers and inventory when three armed gunmen stormed inside and confronted him. Palazzo fought back, killing two of his assailants with a shotgun. Palazzo then fled the scene down 12th Street in the snow, before a third man shot him in the head."

"Where'd you get that information about the shotgun?" Terry asked.

"From a reliable source inside the police department," Rachel said with a sly smile.

They stopped the camera and repositioned on the corner of 12th and Avenue C. There, Rachel continued the narrative of how Lou, already shot and bleeding, was executed, attributing the information to an eyewitness who preferred not to be identified. They couldn't get a good angle looking down the street because of the traffic. Terry settled for a wide shot taken when the traffic on the avenue was stopped for a red light. It was dramatic, even if it didn't add any new information.

When the story concluded, Terry instructed Rachel to stand back in front of the shop, angled so that the *Lou's*

Electronics portion was visible over her shoulder. There was no point in emphasizing the *Pawn Shop* side of the placard.

"This is Rachel Robinson, reporting for ACN." Rachel looked at Terry for encouragement. "What do you think?"

"OK," Terry said as encouragingly as he could manage. "Probably the best we're going to get."

"I guess I suck at this," she lamented.

"No, actually, you don't," Terry said without taking his eyes off the street. "You did well on camera. It's tough finding witnesses."

"Thanks," she mumbled, wondering whether Jason would agree. "I'm not trained as a journalist. I don't have any experience. I should just give up."

"Don't sell yourself short," Terry said. "You need a good producer to find sources. Don't get down on yourself. You did alright."

Rachel's ACN-issued phone rang. She composed herself and answered in her best professional video journalist voice, "Rachel Robinson speaking."

"You're the one who reported on the murder on 12th Street, right?" The voice was male, with a solid New York accent, but was hesitant. Rachel had not dealt with enough cold calls from potential sources to know whether that was unusual.

"That's right," Rachel replied encouragingly. When the man said nothing in reply, she continued, "Did you know the victim, Lou Palazzo?"

"Yeah. I mean, I knew who he was. But, um, I'm calling because I think we should, you know, meet. So we can talk. I might have, some, um, information you might want."

"Is it about Mr. Palazzo's murder?" Rachel wasn't sure this was a legitimate tip, but she wasn't going to jump to the conclusion that the caller was a fraud or a nut. After striking out all day, she was desperate for a break.

"Yeah. Like I said, we should talk."

"What's your name, Sir?" Rachel knew that a witness willing to give their name was much more likely to be trustworthy.

"Um, my name is Harry. Harry Chamberlin."

Rachel was skeptical. It was a generic name, and matched at least one celebrity actor. But it could still be real. "OK, Harry, tell me where you live and I can come by so we can chat. I'll bring my cameraman."

"Um . , ." The line was silent for several seconds. "I don't want you to come to my apartment. I'm worried that people will see me talking to a reporter. But I can meet you somewhere. Somewhere public. I mean, I'm not some kook, but I'm not near my building."

"You live near 12th Street?" Rachel asked, motioning to Terry that he should lean in and listen. She didn't want to put the guy on speaker.

"Yeah. Near. But I'm not there now. Maybe we could meet at, like, one of those outdoor tables in Greely Square. By Macy's on 33rd Street. How about that?"

Rachel looked at Terry, who shrugged. "OK. Sure. Why not? How will I recognize you, Harry?"

"Um, don't worry. I know what you look like. So, how about in, maybe fifteen minutes?"

Again, Rachel made eye contact with Terry, who nodded. "Sure. We'll go there now. It should take us maybe ten minutes to get there."

"OK. OK. Great. I'll find you there."

Before Rachel could ask any other questions, the line went dead. "Well, we have nothing to keep us here. Let's see what this Harry Chamberlin has to say. Agree?"

"I'm game," Terry replied as he turned in the direction of their van.

* * *

TWENTY MINUTES LATER, Rachel sat at a tiny, circular metal table on spindly green legs inside the triangular confines of Greely Square Park. Even seasoned New Yorkers might not know the name of the concrete island wedged between 33rd and 32nd Streets where Broadway cut across Sixth Avenue. In the twenty-teens, the space was made into an urban park, with mammoth planters of flowers, semi-permanent food trucks, and outdoor tables and chairs. It was a popular lunch spot for workers from the surrounding office buildings and the staff at the nearby Macy's department store. At least, when the weather was conducive to outdoor dining.

On this Tuesday, the below-freezing temperatures and persistent breeze left Greely Square deserted. A glaze of ice clung to the metal table and a film of crunchy slush covered the pavement, fighting a constant battle with the sodium chloride pellets periodically scattered by city sanitation department workers. Rachel tapped her feet on the pavement, trying to keep the circulation going inside her fashionable-but-not-insulated boots. She pulled her overcoat's collar together around her neck, where a cashmere scarf covered most of the exposed skin.

Terry sat in similar misery at a table ten feet away. He wanted to be far enough away that Harry could not threaten both of them, in case he was a knife-wielding maniac. His phone was recording video and audio as a precaution. He and Rachel both saw a man in a blue down parka, heavy brown hiking boots, and a black wool hat enter the plaza. He stopped and made eye contact with Rachel, who motioned toward the empty chair at her table.

"Harry?" Rachel asked as the man sat heavily on the small chair.

"Yeah. That's me. Nice to meet you, Miss Robinson."

Rachel didn't bother correcting the man regarding her marital status. "Thanks for calling me, Harry. What did you want to talk about?"

Harry looked from Rachel to Terry and back. "Is he with you?"

"Yes. He's my cameraman. I like to have him nearby when I'm meeting with someone I don't know. You don't mind, do you?"

"Nah. No problem." Harry's tense face relaxed. "The reason I called was because you spoke to somebody from the neighborhood who seen what happened."

"That's right. There was one witness I spoke with on Sunday night."

"Yeah. Well, I also kinda saw some things, too."

Rachel leaned forward, intrigued. "Where were you at the time of the murder?"

"Well, I heard it. I mean, I heard a shot. I didn't know what it was, you know. But I looked outside and I heard a dog barking outside on a balcony. I mean, what the heck was a dog doing out in the cold? And I know that little dog. You met the dog, I bet."

Now Rachel was fully engaged. She had not mentioned Mr. Aaronson's little pup, Seargent, in her on-air report. She hadn't mentioned the dog to anyone. If Harry knew Sergeant had been out on the balcony barking the night of the murder, he must have been there. "Sure, but let's focus on what you saw in the street."

"Well, by the time I looked out there, I seen the guy, Lou, lyin' there in the intersection. Then the cops came and I watched them try to help the poor guy and all that mess."

"Did you see the man who shot Mr. Palazzo?" Rachel held her breath, hoping for a true scoop. Jason hadn't mentioned anything about finding a second witness. Unless he was holding out on her, Rachel would have a clue the detectives didn't know about. Before she could decide whether she would share the new information with Jason, her witness responded.

"Nah. I didn't see the guy. By the time I looked out, he was gone."

Rachel's face exposed her disappointment. "Did you see – or hear – anything that would shed some new light on what happened?"

"I don't know. I mean, ain't I, like, corroboration for you if I seen what the witness saw?" Harry didn't show any sign of being as disappointed as Rachel. "I seen the old guy on the balcony. I don't know his name, but I see him out walking that yappy little dog around the neighborhood all the time. Didn't he see the guy?"

"As I said in my report, he didn't get a good look at the killer. What I need is someone who saw the large man with the bald head. Are you sure you didn't see him?"

"Naw. Sorry. I was farther away than the guy on the third floor. If he didn't see the guy, I wouldn't have seen any better, even if I had looked sooner."

Rachel sat back, almost toppling her unstable chair. "Well, Mr. Chamberlin, even though you might not recall seeing the killer, would you be willing to give me a short interview on camera about what you did see?"

"On camera? Oh, no. No. I'm not getting involved. I don't want nobody knowing what I saw. I don't want no guys coming after me. No way. I didn't see nothin'." Harry rose, looking frightened. He turned and walked away to the south.

"Wait! Mr. Chamberlin!" Rachel called after him.

Terry sprang from his chair and intercepted Rachel before she could follow. "Hold on. You can't go chasing down witnesses. It doesn't work that way. He said he didn't want to be on camera. Neither did Aaronson. But he didn't say his comments were off the record. So, we can use what he said, but we're not getting an interview. Let him go. We have a name and some corroborating facts. That's enough."

By the time Terry finished his mini-lecture, Harry was across the street and down the stairs into the subway system.

"Did you get a recording?"

"Yeah. I got it."

Rachel kicked at a lump of crusty snow. "The problem is, he didn't say anything we didn't already know. It's useless. I can't do a stand-up and say we found another witness who can corroborate that Lou Palazzo was dead when the police found him lying in the street with a gunshot wound to his head."

* * *

TEN MINUTES LATER, Taylor Megill got off the downtown N train at Canal Street and pulled out his phone. The Cannon answered on the first ring.

"Did you get confirmation?"

"Yeah, Boss. She says Aaronson didn't see nothin' well enough to ID anybody. So she was hoping Harry Chamberlin saw what happened."

"But she confirmed it was Aaronson?"

Megill paused, carefully formulating a response that would not be incriminating if somebody overheard his end of the conversation. "She didn't use his name, but she definitely talked to him. The dog was the tell. The guy only said it was a big man with a bald head."

"It's still too much," The Cannon responded evenly.

Megill smiled, knowing his boss could not see. "I understand."

Chapter 14
Real Estate Development

ARLY TUESDAY AFTERNOON, Jason got an email with a four-page attachment. After printing it out, he went directly to Mike's desk. "Guess who owns the office building where our mystery SUV parked at 3:32 a.m. Monday morning?"

Mike's desk chair creaked as he leaned back, looking up at his partner's face, which revealed nothing. "Your poker face is improving, Jason. Good. If it's a name I wouldn't know, you wouldn't ask. I'd say that the most likely options are New York University or Fat Albert Gallata. Since Fat Albert doesn't own many Manhattan buildings, I'll go with NYU."

"Wrong," Jason smiled. "It was your second guess. Fat Albert purchased it in a bankruptcy sale during COVID through a company called Queensboro Partnership, LLC, which is owned by the Laborers and Warehouse Workers' Union, Local 112 Pension Fund."

"Which," Mike jumped in, "is effectively the organizational slush fund for the Gallatas. I'm guessing that the real estate deal is a money-maker for Fat Albert."

"Yeah, probably," Jason agreed. "But even if it's a legit investment, it gives our mob friends a nice base of operations. The report I just got says the parking garage under the building is operated by another one of the Gallata gang's shell companies. Nice way to launder money."

"What do you wanna bet the parking garage's security cameras are out of service?"

Jason laughed. "Let's go find out."

* * *

AN HOUR LATER, the almost-winter shadows stretched eastward on the Lower Manhattan streets. Mike and Jason pulled into the ramp leading underground to the parking garage beneath 301 East 9th Street. They had a warrant to search a dark-colored Ford Explorer with the partial plate number gleaned from the ATM's camera. However, they did not want to tip off the building's owners that they were cops and that they knew the SUV was at the scene of the murder. Jason, who was driving, pulled over next to the diminutive, glass-enclosed cashier's office jutting out from the narrow ramp's painted concrete floor. An overhead sign read, *STOP HERE. WAIT FOR ATTENDANT.*

A thick Black man in a bomber jacket and a knit cap rose from a wooden chair outside the office door and took two steps forward to meet the approaching cops. Jason extended a five-dollar bill. "You mind if I park it myself?"

"No problem," the attendant replied. He ripped off a numbered label from a cardboard chit and placed it under the car's windshield wiper. He handed Jason a receipt with the same number, jammed the five and the remaining portion of the chit into his jacket pocket, and stepped back, motioning Jason onward.

As he inched forward down the curved ramp, a large sign on the wall instructed him: *HEAD-IN PARKING ONLY. PARK AT YOUR OWN RISK.*

"Good thing you tipped him," Mike deadpanned.

The detectives predicted that the SUV, if it was in fact a company car for the Gallata gang, would be parked near the exit on the first level. They were not disappointed – their target occupied a corner space with easy egress for anyone needing a quick getaway. It was backed in. Mike jotted down the full license plate number and called it in. Within a minute, they confirmed that the vehicle was registered to Queensboro Partnership, LLC.

"Bingo," Jason said, parking the unmarked sedan several slots down from the SUV. He extracted a flashlight from his overcoat pocket as they walked toward their target, scanning for security cameras on the ceiling. He and Mike shined lights through the tinted passenger windows and through the windshield, but saw nothing suspicious that would support breaking in. The doors were locked and a blinking red light on the dash indicated an active anti-theft device. Jason reached under the rear wheel well and attached a magnetic GPS tracking chip.

The two detectives took an elevator to the lobby. Mike asked the desk attendant for Charles White of Angel Enterprises. Jason suppressed a smile at Mike's choice of a false name. It was a person of interest they searched for during Jason's first big case with Mike. The attendant said there was no Charles White nor any Angel Enterprises in the building. Mike apologized and turned back toward the parking level elevator. The ruse was intended to be cover in case anyone was paying attention to them. It would seem suspicious if they entered the parking lot and then left again without ever going into the building.

Two steps across the black marble lobby floor, Jason grabbed the left shoulder of Mike's sport jacket and stopped him cold. "That's interesting."

"What?" Mike said in a loud whisper.

"By the door." Jason inclined his head toward Mike's right.

As Mike slowly turned his head toward the building's main elevator banks. He watched two tall figures with Chinese features, short black hair, and long black pea coats amble across the lobby. One nodded to the desk attendant, who nodded back. The two were ringers for the Chinese stiffs from the pawn shop, the ones they found lying in pools of blood. The coats were identical.

Jason said nothing, but hung back from the elevator. The two detectives stood in silence, pretending not to notice when one of the two Chinese men pushed the button to take them down. Mike gave Jason a glance with one raised eyebrow.

Mike was startled by a sharp shout from the desk attendant. "Hey! That's the wrong elevator, Sir. The parking garage elevator is to your left."

"Oh, thanks," Mike responded sheepishly, grabbing Jason's arm and moving toward the garage elevator. He watched as the two Chinese men entered the elevator car. The LED display in a black square above the now-closed door flashed *M*. Mike pushed the call button for the garage elevator, which immediately opened. The detectives entered and turned to see the desk attendant watching them with a furrowed brow from across the lobby.

"You want to go back and see if we can find our way to that mezzanine floor?" Jason asked.

"Let's not go back," Mike said. "I'm assuming the desk jockey works for Fat Albert. I don't think he made us as cops and I don't want him reporting suspicious activity to his boss. But let's see if the fire stairs run from the parking level to the mezzanine."

They exited the elevator at the parking level, where their sedan was waiting. The eight-foot ceiling pressed down on them, illuminated by fluorescent light fixtures every eight feet. On the far side, beyond the smattering of other parked vehicles, Mike saw the red lights of an EXIT sign above a metal door with a bar across its middle. They pushed through into a painted cement stairwell with even dimmer lighting. One floor up, a door stood next to a blue plastic sign bearing a large letter M. On the stairway side, the door's opening mechanism was a chrome knob rather than a push bar. Mike tried the knob, but it didn't budge.

"How are your lock-picking skills?" Mike asked his partner.

"Not good enough for this," Jason remarked as he examined the slit next to the knob. "But skill may not be necessary." He pulled out his wallet and extracted a bit of plastic the size of a credit card bearing a green logo Mike did not recognize. Jason stuck the card into the space and pushed while pulling on the knob. The door clicked and swung open.

"Nice," Mike complimented.

"Our local market has a particularly stiff membership card," Jason responded with a smile, tucking away the card.

They stepped into a dull corridor painted pea green. The light fixtures were dirty, but the painted cement floor, matching the stairwell, was spotless. Two inset doorways on the left wall caught their attention. Painted above one was *M1*, and above the other, *M2*. The right wall was smooth and unbroken, abutting the drive ramp leading to the parking level. At the far end of the hallway, they could see the elevator bank. Mike scanned the ceiling and did not see any obvious surveillance cameras.

"Do we try the doors?" Jason asked.

Before Mike could answer, the door marked *M2* opened with a squeak. Mike clutched Jason's coat and pulled him backward through the stairway door, keeping it open a slit. Peering through, Mike saw two white men without overcoats walk away toward the elevators. One man was short and thin, with long, flowing brown hair. While they waited for the elevator, Mike quietly closed the door and the two detectives retreated to their sedan.

"If we check registered businesses with addresses in this building, we might find out if one of them has an address on the mezzanine level," Jason suggested.

"Good call. It would be great if we could trace them. If there's nobody registered, then it's pretty certain the Gallatas are using the space for whatever operation they're running. Either way, we should let them proceed without tipping them off that we're watching."

After paying their $24 fee for a stay of up to one hour in the garage and obtaining a receipt for expense reimbursement, Jason navigated them around the corner to a parked NYPD cruiser. Officer Roxanne Dupuis confirmed that her phone app tracking the planted GPS unit was active. Mike gave instructions for Dupuis to call if the car moved.

* * *

AT 4:30, BACK AT THE PRECINCT, snow settled in the corners of the windows facing 94th Street. Mike slogged through his departmental email and paperwork – not his favorite activities, but a decent way to spend the last half hour of the day if nothing was hopping.

When Roxanne rang Jason's mobile, Jason popped up the GPS tracker app. He and Mike watched a tiny purple car icon move across a map of New York City. It crawled across the Queensboro Bridge (Mike refused to refer to it as the Ed Koch Bridge) while Mike finished up the case report. Finally, as Mike cleaned up his desktop and prepared to leave for home, the icon stopped in a residential neighborhood in Brooklyn.

"Let's get an ownership record on that address," Mike said.

"Already on it," Jason replied.

Chapter 15
Play it Again

WILL AND RYAN PLAYED *Blades of Karma* virtually nonstop after Ryan discovered his uncle's message. They were sure that they would find the secret path and the falcon somewhere inside the game. They weren't sure if it would be an actual bird of prey, or a statuette like in the movie, or some other object, but whatever it was would surely point them toward their treasure. Maybe it would merely be a hint or a puzzle that only they could solve. They took to calling their unknown prize the *dingus*, mimicking Sam Spade's voice as performed by Humphry Bogart. Finding the dingus was all they thought about. It helped them avoid thinking about Uncle Lou's brutal murder and how much danger they might be in if they managed to find their prize.

All day Tuesday, they were stuck on one particular level with a devastatingly tough boss. Ryan was excited because the graphics included a large bird that flew into the sky and circled around when the boss emerged from his forest castle.

"It's not a falcon, dude," Will scolded.

"It's a freaking bird!" Ryan shot back. "Move around to the left and see if you can get behind him while I draw him over to me."

Will directed his avatar to a position where he could shoot at the boss from behind, but the bird swooped down and attacked him as he attempted to fire. "Shoot the bird!"

Ryan attempted to comply, but his arrows missed. The bird returned to a high altitude and resumed circling. "We need Lou," Ryan lamented.

"Yeah. I know. I'm used to having three attackers. We need somebody to distract the bird."

"Or kill it."

"Damn!" Will tossed his controller to the floor when the boss landed a finishing blow with a spiked club. "Let's knock off for today. I'm spent."

"OK," Ryan replied. "Star's coming over, so I need to get ready."

"We'll try again tomorrow. I know it's there." Will signed out of the game. He had been neglecting his studies, but they didn't seem as important anymore.

* * *

THAT EVENING, RYAN AND STAR BUNDLED against the cold and went to a local independent theater to see a movie. It was Star's choice. Rom-coms were not Ryan's favorite, but he made compromises for his girlfriend. He still got a thrill out of saying the word: girlfriend. After the movie, they went to a diner for a snack. They shared a chocolate egg cream. It always made Star laugh to order the frothy New York drink, which contained neither eggs nor cream.

While they ate, Ryan filled Star in on his frustration about the video game and his and Will's lack of success getting past the "falcon boss," as they called him.

"We always played with Lou. We developed a great three-man strategy for attacking. But with just the two of us, we can't seem to get it done."

"I could be your third," Star suggested.

Ryan scoffed. "It wouldn't be the same."

"Why not?" Star sat back in the booth and pushed the empty glass away. "Because I'm a girl?"

"No, no!" Ryan tried to salvage the situation. "I mean, it's not you, Star. Really. It's like the three of us knew each other's moves. We played for a long time together. Nobody could fill Lou's shoes."

"Why not try?" Star persisted, crossing her arms across her chest. "You said you can't do it. So why not try bringing in a third player? I'm pretty good at video games."

Ryan was stuck. He had played a few games with Star, and agreed that she was not bad. But *Blades of Karma* was on another level. But he couldn't say anything negative to Star. She was his *girlfriend*. And he wanted it to stay that way. "I'll talk to Will about it."

"Great." Star's pouting face brightened. She reached a soft hand out and rested it on top of Ryan's. His heart rate increased by thirty percent.

* * *

AS THE CLOCK APPROACHED MIDNIGHT, Will and Ryan were again playing *Blades of Karma*. Will's homework sat partially completed on his desk. As they talked each other through the gameplay, Ryan brought up the idea of bringing in Star as a third.

"I know what you're saying," Will said, "but I'm not sure. Don't you think we can find it on our own?"

"Maybe we're searching in the wrong places," Ryan suggested.

"What about using Lou's account? Maybe we can check the place where he last saved."

Ryan paused and screwed his face into a skeptical expression that he knew Will could not see. "I don't know Lou's login."

"I know. But what if we go to the shop and use his console? His password is saved there."

"I don't know, man. It's still a crime scene, isn't it?"

"Nah. No way. It's been three days. The cops have got everything they're going to get out of that place. You still have the key to the back door, right?"

"Yeah," Ryan replied hesitantly.

"Well, what have we got to lose?"

"I guess it couldn't hurt. I bet it's gonna stink over there, with all that blood. You sure you wanna go there?"

"Hell, yeah!" Will replied. "What's a little stink compared to finding the file? Plus, maybe if we find it, the cops will be able to use it to find the creep who shot Lou."

"That would mean us turning it over," Ryan noted.

"Well, maybe we would. Who knows? Let's go try and see if we can find something. We'll worry about what we do with it later."

Ryan agreed, wondering what might await them back in the shop of death.

Chapter 16
Morning Walk

JOE AARONSON EMERGED from the exterior doors of his apartment building on 12th Street Wednesday morning. A faint magenta glow over the East River portended the approaching dawn. The ever-present glow of Manhattan and the lights from doorways illuminated a sidewalk pockmarked with white sodium chloride pellets. Despite the chemical treatment, a thin glaze of ice covered the concrete, making the walk treacherous for Joe.

His Maltese-Bichon mix, Sergeant, charged forward, pulling his extendable leash toward a birch tree in a square patch of brown dirt abutting the curb. A one-foot barrier of decorative iron fencing surrounded the thin trunk on three sides, but Sergeant circled around it and lifted his left hind leg. Joe waited patiently for the morning routine to play out. He wore a dark brown sheepskin bomber jacket with a white wool collar against the winter cold. His ears were uncovered below his VFW ball cap. The morning walk seldom lasted more than a few minutes. Joe could handle it if Sergeant could.

Having emptied his bladder, Sergeant proceeded down the usual route, stopping at each urban tree to sniff the morning doggie newspaper. At 6:55 a.m., the street was normally populated exclusively by dog-walkers, a few runners, and the occasional resident with an early work shift.

The bitingly cold wind this morning left the darkened sidewalk deserted.

Upon reaching the last tree before the intersection of Avenue B, Sergeant paused and circled, arching his back in a dance routine that always made Joe smile, before crouching on his hind legs to release the morning poop. Joe dug into his pocket to retrieve a plastic bag bearing an A&D Deli logo.

Focused on Sergeant, Joe barely noticed the man in the tan overcoat with the black faux-fur hat walking briskly in his direction. The walker's black scarf shielded his face from the bitter wind. His hands were in his coat pockets until he pulled one out, holding a black pistol with a three-inch sound-suppressing cylinder attached to its muzzle. Stopping behind Joe, the man pushed the end of the extended barrel against the base of Joe's skull and fired one muffled shot.

The shooter quickly scooped up a still-hot shell casing, returned the gun to its hiding place, and took two strides away before Joe's body came to rest on the frosty pavement. Sergeant barked twice, then circled around his master's body. The leash's handle was wedged under Joe's torso, limiting Sergeant's range of motion. After licking Joe's face, Sergeant scanned the lonely sidewalk in search of a canine pal. Finding none, the dog climbed onto the prone man's back and curled into a ball on the relatively warm fabric of the sheepskin jacket.

Chapter 17
No Coincidence

JASON INTERCEPTED MIKE at the station house before he could even remove his coat on Wednesday morning. "Don't get comfortable, we're on the move. I'll fill you in on the ride. There's a squad car waiting for us." Once settled into the warm black-and-white, Jason gave Mike the quick version. "You remember the witness we talked to Monday, Joseph Aaronson?"

"Sure," Mike said, "the old guy with the dog. He was the one Rachel found before we did, right? What about him?"

"This morning, while he was out walking the dog, somebody whacked him."

Mike snapped his head toward his partner. "The hell?"

"The responding officers' report says there were no witnesses, but they're knocking on doors now. Looks like somebody came up to him on the sidewalk on 12th Street while he was holding his pooch's leash and popped him in the head. Clean kill."

"Let's not make any assumptions based on the opinion of on-scene uniforms," Mike said. He leaned forward to the right of their driver. "No offense, Officer Ellison."

"None taken, Sir," he replied crisply.

"Quite a coincidence," Jason said softly once Mike sat back. "The sole witness to a murder that may have mob connections gets shot on the street three days later."

"The poor guy didn't see the killer well enough to ID him."

Jason turned his head away. "We know that. But the bald man doesn't. Could be somebody trying to make sure."

"I know. What's Rachel doing today? Should we expect to see her at our crime scene again?"

Jason failed to fully suppress a frown and hoped that Mike didn't see him react. "I certainly haven't told her about it. She was home with JJ when I left this morning. I think she was going into her office later, maybe ten o'clock."

"OK." Mike pulled a cough lozenge from his pocket. "She never disclosed the guy's name in her reports, right? So, if this was connected, then whoever ordered the hit found him on their own. I'm sure Rachel will find out soon enough. We'll see if it makes our job even harder."

Ten minutes later, the two detectives ducked under a ribbon of yellow crime scene tape strung between a garbage can and a light pole at the corner of 12th and Avenue C. They approached two uniformed officers standing next to a white sheet covering a lumpy form next to a square of soil carved from the sidewalk. The thin trunk of a barren deciduous tree poked out from the frozen ground. Mike noticed a small curl of frozen dog droppings and wondered if it came from Aaronson's dog or some inconsiderate resident who flouted the city's pooper scooper law.

"Where's the dog?" Mike asked the officer.

"Why? You think the dog can ID the killer?" Jason quipped, causing Mike to roll his eyes rather than laugh.

The officer in charge of the crime scene, whose ID badge read *TAYLOR*, replied without mirth. "A neighbor took the little guy inside the building."

"Was the neighbor outside when it happened?" Mike retained eye contact with the officer, ignoring Jason.

"No, Sir. She called 9-1-1 when she found him on her way out the door."

Mike surveyed the area around the covered body. Crusty slush covered the sidewalk, indented by the prints of hundreds of shoes. It was impossible to make out which were fresher than others, and none left impressions detailed enough to attempt a match to a possible killer. Looking up and down the street, the intersection cameras designed to capture images of vehicles running red lights were unlikely to cover this area of the sidewalk. "Have you asked Traffic to pull the intersection cams?"

"Yes, Sir," Officer Taylor responded, consulting a small notepad. "We also asked building security to pull their camera images, but they say they have nothing that covers this sidewalk. There are two stores across the street that have surveillance cameras. We asked them both to pull their video. The employees who came to open the stores this morning both said they don't have access, but they would call their management. We should get something later today."

"Nice work, Taylor," Jason said, patting the officer on the shoulder. "Any witnesses?"

"None we have identified, Sir. The woman who took the dog said she knows the man. The dog's collar tag gave the name and address. Joseph Aaronson, lived in apartment 3-R in the corner building. According to the lady," he scanned his notes, "a Mrs. Scapala, Aaronson usually walks his dog early. We were on scene at 7:13. The initial report came in at 7:07. Aside from Scapala, there don't appear to have been any other witnesses out on the sidewalk that early. But we're canvassing the street-facing apartments to see if anybody heard or saw anything. We're also tracking down other dog owners to see if anybody was out at the same time."

"That's a good job, Taylor," Mike said. "We'll take a look at the stiff. Then, I want to talk to the woman who found him. Is she inside?"

"Yes, Sir. We have her waiting in the lobby. She's not happy about it."

"OK. We'll make it quick."

Mike bent down and grabbed one head-end corner of the body cover, motioning for Jason to take the other corner. They pulled back the sheet and spent three minutes examining the corpse. They recognized the man from their Monday interview. He wore the same VFW cap, despite the cold. Jason checked his pockets and retrieved a set of keys and an empty plastic bag. The cause of death was obvious. A bullet hole, now black with clotted blood, scarred the back of his head an inch below his gray hairline. The exit wound blasted through his forehead.

"Any shell casings?" Mike directed the question to Officer Taylor, who was watching the detectives with the attention of a medical student observing his first heart surgery.

"No, Sir. We searched the area for fifty feet and found none."

"Shooter cleaned up his brass?" Jason suggested.

"It would figure if this was a pro hit. It sure looks like that."

Mike stood, stretched his back, and peeled off his crime scene gloves. "I don't expect the woman who found the body will be much help."

After ten minutes with Mrs. Scapala, it was clear she saw nothing important. Joe Aaronson was already cold when she found him. She was fiercely protective of the little white dog. Mike was glad he wouldn't have to tell Michelle that the creature was abandoned and hoped Sergent and Mrs. Scapala could comfort each other.

"So, we add one more stiff to this case we're probably not going to solve, huh?" Jason lamented.

"How about a little optimism?" Mike retorted playfully. "There's a non-zero chance we'll find this man's killer. More likely, though, this development might lead us somewhere on the Lou Palazzo case. I'm not sure where, but anywhere's better than the nowhere we're at now."

Chapter 18
Protecting Your Turf

IN THE AMERICAN CABLE NEWS OFFICE on Twelfth Avenue, Dave Butler pressed one finger to each temple. The discussion, more shouting match than conversation, exacerbated his tinnitus. The ringing in his ears was giving him a headache. Normally, he would have made a decision in the first thirty seconds and been back to working on the rundown for the evening news eight minutes ago. Unfortunately, this problem was more one of politics and social balancing than simply business. Plus, Claire Gluskin from Human Resources was there taking notes like the stenographer at the Nuremberg trials. Dave hated HR more than a buried lede.

The disruptive group in the small office also included Jodi Martell, the ACN shop steward from the NewsGuild union, which represented the network's reporters. Dave was in the union earlier in his career, when he was a reporter at *The Daily News*. Now he detested the union, which wormed its way into his newsroom the prior autumn. Jodi was the worst. She was constantly whining about DEI and pay equity and calling Dave a misogynist. He disliked Jodi more than Claire. Jodi was the one who raised the race discrimination issue.

Rachel was by far the most strident participant in the ongoing argument. She was also one of only two Black members of ACN's on-air staff. She stood arms akimbo with a strand of black hair strewn across her forehead. "I started covering this story. Dave, you gave *me* this story. You can't take it away from me and give it to Gabriel."

Gabriel duBois had joined the network a year earlier after being a local star in Baltimore on a network affiliate. He was polished and had a radio voice. He was smart. He was also incredibly Caucasian. "This is a hard news story, Dave. Rachel did a nice job on Sunday handling the spot news, but now we need to dig in and do some investigating and interviewing. That work needs someone who knows what they're doing."

It had been an easy call. Dave told Rachel that she did a great job as the on-call reporter on Sunday and handled the follow-up on Monday well also. But he was handing the story over to Gabriel to move it forward. Rachel was enthusiastic, but raw, undisciplined, and inexperienced. Now, he realized, taking the Black female reporter off the story would create bullshit blowback that would take up hours of his valuable time for weeks.

It was a good story, but was it truly an important one? The cops were stumped. It looked more like a mob hit than anything else. Even when they solved such cases, it wasn't huge news. The killer would be some low-level grunt in one of the crime families, or it would never be solved and it would fade from the public's attention span quickly. Rachel had the advantage of being much more eye-catching than Gabriel. If he let Rachel finish the coverage, Gabriel would be the only person unhappy. Dave thought he was fighting for the assignment more out of pride than because he cared about the story. Rachel was passionate about the story and desperately wanted it. Siding with Rachel would be the easy road now, but it would make Jodi happy, which he hated.

While these thoughts were circulating inside Dave's head, the people in his office continued to bicker and shout at each other. "Enough!" Dave barked loudly enough for everyone else to stop talking. "I've heard all I need to hear. This is an assignment issue. Nothing else. Jodi, it's not a union issue. It's a management issue."

"If it's discriminatory, then it's a violation of—"

"It's got nothing to do with race!" Dave bellowed, cutting off the union steward. "You have a problem with my decision, you file a grievance. For now, you get the fuck out of my office. This is a business matter and the union has no place here." Dave glared at Jodi, saying nothing, but gesturing with his eyes toward the closed office door.

Jodi rose from her chair. "I don't appreciate your language, Mr. Butler."

"Good!" Dave said. "Don't let the door hit you in the ass on your way out." He waited until Jodi left and the door was closed, then turned to his two reporters. Both had the sense to keep quiet. "Gabriel, you are the best reporter for this assignment, which is why I gave it to you."

Rachel attempted to interject. "But, Mr. Butler—"

"Zip it, Robinson!"

Dave's glare silenced Rachel mid-protest. She had been with ACN for less than a year. She knew she had not earned her reporting chops, but she badly wanted to continue the story. She dropped her head, struggling to keep quiet, knowing that anything she said at this point could only piss off her boss.

Dave turned back to Gabriel. "Like I was saying, Gabriel, you are the best man – person – for this assignment." Gabriel smiled and shot a triumphant glance toward Rachel. "But I'm now thinking this story isn't big enough to warrant a change in reporter mid-stream. It's probably not going anywhere, and I can use you better in other places. Since Rachel here is so determined, I'm going to give her a chance. I'm sorry for dragging you into this shit show. You go back to the corruption at City Hall story. Knock that one out of the park. Got it?"

A surprised Gabriel silently shook his head and furrowed his brow. Then, he stood. "Fine. It's your call." He exited the room without another word, leaving Rachel alone with Butler.

"Sir, I just want to say—"

"Don't say anything," Butler cut her off again. "You're not the winner here, Robinson. You want this story, you say? Fine. You got it. But you'd better run with it and bring in something spectacular. You don't have the experience for this assignment. You're doing a nice job with the health and science features, for a rookie. You wanted the spot news stand-by gig and I authorized it because nobody wants it. I give you credit for being willing to do the shit work to get your foot in the door. Well, it's in the door, but it's going to get bruised unless you punch way above your weight on this one. You bring me something worth airing and you do it without me needing to sit on you. This is your shot, kid. Don't fuck it up."

Dave, as was his practice, broke eye contact with Rachel without another word and looked down at the paper on his desk. He took a blue pencil from a gold-plated holder and scribbled a note in the margin. It was the universally understood signal that the meeting was over and the underling should leave the office and get back to work.

Rachel spent the remainder of the morning huddled with Sandi Risbey, the young producer now assigned to her story, brainstorming angles for her to pursue the next day.

"We need to make Lou Palazzo the story," Rachel said. "His neighbors didn't seem to know him well. We need to humanize him and show people what a tragedy his murder was. Sure, he had a criminal record, but that was a long time ago. If we can make people feel sorry for him, that's where the ratings will be. That's the story. You've been researching him, so what have we got?"

"I wish I had something great for you, Rachel," Sandi said, flipping through a folder of printouts. "He wasn't married. One sister out on Long Island seems to be his only living relative. She's married to an accountant for an aerospace company. Doesn't seem like a high-profile couple. They have two kids. One's in high school and the other is a sophomore at NYU. Palazzo has almost no social media presence and there are no articles about him on Google or Factiva since he was convicted of racketeering and sent away to prison for three years in 2012. That's all I have."

"NYU?" Rachel said quizzically.

"What?"

"NYU. You said he has a nephew at NYU. Maybe that's our angle. Maybe his nephew knew him better than his neighbors. Do you have an address or phone number for the kid?"

"No. Just a name. Ryan Gelb." Sandi searched her papers for her few notes about Ryan, who was only a few years younger than she was.

"Well, see what you can get. I want to find him and talk to him. He's my best chance to show a real person's perspective on our victim. I'm not sure if the police have talked to him yet, so maybe we can get to him first."

"OK, Rachel. I'll see what I find by tomorrow morning."

Chapter 19
Following the Boys

WEDNESDAY AFTERNOON, Ryan and Will took advantage of a three-hour break between their morning programming class and late-afternoon European literature. They skipped over to Lou's closed shop. Will brought along a tube of Vick's Vapo-Rub, which he proudly displayed to Ryan.

"What's that for?"

"For the smell," Will replied as if it was the most obvious thing. When Ryan stared blankly, he added, "You put a dab of this under your nose before we go in. It will prevent you from smelling anything, no matter how foul it is inside. Haven't you ever watched a crime show?"

Ryan said nothing. As they walked up 12th Street, he asked, "What are we gonna do if we get caught inside? What if the cops are still watching the place?"

Will smiled. He spent time the night before working out the plan. "The funeral is tomorrow, right? So, we say there's something in the shop that we want to put in Lou's coffin, like a special keepsake he wanted to be buried with. They can't fault us for that, right?"

"What is this special keepsake?"

"I don't know. He's your uncle. Think of something."

Ryan turned his eyes to the cold blue sky. "I guess we could say it's that steel game controller he used to play *Blades of Karma*. After he won that contest, it's the only one he ever used. We'll be looking for it anyway. It was pretty near and dear to him."

"Excellent!"

They continued to the shop, ducking into the narrow air shaft between the pawn shop and the adjoining building that allowed for rear-facing windows and emergency exits. The space was so narrow that Ryan could touch both sides with his arms outstretched. Twenty feet from the sidewalk, they stopped at a door recessed into the brick wall. Ryan pulled out a thick chrome key and opened the door with an eerie creak, then immediately closed it again.

"Gimme some of that Vick's."

After the boys slathered their upper lips with entirely too much menthol salve, Ryan opened the door again and went into the dark corridor. A plump rat scurried away from the sliver of light. Even with the topical nasal block, the stench brought bile to Ryan's throat. After a few moments of acclimation, he and Will inched forward, allowing the door to close behind them and activating the flashlight function on their phones.

They were too curious not to peek around the carnage inside the shop, so they bypassed Lou's office and walked to the front. The damage from two rounds of pilfering remained obvious. Emptied cases and toppled displays made it look like a storm had blasted through. There wasn't a computer or smart phone in sight.

After a quick peek at the bloody floor near the front door, they retreated back to Lou's office. Here, where there was no blood residue, the odor was more manageable once they closed the door. Ryan snapped on the overhead light and activated an air purifier unit in the corner, a remnant from the

COVID pandemic. Lou's twenty-eight-inch monitor was cracked and on the floor, but still worked. Ryan righted the monitor while Will plugged in the HDMI cable running from a docking station hanging off the edge of the desk by its power cord. Several additional cords ripped from Lou's computer tower were splayed out like the black tentacles of a dead octopus. In the left middle desk drawer, Ryan pushed the power button on the black rectangle that was the PS4 base unit.

Meanwhile, Will retrieved a steel-plated, limited-edition controller from the file cabinet where Lou kept his prize. Ryan watched over Will's shoulder while the start-up sequence for *Blades of Karma* illuminated the damaged screen. They heard no sounds until Ryan located two peripheral speakers in the debris field on Lou's office floor. Ryan got the speakers reconnected and gingerly placed them back on the desk, under the monitor.

The game automatically logged in to Lou's account. Will navigated to the internal mail service. They found Lou's message to Ryan about the secret path in the sent mail box. It was the last message Lou sent. Finding no additional messages there, Will played the game with Lou's character while Ryan looked on, searching for clues. But they found nothing.

"I should have brought my laptop so I could play, too," Ryan said. When the boys came to play the game in person with Lou, they both perched their laptops on the metal desk, creating a bivouac of gamers and a cacophony of conversation.

"It's like Lou's ghost is here playing with us," Will said, not sure why he was whispering. "I know he was your uncle, but I really loved him."

Ryan blinked back a tear before responding. "I know. We spent some great hours in here. I didn't think it would end. I miss him."

After an hour of futility, they turned off the system and left the office. Will took the steel game controller with them. It was still to be their story if anybody saw them enter or exit. Plus, they could use an extra controller back at the dorm. It was right and proper to keep Lou's controller in action, rather than leaving it behind in the empty office.

Ryan locked the rear door on their way out. They trudged across the frosty sidewalks of Manhattan, back toward campus.

* * *

LLOYD CANNON GOT THE CALL from Lenny, who was still monitoring the bug in Ryan's dorm room. He reported that Ryan and Will were going back to Lou Palazzo's shop.

"They're still chasing a clue in the video game they've been playing. They're going to play on Palazzo's PS4 using his account. They think whatever it is Palazzo wants them to find might be more visible in his account."

Cannon was intrigued, although he didn't understand gaming terms and only vaguely understood what a PS4 was. The relevant fact was that the boys were trying to find the missing data file, which meant they didn't already have it. "Is the file still in the shop somewhere?"

"They don't know, Boss. They need the clue Uncle Lou left for them. At least, that's what they think."

Cannon pondered the situation. It was still useless to grab the little twerps and squeeze them for information. Was it possible the file was still in the shop and his crew missed it during their early-morning raid? He didn't see how, but four Chinese Dragons and his four techs working around the clock in the downtown boiler room were still looking for it among the computers and other devices they lifted. He was determined not to miss it again if the boys somehow found it. "I'll put The Dog on 'em. You keep listening and see what they say when they get back. And, Lenny, let's keep this information to ourselves. No need for Yung Ji to be bothered with this. Am I right?"

"You got it, Boss!" came Lenny's enthusiastic response.

Two hours later, Cannon's phone buzzed, showing the number of the burner currently being used by Andre "The Dog" Kaleem. Cannon wasn't certain how The Dog obtained his nickname, but he heard it involved an encounter in a junkyard. Cannon didn't care.

"What's the report, Dog?"

"Not much, Boss," came Andre's high, mousey voice, which was discordant with his nickname. "I seen the two brats go around the back of the shop about an hour ago. I checked and there's a rear door. They came out the same way a few minutes ago. They wasn't carrying anything. You want me to follow them back to NYU?"

"No," Cannon commanded. "We got it covered. Go on home."

Cannon walked over to the listening station and tapped Lenny on the shoulder, startling him. As always, Lenny was wearing headphones that drowned out all the other noise in the room. On one of Lenny's two monitors, Cannon saw a lush forest scene, rendered in impressive 3-D animation. In the background, a giant black spider moved along a gossamer web.

"Look alive, dipshit. The kid and his friend are headed back home. Let me know if they say anything about finding the data file."

"On it," a flustered Lenny replied, shutting down the video game without making eye contact with Cannon.

"What were you watching?"

Lenny squirmed in his chair, but didn't want to withhold from his boss. "It's called *Blades of Karma.* It's the game the kids are playing. I want to see what they're seeing so I know what they're talking about."

Cannon walked away, muttering to himself. "I'm dealing with children. But if those idiot kids get that file, they ain't gonna keep it very long."

Across the room, Yung Ji and one of his boys were on their phones, carrying on a conversation in Chinese. Cannon told them to speak English in his room, but they pretended not to understand the instruction. Cannon would not complain to Fat Albert about such trivialities, but it bothered him. It was clear the Corporate Dragons did not view Cannon and his men as colleagues. More like annoyances. He felt the same way about them.

Cannon knew for a fact that Ji could speak English pretty well when he wanted to. He was sure his counterpart was saying something important he wanted to keep secret.

"Yes, General," Ji said in Chinese, glancing toward Cannon. "We understand the importance . . .No, we have not found the file within the devices the Americans brought back from the dead shopkeeper's store . . .I will tell my men. Five million Yuan should be a fine incentive to our team . . .Between the local agents, the police, and the two students, someone will surely find the file . . .Of course not, we will erase any links back to you and the syndicate. No one will know where the file went . . .Do you think that is wise, Sir? . . .Yes, Sir. I understand. It will be done without hesitation if necessary. . .Yes, the American students also."

Chapter 20
Working the File

BACK AT THE PRECINCT, Mike and Jason received a report on Lou Palazzo's finances. As was their normal process, Mike let Jason review the information first. Jason was more experienced after two years working in the white-collar crime division and was generally more comfortable with numbers and spreadsheets.

"Anything good?" Mike asked after a half hour.

"The guy was getting by, but not living a lavish life," Jason said. "He had small balances on three credit cards and slightly more money in his bank account than you would expect from somebody running a piss-ant pawn shop. We know he was active in the Gallata organization a decade ago. He might have still had a few irons in the fire. But he lived like a hermit. Shitty apartment, run-down shop with outdated tech, crappy clothes. He accumulated some money and then he spent most of it."

"What was he buying?"

Jason paused. "There are several pretty large electronic payments to New York University. Maybe they were donations. The report doesn't know the reason. Just the payments."

"NYU? Was he an alumnus?"

"Not that we know about," Jason said.

"Anything else?"

"Semi-regular cash deposits, always small amounts. Maybe he was laundering money for his old bosses. Not big money. But there are no records of large cash withdrawals or electronic transfers. So, if he was laundering it, the organization was not getting it back from him."

"Fine. So, nothing to suggest he was sitting on a mountain of treasure that the Gallata gang and their Chinese helpers would have wanted to kill him over." Mike went back to his desk.

The next call came in from the medical examiner's office. Michelle sent the full tox screen report in an email, but she always called to give an explanation of the medical information.

"Is there anyone else with you, besides Jason?" Michelle asked.

"No," Mike said, setting his cell phone on the conference room table. Jason closed the door and leaned against the jamb, looking through the lone window into the busy bullpen.

"Fine. Detectives, the tox screen doesn't tell us much. Palazzo had nothing of note in his system. He was taking a statin for cholesterol control, probably, and there was a load of antacid in his stomach."

"Maybe he was nervous about something," Jason suggested.

"Sure, but nothing the science can say for sure," Michelle's tinny voice responded. "The two Asians both had cocaine in their blood. Otherwise, nothing significant."

"Is there any ID on the two Asian guys?" Jason asked.

Michelle's voice brightened. "There is. I sent photos of their faces to the feds and got a hit from the ICE database. They were Chinese nationals who entered the country on tourist visas three days ago in Boston. I would try to tell you their names, but they're in Chinese. The feds had no specific information on them. Maybe your law enforcement boys can help you figure out where they came from."

"Thanks, Dr. McNeill," Mike said. "We'll let you know if we have any other questions." He turned to Jason after the call disconnected. "It still leaves us with the big question: What were the two Asians and the bald man looking for?"

Jason answered with another question. "Could Palazzo have been mixed up with the Chinese in some operation that went bad?"

"Anything's possible. He had a record, but it's all ancient history. Just because he hadn't been arrested in ten years doesn't mean he was fully legit. If he screwed over the Chinese and they came calling for him, then it's not likely we'll figure it out unless we find whatever it was the bald man was looking for. But there's not much chance they missed it. That has to be why they came back later that night. They cleaned out the place."

Jason's phone and Mike's phone both buzzed. They simultaneously scrutinized their screens and saw a message that the video team was ready with their report on the next level of surveillance camera review. Without a word, they left the conference room and walked up to the fourth-floor video room, where Officer Cheryl Ridgeway greeted them with a smile.

"Detectives. Good. I want to show you what we've got."

"Tell me you have the bald man on camera with a clear shot of his face and that you've already run an ID on him," Mike said in his most serious voice.

"Oh. No, Detective," Cheryl stammered. "Was – was that – were you expecting—?"

Mike broke into a smile. "Sorry, Officer. I'm busting your chops. I know we never get that lucky. What about those two young men who visited the shop in the afternoon?"

"We couldn't find them on any of the other cameras we reviewed from the neighborhood. They were on the sidewalk with a lot of other pedestrians and we couldn't track them. The street cams are focused on the roadway."

Jason said, "You think they're important?"

"Maybe not," Mike responded, "but we don't have much else. Can we get a few officers to try to find other cameras down the street? Maybe we can find them?"

Cheryl straightened her back upon receiving this new assignment. "OK. We can do that."

Mike got back to the meeting's main point. "What about the other guys who visited the shop that day?"

"Yes," Cheryl said. "We got a decent image of the man who arrived and left in the taxi. Not good enough for facial recognition, but we got the cab's medallion number. We called the cab company and they tracked the payment records and destinations and we got a credit card. The passenger's name is Adam Erickson. He's a deputy mayor. Works for Frederick Douglass, handling housing and social services."

"Well, that's very interesting," Mike said. "Good work, Ridgeway. Nice initiative. Jason and I will pay the guy a visit."

"I'll call downtown to get a meeting set up," Jason said, walking toward his desk.

"Great. Afterward, we need to talk to Sully."

* * *

TWENTY MINUTES LATER, Mike and Jason sat in the uncomfortable chairs in Captain Sullivan's office. Knowing that Sully was already sensitive about Jason's wife covering the Palazzo murder for ACN, Mike handled the debriefing on the Joe Aaronson murder and on the new information about the Deputy Mayor.

"We'll wait for the ME to be sure, Cap, but it looks like a pro hit on Aaronson, the witness. Single shot, gun pressed against the base of the guy's skull. Most likely using a suppressor. They approached Aaronson sometime before seven this morning outside his building while he was walking the dog. No sign of robbery. Left the dog. No witnesses and no helpful video so far. If it was a pro, their face would have been covered, which would not have attracted any attention since it was cold as the Antarctic outside. We'll stay on it, but don't have any leads as of now."

Sully kneaded the skin on his forehead with two fingers from each hand. Mike and Jason recognized the behavior and knew to keep quiet while their captain was thinking. "You interviewed the guy Monday, correct?"

"Yes." Mike's standard procedure in these meetings was to keep things short and simple. "The uniforms talked to him Sunday night. Jason and I met him on Monday."

"Did he give you the impression he was connected?"

"No. He was a vet. A straight shooter. But he was nervous about having talked to a reporter about what he saw."

Sully gritted his teeth. "I suppose we know who that reporter was?"

"Yes, Cap. But it's really not relevant. Aaronson's name was never used."

"But somehow, somebody figured out who he was and decided to whack him because he was a witness to the Palazzo murder. Is that what you're thinking?"

"It certainly would fit the facts, Sully. The perp might have seen Aaronson when he was standing out on his balcony and been worried he could make an ID. He had a yappy little dog. He said the perp looked up when the dog barked, but he still didn't get a good look at his face. The shooter might have thought otherwise."

"Did we offer to protect him?"

"No, Cap. He didn't have anything useful aside from a general description of the guy as large and bald. He was never going to ID the shooter. We didn't flag him as a material witness."

Sully tipped backward in his desk chair, looking at the white foam tile ceiling. "OK. You stay on this on the assumption it has a connection with the Palazzo case. If we make an arrest there, the DA can decide whether to charge in this witness murder. It does sound like a pro job, which means you have a tough row to hoe. If it is connected to Palazzo, it means we're for sure dealing with organized shitheads." He paused and looked at Jason. "You two deal with it. Keep me informed. The commissioner won't want any surprises. Especially since the press is still all over it." He glared at Jason with this last statement, like it was Jason's fault that Rachel was covering the story. All the other local media were also on the story, but Sully was focused on Jason's wife.

"There's one other thing," Mike added.

"Am I going to hate it?" Sully dropped his head.

"Only a little, Cap. The video team found a man who visited Palazzo's shop the day he died. He's a deputy mayor named Adam Erickson. We're going to want to talk to him. We figure you might want to give the Commissioner a heads up. We don't know whether Erickson is connected to the murder. It could be a total coincidence. But we need to follow it up. It might get a little sensitive, especially if people find out that he's been questioned by two homicide detectives."

"By somebody, you mean the press," Sully said, not as a question.

"Yeah. Of course. We should set it up to be a private discussion. Agree?"

"Hell yes," Sully replied. "I'll take care of it and let you know."

Jason and Mike left the office without any further comment.

Chapter 21
An Unpleasant Surprise

RACHEL WAS AT THE ACN OFFICE when she heard the news. Another reporter asked her if she heard about the shooting a block away from the Sunday night triple murder.

"Is there a name?" Rachel asked.

"Yeah. It was Amundson, or something like that. You think it was connected to the murders you're reporting on?"

Rachel shivered. "Was it Aaronson?"

"Sure. Might have been. Why?"

"I talked to a guy named Aaronson. Old guy. White hair. Had a little dog."

"Oh, yeah. That's probably him. He was killed on the sidewalk this morning while walking his dog."

"I gotta go," Rachel called over her shoulder as she raced away to find Terry.

While searching for her cameraman, Rachel reached for her phone to call Jason, but immediately put it away. The last thing Jason needed was her interrupting him during the investigation and creating a record of a phone call that could be misinterpreted later. She wasn't asking him for information. She knew all the relevant information.

She turned into the editing room and stopped, fighting to keep her anxiety in check. "Terry, did you hear about Mr. Aaronson?"

"I did. Looks like somebody didn't want him to be a witness to a murder." Terry's voice was light, almost comical.

"It's not funny!" Rachel shot back.

Terry frowned. "I know it's not funny, Rachel, but it's a fact we can't change. You haven't been in this biz very long, but sometimes you have to make a joke out of awful things. Otherwise they'll eat you up. You must have dealt with similar behavior when you were an EMT, right?"

Rachel dropped her chin. "Yes. We did. We made jokes about the clothes a drug overdose victim was wearing or the bad home décor of a rich guy who had a heart attack. If we didn't laugh, we'd cry."

"Yeah. Figures. Same applies here. You cover news and you cover tragedy and pain. A lot. So you have to let it go and not take it too seriously. You're the reporter. You didn't cause the situation. It's not like you could have prevented it from happening."

Rachel stood on unsteady legs and looked down at her shoes. "What if I could have?"

"Could have what?"

"Prevented it!" Rachel snapped. "I mean, what if it was my fault?"

Terry raised his right eyebrow. "How do you figure that?"

"That guy I interviewed. You remember, Harry Chamberlin, if that was his real name. He was kinda weird. Remember, he asked me about Mr. Aaronson. Do you think Chamberlin was involved in the murder?"

"Rachel, you're talking crazy. You didn't tell that guy shit about Aaronson. As a matter of fact, I remember you said Aaronson couldn't identify the killer. Right?"

"Yeah. Yeah. That's right."

"So, you made it *less* likely that anyone would want to whack the guy to keep him from being a witness."

"You're right. It has to be." Rachel's voice trended toward normal.

"Plus," Terry continued, "Chamberlin knew about Aaronson and his dog being out on the balcony. You didn't tell him that. He knew it already. So, if you think somebody tipped off the killer about Aaronson, it was probably weird Mr. Chamberlin."

Rachel was still shaking. "Do you still have the video of my interview with Chamberlin?"

"Sure. I keep everything until the story's over. Why?"

"I think we should turn it over to the police."

"Whoa!" Terry held up both palms in front of his chest. "Wait a big minute there, Rachel. You're going to have to talk to Dave about that. We don't share our reporting with the police without a court order, and sometimes not even then. You can't give it away. The cops wouldn't give a video of a witness interview to you, right?"

"No," Rachel conceded. "But what if it's important?"

"If it's important, they'll figure it out on their own."

"But—"

"Plus," Terry interrupted, "if you tell the cops about this guy Chamberlin, they're going to want to know how to contact him. What will you tell them, huh? You didn't get an address for him, or an ID. You're not sure Chamberlin is even his real name."

Rachel pulled out her work phone, scrolled through the call log, and called Chamberlin's number. Fifteen seconds later, Terry heard the caustic warning tone and the message, "The number you have dialed is no longer in service."

"So, it was a burner phone and now he's ditched it. You have nothing to give to the police even if Dave would let you."

"I know." Rachel sulked. "But don't you think calling from a burner phone is suspicious?"

"No." Terry responded. "Half our sources use burners when they call us. It's pretty common. It doesn't mean anything."

"OK. Fine. But it's still freaking me out that Aaronson got killed."

"I get it." Terry took on a soothing tone. "It's freaky. But we have to keep going or abandon the story. Which do you want?"

Rachel put on a stoic face. "We keep going."

"Atta girl!"

Chapter 22
Home Front

WHEN JASON GOT HOME, later than usual because of all the activity on the triple murder case, Rachel was holding JJ in the plush rocking chair next to the living room sofa. *Jeopardy!* was on the television, but muted. Jason hung up his coat on a hook by the door, slipped out of his wet boots, and put his hat and gloves on a thin table against the wall. He saw that Rachel was reading JJ his favorite book, *Goodnight, Moon.*

Rachel looked up for a moment and smiled, acknowledging her husband's arrival, then resumed her reading. JJ pointed excitedly at the illustrated images on the page as Rachel mentioned them. Jason watched in proud silence. JJ was so enthralled by the book, he did not notice his father's presence.

When Rachel closed the last page, JJ clapped his hands and turned up his face, seeking a congratulatory kiss from mom. After getting it, he turned and saw Jason.

"Daddy, daddy!" he squealed, launching himself from Rachel's lap and careening across the area rug toward Jason, who squatted to receive his son's enthusiastic hug. Jason rose with JJ in his arms, holding him up over his head until the boy's denim jumper nearly brushed against the ceiling light. "More!" JJ pleaded when Jason lowered him to the floor.

"Not now," Jason soothed. "You know what comes after story time, right?"

"Baff time!" JJ said, then scurried up the stairs. Olivia was waiting with a warm bath. Jason and Rachel could hear JJ's enthusiastic noises, indicating that his grandma was undressing him. He loved his bath time.

Jason sat on the sofa near the rocking chair. "Did you hear about Mr. Aaronson?"

"Yeah," Rachel replied sullenly. The happy mood melted away like a puff of steam from a subway grate. "I don't suppose you can tell me whether you know anything about what happened?"

Jason sat back. "I'm pretty sure there was a release to the press a little while ago. We identified the victim after we contacted his sister, who seems to be his only local relative. The official information is that he was shot and killed while walking his dog along 12th Street this morning. We didn't give details, but it was a single shot at close range to the back of his head. No witnesses. No video yet. We don't expect to get much. It looks like a pro job. No sign of robbery. No apparent dispute or struggle. No motive."

"That sounds like more information than you would put in a press release," Rachel said, sitting forward and reaching out to rest her hand on Jason's. "Thank you. We both can think of one motive."

"We have no evidence to support any theory," Jason replied.

Rachel moved to the sofa and leaned against Jason's shoulder. "I feel awful – like it's *my* fault. If I hadn't found him and reported about there being an eyewitness, they wouldn't have found him." A trickle of tears slid down Rachel's cheeks.

"You can't blame yourself for that, honey. You never used his name or provided any identifying information about him in your report. If the killer or his gang decided to take out a potential witness, they would have found him. They didn't need you and you didn't do anything wrong. You can't beat yourself up over doing your job."

"That's what Terry said," Rachel mumbled.

"Who's Terry?" Jason cocked his head and looked down at his wife, trying to make eye contact.

"He's my cameraman. He's good. He has taught me a lot. He said I need to let it go and not blame myself. How do you handle it, Jason? When something happens during an investigation and you may have contributed to it, how do you keep going?"

"I have Mike. He helps. He's been through it all. Then we dig harder and try to bring bad people to justice, and we console ourselves because we're the good guys."

Rachel snuggled harder against Jason's warm body. "You *are* the good guys. I know that. I wish I knew for sure that I am, too."

"You are. I'm not sure about some of your colleagues." He laughed, but Rachel did not reciprocate.

Instead, she sat up, turned toward Jason, and said, "I'm going to share something with you. You shared with me, and I know you're in a tough situation. I'm not supposed to share with the police. But I can't help thinking that it might be more important than Terry thinks, so I'm going to tell you."

"You've been holding out on me?" Jason said playfully.

"Not as much as I'm sure you're holding out on me. But it doesn't matter. I met with a man who said he was a witness to the murder, except it turned out he wasn't. He didn't see anything. He didn't see the killer. But he said he did see Mr. Aaronson out on his balcony with his little dog. He seemed like he was interested in Aaronson. I told him that Aaronson didn't see the killer's face. He could only say the guy was big and bald. You could probably see that on the traffic cameras, so it's not anything helpful."

"The traffic cams didn't give us a clear image," Jason said, "but we did notice the big, bald head."

Rachel nodded. "Anyway, this guy, who said his name was Harry Chamberlin, didn't see anything new."

"When did you meet with him?"

"Yesterday afternoon."

"Do you have contact information for him?"

"No. That was a little weird. I tried calling his number, but it was disconnected."

"Probably a burner."

"That's what Terry said." Rachel stood up and paced in front of the sofa. "But if it was a burner, maybe it was all just a sham. Maybe Harry Chamberlin wasn't his real name. Maybe he was trying to get information from me about Mr. Aaronson so he could murder him."

Jason grabbed Rachel's wrist as she passed and pulled her into his lap. "Sweetheart. First, thank you for sharing this information. It may be helpful. I may need you to give me a description of this guy Chamberlin. I know your boss would probably fire you if he knew you were giving me this. So, thank you." He pulled her in for a soft kiss. "You said the witness already knew about Aaronson and his dog. When we talked to Aaronson, he said the killer looked up when the dog barked. Aaronson couldn't ID the guy, but the killer saw Aaronson on his balcony. If they decided to take him out just in case, they didn't need your report, or your conversation with this creep, to do that."

"Then why bother to call me and meet with me?" Rachel retorted, sniffing.

"They were making sure. If you hadn't been available, they would have found some other way. They're not stupid – assuming you're correct about why they contacted you."

"What else could it be?" Rachel pulled away from Jason's embrace. "It's not a coincidence."

"I'm not going to argue that with you." Jason guided her back to his shoulder. "It's not your fault."

"If that's true, why do I feel so guilty?"

Jason squeezed her gently. "Because you care about people. All your life you've been helping people. Saving their lives as an EMT. It's your nature. You hate it when anyone dies and you believe you could have done something to save them. In this case, there is nothing you could have done."

Rachel was silent until a splashing sound from upstairs and a squeal signaled that JJ's bath time was over. Bedtime was next on the schedule. *Jeopardy!* had given way to *Wheel of Fortune.*

"You're up, Dad," Rachel tapped Jason's knee. "I'll get supper ready for us while you put him down."

* * *

A HALF HOUR LATER, over a dinner of leftovers, Rachel regaled Olivia and Jason with the story of how she fought to stay on the triple-murder story, despite Dave trying to reassign it to somebody else.

"Now I have to deliver on this story or my ass will be busted back down to fluff features for the foreseeable future," Rachel lamented. "What I really need is an angle for the story to give Lou Palazzo some personality. I'm trying to track down his nephew, who is a student at NYU. Hopefully, he'll be able to give me some sadness and humanity that viewers will connect with."

"What do you think about that, Jason?" Olivia said to her son-in-law as she popped a forkful of mashed potatoes into her mouth.

"It makes sense," Jason responded without emotion. Normally, he kept Olivia and Rachel fully entertained with stories about the cases he was investigating. The details of each murder, funny anecdotes about witness interrogations, and brainstorming sessions when he needed ideas from the women in his life were standard fare in the Robinson dining room. But on this case, he was keeping things confidential.

"Have you and Mike spoken to the victim's nephew yet?" Olivia pressed.

"I can't comment on the investigation," Jason said, looking at his wife.

Olivia, however, was not taking "no comment" as an answer. "Didn't you hear what Rachel was saying just now? She needs a little help here. Have you spoken to the victim's nephew? Yes or no? That's not confidential, for heaven's sake."

Jason turned to Rachel, but saw he was getting no support in maintaining separation between his and Rachel's work. He had already shared more about the Aaronson murder than Sully would want. He heaved a sigh. "No. We have not. The kid is not part of the investigation."

"Do you have an address for him?" Rachel quickly asked.

Jason hesitated.

"You just said the nephew was not part of the investigation. I'm not asking you to do research for me in the police database. But if you have the information already, and it's *not* part of the investigation, what's the harm?"

"It's just—"

Olivia's sharp tone interrupted Jason's waffling. "She's your wife, Jason. Don't you think she deserves some support?"

"Fine," Jason conceded. The chances of successfully stonewalling his wife and mother-in-law while maintaining domestic tranquility were minimal. "I recall seeing information about the victim's family in the file. After dinner, I'll log in and get the kid's address. Will that make you both happy?"

Olivia nodded silently. Rachel beamed. "Did you get anything more from the security cameras?"

"Rach! That's exactly the kind of information you know I can't give you."

Rachel reached out for a spoonful of a reheated Mexican casserole. "Darling, I'm not asking you to give me details, I'm just asking whether you got anything useful. If it's yes, then great. I hope it helps you find the killer. If it's no, then that's too bad. I'd love to know the details, but I understand. You can't share everything with me."

"OK. Sorry." Jason reached across the table and caressed Rachel's hand. "I'm going batty trying to walk this line. I'd love to help you with your reporting. I want you to nail it, but if I give out confidential information and Sully finds out, I'll be in front of Internal Affairs in a New York minute and Sully will have my ass in a sling. So I'm being careful. I told you about the shotgun. But no, there was nothing on the security cams that seems to be helpful. Just..." Jason trailed off, a puzzled look on his face.

"What else can we talk about?" Olivia said. "Have you two made any plans for New Year's Eve yet?"

Jason did not respond, seemingly deep in thought.

"Jason?" Rachel waved her hand to get her husband's attention.

"Sorry," Jason startled. "I was just thinking that we may want to talk to Palazzo's nephew after all."

"What?!" Rachel cried out. "I told you I wanted to talk to him and now, suddenly, *you* want to talk to him? That is so not fair! I suppose now you're not going to give me the kid's address, either?"

"Listen, Rachel—"

"No, Jason, *you* listen to *me!*" Olivia interrupted. "This is nonsense. You talk to Rachel about your investigations all the time. Most of the time you're divulging at least some sensitive information. The two of you brainstorm about your theories and she helps you. That's what wives and husbands do. You owe her for plenty of good ideas that I bet you took full credit for back at the station with Mike and Sully. Why, it was Rachel who gave you the information about that witness to the Palazzo murder on Sunday night, didn't she?"

"She did," Jason said softly, looking at Rachel, "that's true."

"And she told you about the witness who called her yesterday."

"That guy didn't have any useful information." Jason worked hard to maintain a calm tone.

"The point is that Rachel helped you. I bet Mike talks about his cases with Michelle, too. You men never give your women any credit, but you'd be lost without them. Now, it's time you started trusting my Rachel. She's not going to go telling people what you talk about. Unless you want to go live by yourself as long as this case is on so you never have to talk to us, you might as well trust us to be discreet." Olivia turned to Rachel. "And, honey, you know you can't use anything Jason tells you. He can't be your source. So can we stop walking on these eggshells?"

Jason blew out a breath, his cheeks expanding like Dizzy Gillespie playing his trumpet. "OK. I get it. There are still things I can't tell anyone and I don't want to put Rachel in a position where she has important information that she can't report. But you're right, Olivia. I can trust Rachel. I always have. I'm sure she's not going to say anything on air that will get me in trouble. Right, honey?"

Rachel looked her husband in the eyes and threw a napkin at his face. Jason dodged the paper projectile and smiled. "You'd better trust me, you big, dumb cop."

The tension seeped from the room like air from a punctured tire. After a sip of wine, Jason said, "The thing is, when I said we got nothing off the security cameras, I meant we got nothing that seemed important. There was a guy who arrived in a cab and we tracked him down, but he doesn't figure to be connected, although we're checking. He's a deputy mayor for the city, a guy named Adam Erickson. We don't have any reason to think his visit was connected to what happened three hours later. But that is not public, so you can't use it."

"I know." Rachel flashed a momentary pout, but immediately pivoted. "Thank you for sharing."

"There were also a couple of young men who visited the shop for an hour in the early afternoon. We don't know who they are. They didn't bring anything in and didn't carry anything out, so we haven't been focused on them. But if Palazzo had a nephew at NYU, I'm wondering if one of those young men might have been him."

"What if it was? If the kid came by to visit his uncle, that seems pretty innocent."

Jason tilted his head left, then right. "Probably. But what if his uncle said something to him about what he was involved with or why someone might be looking for him? The kid might not even realize he heard something important. We'll have to talk to him and see."

Rachel slapped her hand on the table. "I have dibs on talking to him first!"

"There's no such thing as dibs on a witness," Jason chided.

"I want to talk to him first, before you scare him with your cop questions."

"I don't scare witnesses." Jason's response was met by two skeptical faces. "I mean, not unless I'm trying to scare them."

"Why does it matter who goes first?" Rachel asked. "We don't even know for sure whether he was one of the guys you saw on the camera. I need to get him to say sad things about his uncle and tell me what kind of person he was and that he loved him. Once I'm done, you and Mike can quiz him about whether he was even there, and if he was, what his uncle said to him."

She paused to see if Jason agreed, but couldn't read his face.

"First you need to talk to Mike and tell him your brilliant idea that the dead guy's nephew may have been one of the two young men who visited him, and how it would be a good idea to speak with him. Then you'll need to contact the kid and set up an interview. By the time you get to him, it will be afternoon for sure. I can catch him in the morning and be done with him long before you get there. So, it makes the most sense for me to go first. Right? Besides, I wanted to interview him way before you."

Jason could not come up with a good argument. "Fine. Mike and I have another witness we can talk to in the morning. But I want you to send me a text when you're done with the kid. That way there will be no chance of us bumping into you. Say you're done shopping. That will be my signal. OK?"

"OK. Thank you, sweetie."

"Now *that's* more like it," Olivia said.

Chapter 23
Tangled Webs

WHEN MIKE SWUNG through the apartment door Wednesday evening, he saw Michelle through the pass-through kitchen on the far side of the dining table. It was her favorite spot for phone calls, next to the window overlooking 68th Street. Even with the cold December weather, the window was cracked open to allow fresh air to enter. The apartment's management group ran the heat full bore all winter through the old-school radiators, so it was always better to allow some cold in to temper the blast furnace atmosphere.

When Michelle raised her eyes toward Mike, he immediately knew things were not well. "Yes, I know, sweetie. It's hard not to worry. Look, Mike just got home. Let me talk to him about it and I'll call you back later. . .No. You should not get on a bus. I have it under control. I promise."

Michelle opened her eyes wide and flashed Mike a look of disapproval that would have sent a wayward teen running to their bedroom. He searched his memory, wondering what he had done to upset his wife of three years. As the county medical examiner, Michelle dealt with stress constantly. It took a fair bit of wrongdoing to make her visibly annoyed, let alone angry.

Had he forgotten to bring home dinner? No, he was sure Michelle was picking up salad makings to go with the leftover rotisserie chicken from Monday. Was he supposed to pick up Michelle's dry cleaning? He wasn't late. Who was she talking to? A bus? Who did she know who would be getting on a bus? Her sister. Her sister from Atlanta. Worrying about what? It had to be Star, Michelle's niece, who was a first year at NYU. Michelle's sister, Rosie, expected Michelle to be Star's guardian angel.

Shit, he thought.

Mike hung his winter coat on the hallway peg, strode through the kitchen, and leaned down to kiss his spouse. Her lips were pressed together. As soon as he resumed a standing position, Michelle's dark eyes bored into Mike's. "That was Rosie." She did not offer any additional context or explanation.

Mike chose to play the small percentage that the problem with Star was her grades, or a boyfriend, or something else. Anything but the events on a September night in the alley behind *The Scampering Squirrel*. He put on his best poker face. "How is she?"

"She's extremely upset, Mike. I took Star to lunch today. We went down to the bar where she works. I'd never been there. It wasn't as bad as I imagined. There was a delightful bartender there named Jade who told me how wonderful Star is."

When Michelle paused, Mike jumped in to say, "She certainly is. You should be extremely proud of her."

"That's what Jade said." Michelle stared up at her husband, as if waiting for him to speak again. When Mike remained silent, Michelle continued her story. "Jade described Star as a bad-ass. She was impressed by the way

Star handled her encounter with a man with a gun in the alley behind the bar back in September."

"Oh," Mike said in an ode to understatement. He didn't know what story Star told her aunt, so he continued to play dumb.

"Yes, *oh* is right. I had to ask Star about it and she didn't want to tell me. She told me she made *you* promise not to tell me. Is that true, Mike?" Michelle's eyes were cold. "Did you lie to me?"

Mike could hide his true thoughts from anyone at the poker table, but after five years of dating and then marriage, Michelle could read him like a romance novel. He withheld information, which was different from lying, at least in Mike's head. He was protecting Michelle, and Star, from unnecessary anxiety. He had hoped the whole episode was now ancient history. Apparently not.

"Oh, sweetheart, I didn't want you to be upset for no reason after—"

"No reason! No reason for me to know that Star was almost killed!"

"She was not almost killed." Mike was immediately defensive, but instantly realized that was the exact wrong way to handle the situation. He dropped his arms and sank into the straight-backed dining chair nearest to the window. "I'm sorry I didn't tell you. I never lied to you about it. But I never told you. Which is just as bad, I know. We didn't want you and Rosie to freak out. She had only been in New York a month. It was a total accident and it all came out fine. I thought it would be worse for you if you knew, but had to keep it from your sister. Now I'm sure I made a mistake."

"Star told me that psychopath actor held a gun against her neck that left a mark! I had to tell Rosie. Now she wants to come take Star back to Atlanta. She's distraught."

Now Mike saw a slight opening. "You see? Star didn't want her mother to know because she knew Rosie would overreact. And I knew that if you knew, you'd tell Rosie. Star doesn't want to go back to Atlanta. She loves it at NYU. She's starting her internship at the theater in a few weeks. Do you want her to leave?"

Michelle's anger softened. "No. But you should have told me. I could have kept the secret from Rosie."

"But you didn't. You just told her."

Michelle balled her fists. "You still should have told me!"

"It was over. I didn't want you to have to carry that secret. And I didn't want to upset you."

"Don't you tell me what I deserve to be upset about!" Michelle's fist pounded on the table. She was trembling.

Mike covered Michelle's hand with his. "Let me tell you the whole story."

Fifteen minutes later, Mike held his palms open. "I'm sorry. I thought it was best if we moved on and didn't make a big deal about it. Star agreed. But it wasn't her idea. She was pretty shaken up and I put the idea into her head. Don't blame her. It was my doing."

Michelle was silent during Mike's recitation of the full story. This was more frightening to Mike than any outburst. "Don't you think I can handle the truth? After all we've been through together?" She struggled to get out the words. "I told you once that I don't want you to try to protect me. Do you remember?"

"I remember. But I guess I forgot."

Mike had interrogated mob lieutenants, serial killers, and hardened criminals. He stared down mayors and congresspersons and Wall Street tycoons. But in that moment, at his dining table, his stomach turned inside out and his resolve melted. He was guilty and he knew it. He took a risk with all the best of intentions, knowing the consequences. He wanted to shield Michelle from the reality of the events. She would have been upset. She would have been worried about Star. She would have been compelled to tell her sister, who would have held the entire episode against her, despite Michelle having had nothing to do with it. Michelle had advocated for keeping Star entirely out of the plan. Mike poo-pooed Michelle's concerns. He said there was no risk to her, and there should not have been any. It was a fluke. But he made a decision to withhold the truth. Now, he had to face the consequences.

"It's in the past now," he said. "She's fine. She handled it like a trooper. I'm sorry."

"You're sorry?" Michelle stood and looked out the window, the breeze ruffling her cream blouse's sleeve. "You mean you're sorry I found out."

"Yes. That's true. I'm sorry you found out. I'm also truly sorry I made the decision to keep the facts from you. I thought it was best at the time. But now, I'm sorry."

Michelle spun around and marched to their bedroom, slamming the door behind her.

Mike remained at the table, his palms pressed against the unyielding maple surface. He had faced the music and it was a slam-down. He figured that pleading for forgiveness through the bedroom door would be futile. She was pissed at him for good reason. He needed to own it.

Rising from the chair to a creak from his knees, Mike opened the tiny closet next to the stove and removed an apron bearing a New York Mets logo and the phrase *Ya Gotta Believe*. Extracting a carton of Egg Beaters and a container of skim milk, he began preparing omelets. It was one of the few things he could cook well that didn't involve a charcoal grill. He hoped when the onions and garlic filled the apartment with their enticing aroma, Michelle's hunger would overcome her anger. It was worth a try. If Michelle never emerged from the bedroom, at least he would have a decent dinner.

Topsy, their COVID rescue cat, leapt onto the counter, sniffing at the simmering onions. A soft meow made Mike wonder if Michelle fed her before taking the phone call from her sister. The cat generally avoided Mike, suggesting that her close presence was not merely a ploy to get a second dinner.

"You don't eat until Michelle eats," Mike said, as if Topsy understood.

The cat meowed louder, then jumped to the ground and scurried away toward the bedroom. Mike heard scratches on the wooden door, followed by a click and a squeak as Michelle let her comfort pet inside. He smiled, knowing that having Topsy to cuddle with would help Michelle get over her anger. He also hoped that Topsy's feeding schedule would draw her out of the bedroom – eventually.

* * *

"I COULD HAVE HANDLED IT," Michelle said when she tucked a napkin into her lap and dug into her omelet. She had meticulously measured out Topsy's dinner without speaking to Mike. With the cat fed, Michelle sat across from him. "Thank you for cooking, dear."

"I know you could have handled the truth," Mike said softly, raising his fork. "I didn't want you to have to. I made a choice in the moment. Now I regret it."

"You damned well better regret it." A tiny hint of a smile played at the edges of Michelle's mouth.

Mike put his fork down without eating. "Saying I love you doesn't mean shit at a time like this. But I love you. Tell me what I can do to earn your forgiveness."

Michelle sat in silence, chewing. Topsy jumped into her lap and purred while Michelle stroked her ears. "I'll let you know if I think of anything."

Mike dropped his head. "I owe you."

"You absolutely do." Now Michelle's smile spread across her face.

"Am I sleeping on the couch?"

"No, silly. Why should I be punished for your transgression?"

Mike's smile matched Michelle's.

Chapter 24
Blades of Karma

THAT EVENING AFTER DINNER, Ryan and Will spent two hours playing *Blades of Karma* in Ryan's room. Will logged into his game account from Ryan's laptop, while Ryan connected directly to his PS4 console. Ryan suggested that they invite Star to help them again, but Will wanted to try without a third.

"We're here. Let's keep going," he said.

Ryan wasn't going to press the point, although he made the occasional comment when having another player would have been helpful.

After more than twenty attempts, they finally defeated the boss and cleared the level where they had been so stuck. They waited, anticipating a clue to the whereabouts of the dingus at the end of the level. But nothing presented itself. There was only a portal allowing them to reach the next level, a dense forest intersected by a narrow path.

"Do you think this is the secret path?" Ryan asked.

"It's not hidden, so probably not. But maybe there's a side path inside this forest. We have to find it, so let's try to veer off whenever we see anything that could be a secret entrance."

They spent the next hour exploring the forest path, battling challengers that popped up to block their progress.

After defeating a group of giant spiders, Will fell backward on Ryan's bed. "Where the hell is the clue?"

They played in silence, save for shouted instructions to each other. On the far side of the forest, a flat, dry plain ran across the landscape for fifty feet, ending in a sheer cliff of gray rock. On the ground at the foot of the rock face, several skeletons lay in impossible positions. Skulls, separated from the rest of their former bodies, were piled up against a boulder like a warning for future travelers to avoid the area. About twenty feet up the wall, a horseshoe-shaped opening marked the location of a cave. Undoubtedly, some monster lurked inside the dark expanse. Since they saw no enemies between them and the mountain, Ryan and Will advanced their avatars, moving carefully while they scanned the virtual landscape for hazards.

Then, Ryan called out, "Look up!"

When Will's character looked at the sky, he could faintly make out the top of the edifice. Thin white clouds drifted by the peak. Then he saw what had caught Ryan's attention. A brown cross flashed across the high rock pinnacle. A bird. A hawk. Maybe a falcon!

"You think?" Will asked.

"Hell yes!" Ryan responded. "It has to be. Maybe there's a nest. Whatever it is we're looking for, it could be up there."

"So, we bypass the cave?"

"Yeah. For now, at least. If we can't climb up the cliff, we'll have to go through the cave. Maybe there's a way up from inside, but let's not disturb whatever is in there until we have to."

The boys' avatars carefully crept up a narrow path they found at the far edge of the mountain. It took them to a flat shelf of rock in front of the cave, no more than three feet deep. With no other obvious route (and after several failed attempts to climb the sheer rock face), they moved past the cave opening, not making any move to enter. Two strides past the dark doorway, Ryan spun around when he heard a low growl. He drew his sword and confronted an ogre, a creature ten feet tall with four arms and skin the color and texture of boulders.

"Look out!" Will shouted, but it was too late. The ogre emitted a guttural shriek and swung a wooden club, throwing Ryan's avatar off the cliff and onto the ground below. Dead.

"Fuck!" Ryan exclaimed, tossing his controller onto the bed. He watched as Will struggled with the monster, but it was far too strong, fast, and resistant to slashes from Will's sword. In two minutes, Will's avatar lay on the barren brown dust at the foot of the cliff, on top of the now-crushed skull of the boss' former victims.

Ryan splashed down on his dorm bed while Will tipped back in the threadbare desk chair, putting his feet on a white radiator.

"Wanna try again now?" Will asked. "We gotta find a way around that ogre."

Ryan rubbed his wrist. "Nah. Not enough time. We'll try again tomorrow. At least we have something to push for. If that bird was a falcon, it could be what Lou wanted us to find."

"I know. Let's hope. A clue to the dingus has to be there."

"Will, what if the guys who killed Lou found the drive in the shop? They did a pretty good job of picking through his inventory. If they found it, then we're chasing a ghost."

Will hurled a pillow at his friend's head. "Shut up. If the guys who killed Lou got the drive, then it's game over. Unless they never use the NYU data, or the university never notices that their data got breached."

Ryan grunted. "If there's a breach, they are sure as shit going to blame us – well, blame me. They'll blame me for sure. The hackers used my account to get into the university server."

Will's face drained of color. "If they find out I was involved, they could pull my scholarship. Dude, that can't happen. Promise me. No matter what, we won't tell them what we were doing when the hackers got in."

"You really think they'd expel us?" Ryan's stomach did a somersault. "It was an accident."

"Yeah. Sure. But if there's a data breach, they'll have to blame somebody. And we're actually the ones to blame. They won't take mercy on a couple of underclassmen. No way. So, we have to make sure they never find out. I'll never tell. You won't, either. Right?"

"No. I wouldn't." Ryan softly banged his head on the wall behind his bed. "What I really want is to find that file and turn it over to them so they can burn it."

"You think they killed Lou over the dingus, and not something else he was involved in?"

"We can't know for sure." Ryan struggled up from the bed and gazed out the window, where a truck rumbled down MacDougal Street. "But it happened three days after we gave him the drive. That's too much of a coincidence for me."

"OK. I'm out of here. See you in programming in the morning." Will grabbed his backpack on his way out of Ryan's room. The door closed with a *ker-chunk* as Ryan turned up the volume on his miniature speakers, which were connected to his phone via Bluetooth. As "Uptown Funk" filled the space with its hypnotic beat, Ryan sat down at the desk and opened his academic laptop.

* * *

LENNY WAS TIRED AND HUNGRY, and thrilled that the conversation in Ryan's dorm room was finally over for the night. Once Will left, it was unlikely Ryan would start talking to himself about the data file, which he didn't have and didn't know the location of.

The Chinese tech crew was still diligently working on the remaining devices from the pawn shop, mining the hard drives for any sign of the "dingus". Lenny had taken to calling it that, partly because the Dragons didn't know what he was talking about. Yung Ji brought in Mexican food for his crew, which was stinking up the boiler room as far as Lenny was concerned. Why couldn't these jerks eat Chinese food? It was clear neither they nor their Gallata counterparts had found the prize. That was fine with Lenny. The Dragons were rude and unfriendly and he secretly hoped they never found the dingus.

He called The Cannon and spoke in a hushed whisper Ji couldn't hear. "Hey, Boss. Will has left for the night and Ryan's done talking. They're still playing *Blades of Karma* and have definitely not found the file. They still think there's a clue in the game, but they haven't found it yet. I'm going to knock off for the night and get some food and sleep. I'll be back here first thing tomorrow. That OK with you?"

After a pause, Cannon said, "Sure. Fine. Why are you whispering?"

"Sorry, Boss. I don't want the Chinese idiots to hear me."

"OK. I get that. They're creepy as hell. Fine. Knock off. But keep listening tomorrow. If they find the file, I need you on 'em like white on rice."

"You know it."

"What you know?" Ji's voice snapped Lenny's attention away from his phone as he punched the END button. The Dragon boss had crept up behind Lenny while he was on the phone.

"I know shit," Lenny responded.

"Who you talking to?"

"I was talkin' to The Cannon. My boss. Giving him a report before I knock off for the night. You have a problem with that?" Lenny raised his voice, getting the attention of two of the Gallata techs sitting at the long work table across the room. They stood up to observe the commotion. The four Dragon techs looked up from their work in response. Within seconds, all eight techs were standing and staring across the tables like rugby players getting ready for a scrum.

"You tell me. So I know what you know." Ji pointed at Lenny.

Lenny, although short and thin, was a better fighter than his opponents usually figured. But this was not the time. He took a step back. "I told him it was a quiet night and nothing much happened in the kid's room. Now his friend has left and he's studying. Alone." Lenny could see over Ji's shoulder that all his Gallata colleagues were looking at him. Emboldened and also embarrassed by his meek response, he quickly added, "You got a problem with that?"

"I have problem if you keep secrets." Ji pointed at the listening table. "Maybe I have my man listen, too."

"Go to fucking town," Lenny responded, bowing sarcastically and gesturing toward the rickety cluster of tables.

"What town?"

"Stuyvesant Town," Lenny responded with a straight face, referring to the massive public housing project several blocks away.

"Where is that?"

"Up your ass!" Lenny said, prompting laughter from all the Gallatas.

A Chinese tech named Huoban took offense. He picked up an already-searched iPhone and hurled it at close range into the nose of his closest Gallata counterpart, who was known in the room as Little Tony. By the time the first drop of blood from Little Tony's nose dripped onto the white table, the other three Gallata techs had crashed across the plastic and metal barrier. They engaged their Corporate Dragon counterparts as equipment spilled from the toppled tables with a metallic squelching sound.

The Gallata men may have been on the tech team, but they were still part of a tough-as-nails crime organization and had all been in their share of fights. Punches and kicks, accompanied by curses in English and Mandarin, erupted with the speed and force of an avalanche. Little Tony shook off the pain in his face and stepped toward Huoban.

Then, all the combatants froze as a gunshot exploded nearby. Ji stood ten feet from the melee, smoke drifting up to the low ceiling from the muzzle of his black Glock G-17. A hole slightly larger than all the others appeared in the foam ceiling tile. All eyes swung to Ji and his gun.

"Back off!" he yelled in English, then barked an order in Chinese. His men pushed away from their wrestling partners and stepped back. The Gallata techs did the same.

Little Tony picked up a power cord adapter and threw the black rectangle at Huoban, shouting, "Fuck you!" The trailing cord caught on its plug, causing the adapter to fall harmlessly to the ground. Huoban stepped back involuntarily upon seeing the black brick heading toward his head.

Another shot engulfed the room. Little Tony screamed, hopped on one foot twice, then crumpled to the ground, blood oozing from both his nose and his right sneaker.

"Enough!" Ji shouted. He barked another command in Chinese, prompting Huoban to scowl and turn away. Ji pulled out a phone and held it to his face. "Car is coming. You go fix foot." He motioned toward the other Gallata employees. "You go with him."

The three men picked up Little Tony and helped him limp to the door. One of his colleagues grabbed a roll of paper towels from the kitchen area and wrapped his bleeding foot.

The Dragon techs rolled the fallen tables back into place and picked up the jumbled equipment in silence.

Lenny, not being inclined to trade barbs anymore, closed down the listening station and donned his coat. He tossed his trash into the can next to a pillar and walked past Ji without a word.

Chapter 25
Interrogation

RYAN JOLTED AWAKE at the sound of his generic ringtone. He groped for the phone and was surprised and unnerved by an unfamiliar female voice. The woman said Ryan was required to attend an urgent meeting at the NYU Security office. His stomach did a double somersault with a half twist. He called Will, who attempted to calm down his friend. They had discussed the possibility that the university would be able to trace the hack back to Ryan's account. Ryan knew what his story would be. It was a good story.

He dressed without showering, making sure to pick out clothes he had not worn since his last trip to the laundry room. Trudging across the street in the cold morning air, he practiced his statement. By the time he reached the building housing the university security office, he was confident.

After he showed his university ID, an NYU security officer in a blue uniform escorted Ryan to his meeting. The guard held open a heavy oak door and beckoned the student inside. Ryan immediately locked eyes with Jan Yates, Head of Security for the university.

"Mr. Gelb, please have a seat."

Yates came from a Norwegian family. He had long since jettisoned the old-world pronunciation of "Yan" and accepted the Americanized name of Jan. He was a solid man whose broad shoulders were obvious even under a suit jacket. Blue Scandinavian eyes without glasses gave him an intimidatingly athletic appearance. A buzz-cut marked him as former military.

The office was much more impressive than the spartan work space through which Ryan traversed on his way to the meeting. Outside, the banks of video monitors and rows of cubicles resembled a telemarketing workspace. Inside, the boss' office was lined with plush carpeting and sported paneled walls hung with photographs and an original oil painting. The furniture was dark wood. An overstuffed sofa dominated one wall, where a woman wearing a pleated business suit and a younger man holding a clipboard sat with stern expressions. Ryan's throat contracted involuntarily. Yates directed him to an uncomfortable straight-backed chair.

Yates sat on the edge of his desk chair, hands clasped on the black blotter, which was devoid of any papers or folders. "Mr. Gelb, I assume you know that it is your obligation to report any breach of NYU cybersecurity."

Ryan swiveled his head toward the two figures on the sofa, then back to Yates. Despite spending the entire walk to the security office rehearsing his story, he found it difficult to speak. A bead of sweat trickled down the back of his neck. He cleared his throat. "Ahem. Um, I – yeah, of course I know. Is that why I'm here?"

"What do you think?" Yates fixed a stare at the obviously intimidated student before him. It was standard procedure for him: Present a menacing presence and let the terrified students incriminate themselves. Guilty people who were not practiced liars often spilled their guts without the need for interrogation. Ryan's eyes darted around the room. A bead of sweat slid from his ragged sideburn to his neck, where his carotid artery throbbed.

"I don't know," Ryan said. He knew he should keep quiet, but he was so nervous he worried that he'd puke on the man's desk. "I had a hack on my personal laptop the week before last, but I'm not supposed to report that, am I?"

Yates maintained his death stare for another ten seconds. "Miss Lang," he turned his head toward the woman on the couch, "would you please let Mr. Gelb know the results of your investigation into the security breach?"

Miss Lang's black hair was pulled back into a tight bun above black-rimmed glasses. Her voice was deep and throaty. Ryan wondered if she was as nervous as he was. "We traced the breach to your student account, Mr. Gelb."

Ryan did a credible job of looking stunned. "What? When?"

Lang stole a quick glance at her boss, who nodded. "Access occurred at 1:32 a.m. eleven days ago. The breach was active for fourteen minutes. The intruder bypassed a firewall and downloaded files that you did not have authority to access."

"Mr. Gelb!" Yates' voice snapped Ryan's head back to the man's penetrating blue eyes. "Did you hack your way into files for which you did not have access?"

"No!" Ryan said, more loudly than he intended. This was the absolute truth, so it didn't take much effort to be sincere. "That sounds like the same time my laptop was hacked. I was working on some internet research. It was a new machine – well, it was used, but it didn't have anything on it. That's why I was using it for the research. I was working in the computer lab on a hard-wired connection. When I noticed the hack, I disconnected from the internet and shut down the machine. Later, I ran a virus scan and it found a file I couldn't clean. I tried to open it to see what was in it – which was part of the research I was doing – but it was encrypted and I couldn't open it. So, I copied the file to a thumb drive and took it to my uncle, who is amazing with computers, to see if he could help me open it. Then, I reformatted the laptop's drive to clear it off. I had no idea that the hackers accessed NYU files. I don't understand how that could have happened."

When Ryan finished his speech, he looked around the room, hoping to get some sympathy from Lang or the guy next to her. They both looked at Yates.

"Miss Lang, is that explanation consistent with the facts as we know them?"

"Yes, Sir," she responded tersely.

"I'm curious, though," Yates continued. "Why copy the virus file and engage your uncle when you could have deleted everything?"

Ryan tried to swallow but his throat was bone dry. "Um, well, I'm in a cybersecurity class, so I thought maybe there was something in the hack file that might be interesting."

Yates stared skeptically at the obviously nervous student. "Well, Mr. Gelb, for now we'll assume you are telling us the truth. For now. We will need to get the thumb drive for further analysis. When can you get it to us?"

"Well," Ryan hesitated, "I didn't get it back from Uncle Lou. So, I don't have it. I think he erased the thumb drive."

Yates sat back in his chair, assessing Ryan's answer. He snatched a pencil from a chrome holder and swiveled it between two fingers like a helicopter blade. "OK. That makes some sense. In that case, I'd like to have a talk with your uncle. What's his number?"

"Um, Sir, that's not going to be possible. You see, my uncle died."

"Died, you say?" Ryan would have sworn the man's buzz cut literally bristled. "That's an amazing coincidence. I don't suppose you have a death certificate?"

"You won't need one," Ryan said. "It's been all over the news. My uncle is Lou Palazzo. He was murdered on Sunday."

Chapter 26
Excuse Me, Your Honor

ARRANGING AN INTERVIEW between two homicide detectives and an official in the city government was a delicate dance. If the cops barged into the politician's office and demanded to speak with them, it created the appearance that wrongdoing was afoot. The optics were terrible for the mayor's office, and that would blow back on the NYPD if it turned out the interviewee was fully innocent.

On the other hand, giving the potential witness advance notice that the police wanted to speak with them would allow the person of interest time to prepare their answers. If there was any criminal conduct involved, the police gave up the critical element of surprise.

The compromise was to get the witness somewhere the cops could corner them and conduct the interview without many other people around. For Deputy Mayor Erickson, the path started with Sully, who called Police Commissioner Earl Ward and explained the situation. Ward called his good friend Mayor Frederick Douglass and gave a somewhat opaque explanation about needing to meet with Erickson but not wanting to attract attention – for the deputy mayor's benefit, and for the mayor's. The mayor called back half an hour later, and after another game of telephone, Mike and Jason left the precinct for City Hall.

Adam Erickson was in a morning meeting in a conference room near the mayor's office when the detectives arrived. The chief of staff, an elegant Black woman named Mildred, escorted the cops to a sitting room the mayor used for one-on-one press interviews. After a few minutes, the deputy mayor came through the door.

"Mr. Erickson," Jason began softly, "I'm Detective Jason Dickson. This is Detective Mike Stoneman. We're involved in a murder investigation and need some information from you." Mike preferred to hang back, partly because Jason would have a better chance of establishing a report with the Black deputy mayor and partly because he wanted to observe the man carefully during the interview.

"Of course, Detectives. I know who you are. You're working the Lou Palazzo murder, right?" Erickson wore a well-tailored gray suit with a conservative tie. His shirt had standard cuffs and no monogram. The look contrasted with Erickson's boss, Mayor Douglass, whose French cuffs, gold cufflinks, and suspenders with matching ties and pocket squares made him stand out as a fashion icon. Erickson was more of a working man's politician.

If he were in a deputy mayor job, Jason mused, he would dress better. "That's right, Sir. What can you tell us about Lou Palazzo?"

Erickson's placid face morphed into a puzzled frown. "I'm sorry. You're asking me about the victim?"

"Yes." Jason said, then fell silent. It was one of Mike's principle interrogation techniques: Especially when you suspect the witness knows something and you want them to talk, you shut up. Let there be silence and let the witness fill it. The room was padded and soundproofed. There were no windows to let in street noise. Jason could hear his pounding pulse.

Erickson stared at Jason. "Why would you think I know anything about the man?"

"You knew him, didn't you?" Jason calmly returned the volley.

After a pause, during which Erickson's eyes darted back and forth between Jason and Mike, he said, "A man like that doesn't frequent the same professional or social circles as I."

"Probably not," Jason agreed. "And yet, you did know him."

"What makes you think that?"

Jason showed no anger or annoyance with his witness. "Can you perhaps answer my question, first? Sir?"

"I did not have anything to do with the man's murder, if that's what you are implying." Erickson's smooth demeanor cracked a bit as he answered, appearing defensive and a bit hostile.

"I'll take your word on that for now, but I still would like you to tell me how you knew Mr. Palazzo."

The deputy mayor fixed his eyes on Jason's. "I have had occasion to use Mr. Palazzo's professional services. His shop is in the neighborhood where I grew up. I needed some help with a computer and I gave him some business. Nothing more."

Mike scrutinized the man's answer. It was delivered calmly, but it made no sense that he would have avoided answering so persistently if the answer was as innocent as it seemed. It was more likely he had spent the duration of the questioning composing the answer.

Jason continued, "When was the last time you saw Mr. Palazzo?"

This time, Erickson did not hesitate. "It was on Sunday. The day he died."

"So, Sir, you can understand why we're asking."

"I can. And you can understand my reluctance to be connected to such a crime. I did not know Mr. Palazzo well. We had only a few interactions. But he seemed like a hard-working man and I like to support people like him. Lou didn't deserve to go out like that. But I don't have any relevant information for you."

"With all due respect, Sir, you never know when some bit of information is going to prove important to an investigation. What sort of work was he doing with your computer?"

"I didn't say it was *my* computer," Erickson quickly responded. "It was a private matter I would prefer not to discuss. Suffice to say that the computer was damaged and needed some repairs and I asked Lou to see what he could do."

"Was he finished with the work? Is that why you visited him Sunday?"

"No. He needed a fingerprint image in order to unlock the machine. I had to go in person to do that. I was only there for a few minutes."

Jason raised an eyebrow. "You said it wasn't your machine."

"I did. And it wasn't. But I tried to deal with the problem myself and had locked the machine with my fingerprint while it was in my possession."

"OK, Sir. Can you tell us anything about Mr. Palazzo's behavior that afternoon? Did he say anything unusual? Did he seem to be in any trouble?"

"No. Our interaction was very brief and simple. He called me to say he needed my fingerprint earlier in the day. I agreed to dash over and give it to him between meetings. I was in and out in just a few minutes. We didn't talk much. I was in a hurry and didn't notice anything unusual. That's all I know."

Jason glanced at Mike, who shook his head almost imperceptibly, letting Jason know he had no additional questions. "Thank you, Sir. We appreciate your cooperation. If we have any other questions for you, we'll certainly let you know." Jason held out a business card, which Erickson took and stuffed into his shirt pocket.

"And, Detectives, I do appreciate your discretion in handling this interview. It would have been awkward if you had come to my office for this. Thank you."

"Of course," Mike said, his first words since Erickson's arrival. "We always try to take the optics into account. Commissioner Ward wants to maintain good relations with the mayor's office."

Without another word, Erickson walked from the room.

"Why so evasive?" Jason asked once the two detectives were alone.

"Don't know." Mike circled his neck, which popped loudly. "He's hiding something. He knew Palazzo better than he's letting on. Did you notice how he kept calling him 'Lou?' He doesn't want to talk about what he was really doing there. Of course, it may not be connected to the murder."

"But it could be."

"Yeah," Mike said, moving toward the door. "But until we have more, we keep our hands off the mayor's office. He's not off the hook yet, though."

Chapter 27
Everyone Has a Boss

TWO HOURS LATER, Jan Yates sat in an office more impressive than his own. University President Sharron Henry sat in a maroon leather armchair, flanked by Jameson O'Shaughnessy, the university's general counsel, and the chairperson of the university's Board of Trustees, Walter Hammond. All the participants understood the stakes. Disclosing a data breach involving financial accounts would require notifying every parent and student as well as any alumni who made contributions to the school. It would be a gargantuan embarrassment for a prestigious university to admit that it could not protect its own data. Federal regulations required such notices, if there was an actual breach.

Yates broke the bad news. "Ms. Henry, we have confirmed that there was a data breach. Confidential information was downloaded onto the student's computer. My team is still trying to catalogue exactly which files were copied, but it looks like more than a thousand. It's possible there was sensitive personal and financial data involved. However, we don't know whether those files were ever transferred from the student's computer to any hostile agent. The student says he disconnected from the internet and shut down the machine, which is consistent with the duration of the access we observed in our investigation."

"Does that mean there was no breach?" President Henry asked in the direction of the university's chief lawyer.

O'Shaughnessy answered, "Sharron, I'm not an expert on this. I can't say for sure whether it is or it isn't."

Yates interjected, "We have no confirmation that anybody other than this one student had access to the data. The kid says he didn't see the data because he couldn't access the file, which he thought was a virus. It's possible the hackers never uploaded the file to another source."

Henry looked back at O'Shaughnessy. He shrugged. "Whether that triggers a disclosure obligation, I can't say. We'll need outside counsel to weigh in on it."

"How long?"

The lawyer, with graying hair that always looked like it had been cut that day, looked back at his boss and looped a thumb in his suspenders. "I'd say at least a few days. Maybe not before Monday."

"OK. Let's get that opinion as soon as possible. Until then, we keep this information absolutely confidential. If there was a breach, we'll disclose, as we must. But let's not do it any sooner than necessary. Jan, I want you to monitor whatever sources you have to watch for evidence of an actual breach. If any of our student or alumni financial information turns up on the internet, we'll have to go public immediately. We'll prepare the necessary press releases and letters to the government agencies and the affected students and alumni, just in case. But if we can keep a lid on it, then we keep the lid locked down. Agreed?"

Everyone in the room acknowledged their agreement. Hammond, the university trustee, leaned toward Yates. Speaking with a Texas drawl, he asked, "Do you have any idea how this happened? That data is supposed to be secure. How in the hell did a hacker get in through a student account and past our firewall? That cloud system is certified as fully secure. Even users with authorized passwords need two-factor authentication to get in."

Yates' shoulders and chin slumped simultaneously. "We don't know for sure, Sir. We're still analyzing the hack, but it appears to have been very sophisticated. It was Sunday night – early on Monday morning, actually. We were uploading a system update and a set of new applications that night. The developers shut down the servers during the upload, but this Gelb kid was in the system using a hard-wired connection. The tech team thinks the firewalls may have been compromised due to the upload in progress. It might have been a fluke. Or, maybe these hackers have some new program that beat our security. I don't know. We're still evaluating it."

When nobody else had a question, the meeting adjourned. On his way out, Yates felt a tug on his sleeve. His boss took him aside when the room was otherwise empty. "Jan, is there any chance that the confidential security files could have been accessed?"

"We don't know for sure yet. It's possible."

President Henry blew out a long, slow breath. "The credit card numbers and bank accounts are bad. Embarrassing, but we can weather that storm. Hacks happen. But if we get a leak about the Aswani investigation—"

"I know." Yates turned away, glancing out the third-floor window as if someone might be there eavesdropping. "We kept a lid on it. He has complied with the confidentiality agreement. But we couldn't delete the files in case there's a lawsuit. Each individual document was encrypted, so even if the hackers downloaded the files, they wouldn't be able to open them. And if the hackers were after financial data, they won't be interested in text files."

"You said it was a sophisticated hack, Jan. Somebody that sophisticated could break through the encryption. Right?"

Yates hung his head slightly. "It's possible. I can't say otherwise."

Henry sat behind her desk, as if the meeting was over, then said, "If you have to bend a few rules to monitor this, or contact some people who aren't on the official payroll, you make it happen. This could be Armageddon, so you do whatever it takes."

"I understand, Sharron. And what about the police?"

"You mean the murder?"

"Yes. Mr. Gelb's uncle getting murdered days after getting the file may not be a coincidence. I'm sure the officers investigating the homicide would want to know."

President Henry pursed her lips and stared at a photograph on the far side of the room in which she posed with former mayor Mike Bloomberg. "That's not our problem. If we disclose it, there's no way we can keep it confidential. The police would want to know what data was in the downloaded file. At this point, we don't have any specific reason to think there is a connection, so we are not obstructing justice if we keep quiet. So, we keep quiet. If that changes, you let me know."

"Absolutely." Yates turned and left the office.

Pulling out her personal phone, Henry dialed an alumnus who had a high enough profile to be listed in her private directory. Being able to tap a high-ranking officer at the FBI was a luxury she did not take for granted.

"Chester, it's Sharron Henry. I have a situation that may need some discreet assistance. I need someone who can keep things out of the press in order to protect the university's reputation. Can I call you if the shit hits the fan?"

"You know you can, Ms. Henry. I owe everything to NYU. Let me know what you need."

After hanging up, Henry felt better. It still could get bad, but she had all the pieces in place that she could. There was nothing else to do now, except wait. And pray.

Chapter 28
Why Was He There?

RACHEL AND TERRY WERE WAITING in the lobby of Ryan's dorm building when he returned from the NYU security meeting. They were not sure whether they were trying to catch the student coming or going. They hoped the photo from his high school yearbook would be close enough to let them spot him, which they did as he flashed his ID to a sleepy student desk attendant.

"Ryan Gelb?" Rachel inquired, trying to be non-threatening. "I'm Rachel Robinson, ACN News. We're doing a feature on your uncle's tragic death. Can you spare me a few minutes to give me some memories of him?"

As shell-shocked as he was coming out of his security grilling, Ryan found some solace in talking about his Uncle Lou. For ten minutes, he reminisced about what a great mentor and friend Lou was. The happy stories poured out, along with a few tears. Ryan excused himself, saying he had another class to get to and needed to visit his room first.

Rachel and Terry retreated to the warmth of the ACN van. Over cups of Starbucks, with their producer, Sandi, on the speaker phone, Rachel plotted out her next moves.

"Did you get anything good from the kid?" Sandi asked.

"Not bad," Rachel said. "We need more for a decent report, but he gave me what we needed. He talked about what a great guy his uncle was and how he helped Ryan with his computer programming training. The kid was emotional enough but not a pansy."

"Terry? You agree with that assessment?"

Rachel flashed an annoyed expression at the phone, then at Terry. Her producer didn't trust Rachel to evaluate the substance of her own interview. Life as a rookie reporter, she assumed.

It made Rachel smile when Terry had her back. "Yes," he said firmly. "Rachel knows what she's doing. She cajoled the kid and got everything out of him that we could expect. He was nervous, but warmed up by the end. It was good. Not enough for a whole feature, but solid material." Terry nodded silently at Rachel. She formed her hands into a heart and patted her chest.

"OK, what's the next element of your piece? What do we have on the investigation?"

Rachel sipped her coffee. "I'm working on another angle. I'm not sure it's truly related to the murder, but it's connected to the victim. I should have some more on it later today."

"What is it?" Sandi pressed. "I have to justify keeping Terry out in the field with you. Dave will want to know why he's not available for breaking news. If you can't give me details, I'll have to call him back to the barn and you can chase your lead solo."

Rachel hesitated. She could tell Sandi was serious. Dave seemed to want her to fail. Taking away her cameraman would push her firmly in that direction. She couldn't let herself miss this chance. "There was somebody who visited the pawn shop on Sunday. Somebody who may have some information. The security camera across the street captured him getting out of a cab, going into the shop, staying for a few minutes, then coming out and driving away in the same cab. It looked kind of suspicious. He's connected to the mayor's office."

"Whoa! Well, that could be dynamite. Dave will cream in his jeans if you bring back something that throws shade on Douglass. Connecting one of his underlings to a triple murder would be outstanding. What's the guy's name?"

"Adam Erickson."

"I know who he is!" The excitement in Sandi's voice was obvious. "What can I do to help?"

Rachel had not fully thought through her next course of action. "I guess I need to figure out where to find him?" She immediately kicked herself. This was not how a competent reporter would talk to her producer. Or was it? From what Rachel had observed at ACN, the producers did all the important thinking and the reporters simply held the microphone and looked cute on camera.

"Leave that to me," Sandi responded. "I'll make some calls and see if I can find out his schedule for the day. You'll never get into his office with Terry and a camera, but maybe we can catch him outside."

"Great. So, I'm thinking that I'll try to surprise him and get a reaction when I ask what his relationship was with Lou Palazzo, a known organized crime figure who was murdered a few hours after the deputy mayor's visit." Rachel tingled, thinking about bringing in such a juicy story. She suppressed the anxiety burning in her chest.

"What's your source for the information about the security camera?"

Rachel froze. Jason had shared this information about the case specifically because Olivia egged him on, and on the promise that she would not use it. Now, she was blabbing to her producer. She should have anticipated this question. "Um, I can't say."

"What do you mean you can't – oh. Oh, sure. I get it. That's your secret source, huh? Fine. But make sure you have some corroboration. Unless the guy admits it. I'll let Dave know. He'll want Standards to review it."

"Um, sure thing," Rachel responded hesitantly. She looked at Terry, who shrugged. It was her story. He was just the cameraman.

Sandi hung up without making Rachel squirm any further. When she and Terry were alone again, Rachel took a long drink from her now-tepid Starbucks.

"Thanks for backing me up," she said.

"No worries." Terry tipped his coffee, which Rachel had purchased, in her direction. She had heard from more than one other reporter at ACN that keeping your cameraman happy was the key to success. "Where to now?"

"City Hall, I guess," Rachel suggested.

"You got it." Terry climbed into the driver's seat.

Twenty minutes later, Rachel and Terry were perched on the lowest step of the marble stairs leading up to the city's administrative office building on Centre Street. Fresh cups of coffee and a half-dozen donuts constituted lunch for them both. As they watched a young woman wearing a tiara and a white lace veil charge up the stairs with a man in tow, Rachel's phone buzzed.

Rachel answered before the end of the first ring. "Talk to me."

"He's got a 12:30 appearance at a rally sponsored by the Teamsters union. They're threatening to strike Christmas week if the company doesn't reach an agreement on a new contract. The mayor is a big supporter, as you know. They're big on taking public transportation to show how environmentally friendly they are, so you can bet he'll be heading for the cross-town bus on Chambers Street. You can intercept him when he comes out of the building."

"Great!" Rachel said, motioning to Terry that they needed to get ready. It was three minutes before noon.

Rachel fixed her eyes on the massive brass-and-glass doors above the marble stairs. She did not notice the man who stopped a few feet behind her. "Well, what have we here? The ACN rookie squad?"

Rachel spun around at the mention of ACN. Dexter Peacock was *The New York Times'* most senior reporter covering city politics and crime. He had a reputation for being a pretentious prick, but one who got exclusive scoops. Rachel had seen his name a hundred times in print, and heard Jason talk about how much he and Mike detested the reporter. Peacock was relentless and smart and tended to ask the most annoying questions. The homicide detectives avoided him like the plague, except when they wanted to leak information discreetly to the press. In those cases, Peacock was their go-to reporter. The guy was obnoxious, but he knew how to keep his sources confidential. His tweed jacket and bowler hat identified him. Rachel was impressed that he was on the streets without a heavy overcoat.

"I'm sorry?" Rachel didn't need to disguise her offense. "I'll have you know that Terry is the best cameraman in the business."

"My apologies." The reporter's obsequious tone was more annoying than his original condescension. "I meant no offense to your camera operator. You, however, have not been on the City Hall beat before or I would have noticed you. You are, as I'm sure you know well, rather eye-catching."

Rachel was unexpectedly flattered. She smiled, then remembered that this man was her competition and that Jason despised him. "Flattery will get you nowhere, Mr. Peacock."

"Perhaps not, but it never hurts." He flashed a rakish smile, as if his charm would immediately win over any female in his presence. When Rachel gave him a blank stare, he said, "Is there someone special you are here to see?"

Rachel knew better than to give away any information. "You'll have to wait and see."

"Oh, come now, Miss Robinson, surely you and I are not in competition. I'm print. You're broadcast. There's no need for you to view me as the enemy."

"You know me?" Rachel could not help herself. It was amazing that one of the most decorated print journalists in New York knew her name.

"Of course. You are an up-and-coming personality, and the wife of Detective Jason Dickson. You also look amazing in a ball gown, I must say."

Rachel blushed and hated herself for it. Dexter must have been at the Hero's Ball and a few other formal gatherings where she and Jason were together in a crowd. "Thank you, but I can't give you any information."

"Not necessary, my dear. Let me guess and you can tell me if I'm right. You are perhaps the only person aside from me who has access to information about the images captured on a street security camera near the pawn shop where Louis Palazzo and two other men were murdered on Sunday. It's quite interesting that Deputy Mayor Erickson visited Louis Palazzo's pawn shop mere hours before the murders. I am here to obtain a statement, not that I expect him to say much."

"I-I really don't think—"

Dexter cut her off. "I'm assuming you are on the same scent. My experience is that officials such as Erickson are much more willing to talk when there is a camera recording them. For a mere print reporter, it's easy to shout a 'no comment' and walk away. But when a camera is rolling, a politician feels compelled to make some kind of statement, lest he be captured on video skulking away guiltily. Therefore, I propose we team up. We are the only press here. I will gladly let you take the lead. I'll stay in the background and come forward after you have had your chance at him. Does that sound fair?"

Rachel leaned in toward Terry. "Is this guy for real?"

Terry whispered back, "As long as he stays out of our way, we can't force him to leave, so I say we try to use him to our advantage. When he asks a question, Erickson may feel compelled to answer, like he said, so I'll keep the camera rolling."

Rachel straightened up and turned to Dexter. "Stay out of my way, and we'll be fine."

"Of course," the reporter responded with a half-bow and a tip of his hat.

Less than five minutes later, Rachel saw her quarry leading a group of three men and two women all dressed in business overcoats, scarves, and leather gloves, walking purposefully down the stairs. Rachel signaled for Terry to follow behind her. Microphone in hand, she positioned herself at the bottom of the steps, where the group was compelled to pass on their route to the street.

"Mr. Deputy Mayor!" Rachel called out, "Rachel Robinson, ACN. Can I get a quick word?"

Erickson stopped three steps from the sidewalk. His entourage gathered behind him as Terry positioned himself so that Rachel and the politician were both in frame. Rachel hoped Erickson would assume she was there to ask a question about the UPS strike threat or about workers' rights. She was rewarded by Erickson saying, "Sure. Happy to get the word out in the broadcast media." He ran a hand through his hair and straightened his tie, anticipating his on-camera moment.

"Sir, why did you visit the pawn shop belonging to murder victim Lou Palazzo on Sunday afternoon?"

His smiling face morphed into something between confusion and panic. "I'm sorry. What did you—"

Rachel was ready to pounce. "You visited Lou Palazzo's pawn shop Sunday afternoon about 2:30. Can you tell me why you were there and what you and Mr. Palazzo talked about?"

The deputy mayor spun his head left and right, looking at his aides. "I don't know what you're talking about." The camera was rolling and he knew he looked like a trapped rat. "I'm sorry, but I have an important event. You'll have to excuse me."

Before Erickson reached the bottom step, Peacock stepped forward, holding his cell phone out and recording. "Mr. Deputy Mayor, we know that you met with Mr. Palazzo. Do you deny it?"

Erickson stopped and made eye contact with the well-known reporter. Rachel recognized the question's elegance. If he denied the meeting, he would be contradicted by the video and would be pressed about why he lied. If he admitted to the meeting, he would need to have an explanation, which could be verified. If he refused to comment, he would seem evasive. If the accusation was false, the man would deny it. Anything else was incriminating. Rachel wished she had constructed her question so well, but she was hesitant to mention the security video.

"I – Let me say that I have no comment. There is an ongoing police investigation and I cannot say anything at this time that might compromise the work of our detectives." Erickson rushed forward past Terry and made the turn toward Chambers Street, surrounded by his group, who totally obscured his face.

Terry removed the camera from his shoulder and rested it on the sidewalk.

Rachel turned to Dexter. "That was a well-formed question. Thank you."

"My pleasure, Miss Robinson." Dexter again gave a half-bow and tipped his idiotic hat. "I only regret that Mr. Erickson was quick-witted enough to have a good response. Nevertheless, he did not deny being at the pawn shop. I'll let you draw your own conclusions." He walked up the stairs and disappeared into the building.

Terry tapped Rachel's shoulder. "Let's get a shot with you here on the steps. We can do a lead-in and then an outro. We can cut the video, along with your interview of the kid, when we get back to the barn. That should make a nice report."

"Yeah. Thanks," Rachel replied. She positioned herself in front of Terry's camera, took a deep breath, and held up her microphone.

Chapter 29
Sophomore Blues

AT 11:00 ON THURSDAY, Jason and Mike left City Hall and returned to their waiting squad car. Jason had briefed Mike earlier on Rachel's research that identified Lou Palazzo's nephew. After checking his text messages and confirming that Rachel was finished with her "shopping," he turned to Mike. "What do you think about the nephew? We know Palazzo made big payments to NYU. That has to be connected to the nephew. Unless you have any better ideas, I say we go over to NYU and have a chat with him."

"I'm more interested in figuring out how to get a search warrant for the building where our treasure hunters went with the equipment they snatched from the pawn shop, but we're waiting for probable cause. Sure, I'm in for questioning the kid."

"Alright. Let's go see if we can catch him off guard."

The office of student affairs at NYU proved quite willing to provide two NYPD detectives with Ryan's class schedule without a warrant. At a quarter past noon, Mike and Jason stood in the shade of a scrubby tree growing in a square of dirt carved from the Manhattan sidewalk. They watched students pour out of the double doors of Kimball Hall, a squat concrete structure rising ten floors above Greene Street.

Ryan shuffled out the door. Mike recognized him from the graduation photo they took from Lou Palazzo's office. He wore a black baseball cap with a silver logo resembling a stick figure with horns on its head and a cross for legs. Mike smiled, realizing that the boy was wearing the much-maligned novelty cap of the "Mercury Mets." It was from a throw-ahead promotion sponsored by Major League Baseball in 1999. Only a die-hard Mets fan would know it. Ryan also sported a dark winter coat consistent with the security cam video from Sunday afternoon.

The two detectives moved into an intercepting position. "Ryan Gelb?" Mike called out. As the less threatening-looking detective, Mike made the first contact, hoping the kid wouldn't run from a fifty-plus white guy who looked even older.

Ryan looked up at Mike with a puzzled expression. "Yeah?"

Mike gently guided Ryan by the elbow to the little tree where Jason waited. "My name is Mike Stoneman. I'm a homicide detective investigating your uncle's death. This is my partner, Detective Dickson. Don't worry, we know you had nothing to do with it. But we know you spoke with him the day he died. We'd like to ask you a few questions about what he said."

Ryan's eyes opened wide. "How – what makes you think I talked to Lou that day?"

Jason stepped up close to Ryan, towering over him. "We have you and your friend on a security cam, son. We're trying to find the killer. You want to help us, don't you?"

"Um, sure," Ryan stammered, clearly intimidated by Jason's presence.

"Good." Mike stepped forward as Jason backed away a stride. "Let's go across the street. I'll buy you a cup of coffee while we talk."

Mike pulled Ryan along, keeping a hand on his arm in case he decided to bolt. In a diner where the lunch traffic was beginning to ramp up, Mike flashed his badge and got the hostess to seat them in a corner table next to the window. As the pedestrian traffic flowed past them, Mike ordered a BLT and coffee. Jason opted for a tuna sandwich and a Diet Coke. Ryan accepted the offer of coffee, but said he wasn't hungry.

"I'm sorry for your loss," Mike said soothingly after the waitress trotted off. "I had an uncle, who also happened to be named Lou. He was a terrific mentor to me when I was younger. It hurt when he died. It was cancer for my Uncle Lou, so there was no police investigation. But I understand the feeling. If there's anything you can tell us that will help catch the guy who murdered your uncle, we want you to help us."

"I don't know anything," Ryan said, putting both palms up on the table in surrender.

"You may not think so," Jason cut in. "But there may be something he said to you that could be a clue for us. So, let's start with the day he died, last Sunday. You visited him at his shop, right?"

"Sure. Yeah. I was there."

"Who was the person with you?"

"Me and Will went over there to hang out. There was a Humphrey Bogart film festival on cable. Uncle Lou wanted us to watch *Treasure of the Sierra Madre* together." Ryan's level of anxiety seemed to wane as he talked about the friendship with his uncle.

"Who's Will?" Jason asked, forcing Ryan to shift his focus.

"He's my best friend."

"You're into old movies, are you?" Mike asked, again changing Ryan's attention.

"Lou was," Ryan smiled. "He was always trying to get us to watch films we'd never heard of. Most of them were pretty good."

"Did your uncle say anything about being involved in anything dangerous or unusual?"

"No." Ryan averted his eyes and stared at the coffee cup on the table in front of him. "Nothing that I remember."

"OK." Mike glanced up at Jason, who was seated to Ryan's left and blocking him from dashing for the door. It was a signal for Jason to jump in and be a little bad cop if necessary. "What did you talk about on Sunday? Tell us anything you can remember, no matter how trivial it might seem."

Ryan fidgeted on the metal chair's blue vinyl pad. "Nothing, really. We talked about the movies, and a video game we play together and what level we were on and how we were going to run a triangle attack on the new boss. That was about it. Uncle Lou never talked much about his business."

Jason broke in, using a heavy, authoritative voice meant to intimidate. "What kinds of computers was he working on? He must have talked to you about that, since you're a tech nerd like him, right?"

"I guess. Sometimes he told us about a password he was trying to crack or a coding problem he was working on."

"What was he working on Sunday?" Jason pressed.

"I-I'm not sure. I don't remember him mentioning anything specific." Ryan did not make any eye contact with Jason as he responded, but he glanced across the table at Mike, as if asking for help against Jason's onslaught.

"The shop was ransacked by the guys who killed him. They stole every computer in the store, every laptop and desktop and phone. Anything with a hard drive. They were looking for something – probably a program or a file. Did your uncle mention anything about working on something like that?"

"No!" Ryan's voice raised half an octave. "I mean, I don't think so. Not that I remember."

Mike came to Ryan's rescue, speaking in a soothing voice. "We know this is tough on you, son. It's hard to lose someone you loved. Let's approach things from another angle. Do you remember anything on the work space inside the office? Did your uncle have a desk or a place where he did work on computers?"

Ryan relaxed a bit and kept his eyes on Mike. "Well, I guess he would mostly work behind the counter out front, at his laptop on the shelf behind the cash register."

"So, you didn't notice anything new or unusual last Sunday?"

"No. Not that I remember." Ryan squirmed. "Listen, I have another class and I need to get some stuff from my dorm. How much longer do you need me here?"

Mike and Jason made eye contact, each confirming to the other silently that they were done. "OK," Mike said, "if you can't remember anything right now, we understand." He handed Ryan a white business card. "If you remember anything, anything at all, my number and email are on that card. Please give me a call. You never know, sometimes the smallest detail can help us find the guys who did this. You want us to catch them, right?"

"Sure," Ryan said with increased enthusiasm. "I'll call you if I think of anything." He was already halfway out of his chair, squeezing behind Jason. He rushed to the door and disappeared from the detectives' sight.

Jason said what Mike already knew. "He's holding back."

"Yeah. But why?"

"They could have been involved in something shady with Palazzo. Maybe cheating on their computer programming homework?"

"Could be, I guess," Mike mused. "There was something there he didn't want to talk about. But I don't see why he would want to hinder the investigation into catching his uncle's killer."

"I agree. We know the bald man and the two goons killed him. These two kids weren't involved. Ryan can't be protecting them."

Mike paused as the waitress delivered their sandwiches. The interrogation was over, but they still needed to eat. "So, Ryan is a dead end."

"What about the other kid? His friend, Will?"

"You think he might remember something Ryan couldn't? It's worth a try. Of course, Ryan will be telling him all about our little chat within the next ten minutes, so we won't catch him fresh."

"You're right. Back to square one." Jason bit into his tuna sandwich.

* * *

ACROSS CAMPUS, SECURITY HEAD JAN YATES stared into his computer monitor. On the video call, President Sharron Henry and her general counsel hovered in their white squares. O'Shaughnessy, the lawyer, wasn't actually needed for the discussion, but was there to make sure the contents of the conversation were protected by attorney-client privilege.

Yates said, "The police are questioning Ryan Gelb."

"Now?" O'Shaughnessy asked.

"I don't know exactly when. They showed up at Security asking for his class schedule. They wanted to talk to him as a witness to a criminal investigation."

President Henry held up a slender hand. "How did the police find out about the data breach?"

"Calm down, Sharron. We don't know what the police know or don't know. I doubt Mr. Gelb told the detectives about the computer hack. Remember, the student's uncle was murdered. It's more likely the police are talking to him about that. It probably has nothing to do with the hack. Let's not panic and make things worse."

O'Shaughnessy cut in. "Do you have any reason to think the student was more involved in the hack than he admitted to?"

"I'm not sure." Yates stroked the stubble on his chin. "But there's something about the way he answered my questions. Like he rehearsed his story. You don't do that unless you're guilty of something."

President Henry looked concerned. "I'm still worried about keeping a lid on this breach. I made a call to Chester Miller at the FBI. I can count on him to be discreet. You know him?"

"I don't, but I know who he is. Maybe we should have him come down so we can talk to Mr. Gelb again."

"Maybe. In the meantime, is there any indication that the breached data has shown up anywhere on the internet?"

"Not yet. All quiet on that front." Yates glanced at his watch.

"What about the Aswani investigation files?" Henry lowered her voice involuntarily. "Were they part of the download?"

Yates pursed his lips and nodded. "We confirmed it an hour ago."

"Oh, Lord," Henry dropped her head, exposing the thin patch on the crown of her head to the camera. "The witness statements – from the girls?"

"We can't be sure, but probably. It would also include the Board's recommendation to fire coach Evans and his agreement to retire in lieu of being fired."

Henry's eyes flashed a combination of anger and fear. "Yes, and also the statements that my predecessor knew about the sexual abuse and helped cover it up. We need to get that file back, Jan. Until we have the data back in our possession, it's out there somewhere. It's only a matter of time, unless the data never made it off the kid's laptop. Gelb did the right thing by disconnecting and powering down. It's possible the hackers never got the data."

"Yeah, sure," Yates said without enthusiasm. "But Mr. Gelb said he gave the only copy to his uncle, and now the uncle is dead. Murdered. What if it was stolen from the uncle's shop?"

After a few seconds of contemplative silence, Henry said, "If somebody stole it in a general robbery, they wouldn't know what it is. And Gelb said the file was encrypted. It's unlikely some random criminal would be able to access the data, even if they found it. So, we're OK there, right?"

"I'd rather have it in my lab where I could destroy it for sure," Yates said, "but as long as the hackers don't have it, we may be in the clear."

Chapter 30
Déjà Vu

AS SOON AS RYAN LEFT his afternoon psychology class, he got a call from university security, directing him to attend another meeting. He immediately texted Will, Star, and Sarrie. When he made it to his room, he got on a group video call to discuss how worried he should be. He had already told Star about being interviewed by a TV reporter – the same one who did the live report the night his uncle was killed. Star knew her somehow, although Ryan could not recall exactly how. He had not yet mentioned to anyone that he was also interviewed by two cops.

Will was the calm one in the group. "You told them you got hacked and that you gave the thumb drive to Uncle Lou and reformatted the laptop drive. Then, when Lou couldn't crack the encryption on the file, he reformatted the thumb drive. That's your story, stick to it. It's the truth. Mostly. You don't need to fill in any blanks for them. You have nothing to worry about."

"Not from the university." Star's voice was decidedly more animated and concerned. "But we still haven't told the police that there may be a connection between the hack and your uncle's murder. When are you going to tell them?"

"We're not," Will said firmly. "If they connect the hack to the murder, then we'll end up having to tell the police everything and the university will find out and we'll be expelled for sure."

"That's not necessarily true," Sarrie jumped in, her video square enlarging on the screen as she took the floor. "The hack could have happened just like Ryan told them. He clicked on an email or a link on a random website and the virus downloaded. Why would you have to tell them the whole story about your research project?"

Ryan answered for Will. "Because if it was a random virus and we took the file to Lou because we were curious about what might be on it, there would be no reason for us to think it was connected to the murder. It's only connected if we knew the hack attempt accessed important files that the hackers might want to get back."

"Oh, right," Sarrie said softly.

"Right now, it was just a virus and a random hack. It was an accident. Plus, if we can find the file, then we can turn it over to the university and that will be the end of it. We're not going to turn ourselves in without the file."

"But it *was* an accident," Sarrie chimed in. "You didn't expect the university's accounts to get hacked. They can't hold it against you."

"You can't guarantee that," Will protested. "It's not your future at stake. It's mine. And Ryan's."

Star cleared her throat for attention. "Nobody wants you or Ryan to get in trouble, Will. But it's also about catching the guys who killed Ryan's uncle. Don't you care about that?"

"I don't mean to sound cold, but Lou's dead. We can't bring him back. Maybe he was whacked by his old mob associates. Maybe it was the hackers. Either way, there's nothing I can do. If they get caught, then fine, but they probably aren't going to get caught. I'm not sacrificing my future on the off chance that it might help catch a criminal. No. You're with me, right, Ryan?"

Ryan was quick to have Will's back. "Sure, bro."

Star waved her hand toward the screen in defeat. "Fine. But don't lie to security. Right now you might be in trouble for being careless and allowing the hack to happen, but it was still an accident. If you lie to them, then you'll be expelled for sure."

"Only if they find out," Will said. "But I agree, Ryan. Try to not outright lie. Stick to the story."

When the call ended, Ryan grabbed his backpack. It had been a crazy day. He gave an interview to a TV news crew, was accosted and interrogated by two detectives, and now he was going to face the university security gorilla again. Keeping secrets was not in his comfort zone.

* * *

WHEN RYAN ARRIVED AT THE SECURITY OFFICE, Jan Yates was there with one of his underlings whom Ryan remembered from the last meeting and an older man he did not recognize. The new guy wore a sport jacket with no tie and had a buzz cut in his partly gray hair. He had the same ex-military appearance as Yates and immediately made Ryan more nervous than he already was.

"Have a seat, Mr. Gelb," the security director said, motioning Ryan to the sole unoccupied chair. "I'd like you to meet Chester Miller, a distinguished alumnus. He's an expert in cybersecurity and we've brought him in to consult about the hack of your laptop. He works for the FBI, but this is a private consultation. For now."

Ryan gulped, his mouth dry as the Coney Island boardwalk. Unable to speak, Ryan nodded in the man's direction.

"Son, you understand that this situation may have resulted in a data breach, which triggers certain required disclosures to anyone whose data might have been compromised. It's a very serious situation."

"Uh huh," Ryan affirmed, working to clear his throat.

"Good boy. So, obviously, we need to know exactly what happened in order to determine our obligations. So, I want you to tell me in as much detail as you can, step by step, what you did."

"I did that this morning," Ryan protested.

"I know. But I want to hear it first-hand. Humor me, please," the FBI man said politely, but with an undertone letting Ryan know that compliance was not optional.

Over the next forty-five minutes, Ryan answered questions from all three of the other participants and repeated the events from several angles. He doggedly stuck to the original story.

"Why were you using a clean laptop for this research?" Miller asked.

"I knew there was some chance I would stumble across some websites that might give me a virus, so we wanted to be careful so nothing important got infected."

"You and who else?" Yates interjected.

"Huh?" Ryan swiveled his head toward the security chief.

"You said *we*. Who were the other people?"

"Well, I-I mean, there are a bunch of people in my programming class and we have a kind of study group. So, when I told them what I was doing, we all agreed that there was some risk of picking up a virus or trojan. We all thought it was a good idea to use a clean machine." Ryan looked around the room, assessing whether his answer passed muster.

"Can you give us the names of the other study group members?" Yates asked.

"Oh, come on." Ryan was tired from the lengthy questioning and had no problem feigning annoyance. "They didn't do anything wrong. I don't want to get anybody else in trouble."

"You're not in trouble," Miller noted calmly.

"It sure seems like I am." Ryan's nervous shaking could easily have been interpreted as anger. "Look, I've told you everything I can. I fucked up. OK? I get it. I'm really sorry. I'm pretty sure I shut down before the hackers finished downloading whatever it was that they were hacking into. I hope I did. I don't know what it was. That's why I took it to my Uncle Lou. I don't know what else I can tell you." He looked around the room, hoping he looked as pathetic as he felt.

"Alright, Mr. Gelb. Thank you for your time. We'll let you know if we need any additional information. If the police recover your thumb drive, you'll let us know, won't you?"

"Absolutely," Ryan confirmed, already standing.

The man from the FBI, Miller, fixed his eyes on Ryan's. "So, it wasn't reformatted, then?"

"What?" was all Ryan could get out in response.

"Your thumb drive is missing, isn't it? The police are looking for it. Your uncle didn't really reformat it."

Ryan gulped. What did he say? He couldn't remember. He answered so many questions. "Um – I – I mean," he realized he was caught and looked guilty. "OK. Fine. My uncle said that, if he couldn't open the file, he was going to reformat the drive to destroy the file in case it included a virus. I assume that's what he did, but I'm not absolutely sure. I never actually got the drive back from him before he . . .got killed."

"Why lie to us about it?" Miller pressed.

"I didn't lie. I just assumed it was true. I guess I want it to be true. It might be. I don't know for sure."

Yates stood, getting Ryan's attention. "Son, I imagine you're worried about being in trouble here. You're not, but if you don't tell us the truth, you will be. We need to be sure the people who hacked your computer never got that data. So, like Mr. Miller said, if you happen to get the drive back from the police, whether it's wiped or not, you let us know immediately. Understand?"

"Yeah. I do. Can I go now?"

"Yes," Yates said. Ryan was out the door in ten seconds, since nobody tried to stop him.

* * *

AT SIX O'CLOCK, THE TWO COUPLES GATHERED in Will's room to get the report from Ryan first hand.

"They don't think I did anything wrong, just that I was stupid. I had to tell them that we have a study group."

"What study group?" Star asked.

"There is no study group." Will paced to the door and back. "Why'd you have to make that up?"

"It was that or tell them *you* were the person who suggested I use a clean laptop. Would you have preferred that?"

"Why'd you say anything at all?"

"I slipped up and said *we* instead of *I* at one point. They asked who I meant, so I said it was our study group." Ryan's eyes flashed around the room. "What? You think they're going to start asking around in programming class to find out who was in our non-existent study group? Why would they do that?"

"I still think you should let me tell my uncle about the file," Star said. "He doesn't care about NYU security. The file might be important to the investigation. You guys are withholding information. Isn't that obstruction of justice or something?"

"It's only obstructing justice if you lie to the cops," Will replied authoritatively, although Star doubted he was an expert on the subject.

"Well, not telling them what you know is pretty much the same as lying. I'm having dinner with him and my Aunt Michelle tonight."

"Don't say anything," Ryan said, reaching out and clutching the bottom of Star's sweater. "Please. We're in enough trouble already. Let's keep this to ourselves, like we all promised we would. You gotta be on my side on this, Star. OK?"

Her new boyfriend's pleading eyes melted Star's resolve. She was so happy to have found someone like Ryan. She couldn't refuse him and feared that going behind his back would end their relationship. "Fine. But think about it. Please?"

"Sure," Ryan said, not wanting to upset Star. "I will."

After Star and Sarrie left, Ryan closed the door and turned to his friend. "Dude, two cops came around today and talked to me about Uncle Lou."

"What? Holy shit! Why didn't you tell me?"

Ryan plopped onto his bed and held his head with both hands. "It was such a crazy day. I didn't want to freak out the girls. It was mostly nothing. They wanted to know if Uncle Lou said anything to us on Sunday about what he was working on."

"Sunday?" Will sat cross-legged on the floor in front of Ryan. "How did they know we saw Lou on Sunday?"

"They had us on a security video. I couldn't lie about being there, but I didn't tell them anything. I said we hung out for a while and watched one of Lou's Bogart movies, but he didn't tell us anything about his work."

"Ryan, this is getting worse and worse. Are we totally screwed?"

"No. Not yet. They're looking into Lou's murder. It has nothing to do with the dingus."

Will whispered, "But what if it does?"

Chapter 31
Dinner Table Conversation

STAR HAD NOT JOINED her Aunt Michelle and Uncle Mike for dinner at their Upper West Side apartment for several weeks. During her first month at NYU, Michelle invited her favorite niece to dinner regularly. It gave them a chance to catch up and allowed her to report to Star's mother, Rosie, that the girl was not starving or hooked on drugs and looked great. Privately, Michelle worried that Star was too thin and wasn't eating enough at school. She made sure to send Star home with leftovers.

On this particular day, Michelle had prepared one of her specialties, intended to be healthy for Mike and also a treat for Star. When Mike walked in the door, his salivary glands gushed involuntarily. The aroma of garlic, onions, Italian spices, and shrimp filled his nostrils after the twenty-six-block walk from the station house. Even in the cold weather, Mike took pride in getting his steps. It worked up an appetite, even if the rest of the day was often sedentary.

The small dining table was set with wine glasses. A tossed salad patiently waited in a large blue bowl, adorned with wooden serving utensils and accompanied by a warm French baguette.

Mike called out, "I'm home," and crept noiselessly into the kitchen.

The chrome, non-stick Pampered Chef wok rattled as bursts of steam escaped from the cauldron into the air. Michelle was making her signature seafood risotto. Mike peeked into the bubbling center, admiring the curling squid tentacles and dark squares of portobello mushroom caps swimming in the sea of rice, onions, and cubes of red, orange, and yellow peppers. He reached carefully to pluck a pink shrimp from the surface. As he straightened up, he looked right into Michelle's disapproving countenance.

Michelle wore a tan apron bearing a PBS logo, as comfortable in the kitchen as in her ME lab. Mike shed his coat and sport jacket, marveling at how lucky he was to have this lovely, smart woman making him dinner. He was a stocky, middle-aged cop who was never described as handsome, even in his younger days. It was a miracle and he swore to himself he would never take her for granted.

"Stealing shrimp again?" she accused him with the face of a mother catching her nine-year-old with his hand in the cookie jar.

"Yes," Mike said unabashedly, popping the hot morsel into his mouth and chewing greedily.

Michelle's angry face morphed into a grin as she watched Mike's jaw work the shrimp. He closed his eyes in relaxed pleasure. "I'm glad you like it, Mike. Now, leave some for me and Star."

"Absolutely." Mike covered the entire length of the Manhattan-sized kitchen in two strides, wrapped his arms around his wife's waist, and kissed her gently. "I love it when you get your chef on."

She leaned into him and hummed softly, like a purr from Topsy, who watched curiously from her perch on the window ledge. After a moment, Michelle planted a kiss on Mike's lips, wrapping both arms around his neck. Topsy emitted a scratchy meow and leapt to the floor, nuzzling Michelle's leg.

"That cat never lets me have you to myself for more than a minute," Mike grumbled.

"Oh, Mike. Topsy just wants to be part of the family. Now that you're home, she wants to snuggle."

"She wants to snuggle *you*." Mike disengaged from his amorous embrace and reached for an open bottle of chianti, which Michelle said paired perfectly with the risotto. Mike would have preferred a beer, but that would have more carbs and calories. He would take solace in the wine's slightly higher alcohol content.

When Star arrived, aunt and niece spent five minutes complimenting each other and hugging multiple times. Twenty minutes later, Star set down her fork and leaned back in her chair as she stroked Topsy's left ear. The cat never failed to find Star's lap and was universally rewarded with table scraps. Michelle didn't mind. The glowing smile on her niece's face overwhelmed any contrary considerations.

"When do you start the internship on Broadway?" Mike asked as he sopped up olive oil and risotto remnants from his plate with a thin slice of the baguette.

"My last final is next Thursday. After that, I'll start working at the theater for the winter break. It's so nice of Mr. Matthews to give me the chance." Nathan Matthews promised Mike he would find a job for Star after Mike and Jason's unauthorized investigation cleared the Broadway director of murder charges.

"You must be over the moon to be starting."

Star laughed. "Uncle Mike, nobody in the twenty-first century says *over the moon*."

"Well, Mr. Matthews owes Mike," Michelle said softly. "And he owes you, too."

Star's chin dropped toward Topsy. "I didn't do anything. It was no big deal."

"No big deal!?" Michelle's voice raised briefly, but she realized she was unfairly blaming Star. "Honey, you could have been hurt, or even killed."

"But I wasn't. It was all fine. I was in the wrong place at the wrong time. I told Uncle Mike I didn't want to tell you, because I didn't want you to be worried about me. I was fine. I *am* fine. It's all fine."

"Well," Michelle huffed, "I'm not happy that Mike didn't tell me." She flashed a sternly disapproving stare at her husband, the cop.

"It wasn't Uncle Mike's fault," Star protested.

Mike held up a hand to stop Star from further defending him. "Thanks, Star. I appreciate that. But what I tell Michelle is up to me, not you. So I have to take the blame on this one. I'm just glad you weren't hurt and that it all worked out." Mike winked at Star and they shared a moment of mutual respect. Mike owed her one. Maybe two.

"It must run in the family that we somehow find our way into bad situations, Aunt Michelle," Star laughed. "You got kidnapped by a serial killer, but you came out alright. That must have been crazy."

"It was, but I don't like to talk about it," Michelle demurred. She grabbed their three dinner plates and headed for the sink.

Mike desperately wanted to change the subject. "Oh, I didn't tell you that we tracked down the dead shopkeeper's nephew. He was one of the last people to speak to Palazzo before he was murdered. Jason and I spoke with the kid this morning but he said he didn't know anything relevant."

Star froze. The back of her throat felt like she had chugged two Pixie Stix. Ryan didn't tell her he was interviewed by her Uncle Mike. She was angry at Ryan, but also knew he and Will would never forgive her if anything she said caused them to get in trouble with the university. She understood the anxiety.

She could never afford a school as good as NYU without the scholarship money. At the same time, she didn't want to lie to her aunt and uncle. They had done so much for her. Michelle was like a second mother. She wanted to crawl under the table.

Mike followed Michelle to the kitchen bearing empty wine glasses. He paused at the threshold and looked back toward Star. "Palazzo's nephew is a sophomore at NYU. Named Ryan Gelb. He's a computer science major. You wouldn't know him, would you?"

"Probably not. Um, Aunt Michelle," Star called out, "thanks so much for the dinner, but I need to get going. I have to meet someone downtown."

"Who are you meeting?" Michelle said when she returned to the dining alcove to collect water glasses.

"Um, my boyfriend," Star said, dropping her head as if embarrassed.

"Ohhhh," Michelle purred. "I didn't know you had a boyfriend." She returned to the dining alcove, abandoning the table-clearing chores. "What's he like?"

"Aunt Michelle," Star scolded, "you know I don't like to talk about it. He's a sophomore and he's sweet. That's all I'm going to say." She snatched her red winter coat from a peg on the wall next to the door.

Mike reached out a hand and patted Star's. "I won't interrogate you about your boyfriend, Star. But I have one question."

Star's dinner rose in her esophagus.

"Does he treat you with respect?"

She swallowed hard, then forced a smile. "Oh, yes, Uncle Mike. He does."

Mike took a step back. "Just . . .be careful, Star. Make sure you know who you're getting close with. And remember, if anything ever starts to go crazy, you can call us. We'll always be there to help."

"That's right, sweetheart. We're always here for you. Now, let me get you a container to take home." Michelle disappeared into the kitchen and emerged seconds later with a white paper bag. She handed it to her niece. "Here you go. I'm sure this is much better for you than what you get in the cafeteria at school."

"Thanks," Star said, accepting the bag and hugging her aunt. Without any additional conversation, she blew kisses and waved to Mike and Michelle, scratched Topsy's ear one last time, and disappeared out the door.

Mike strolled into the kitchen to continue the clean-up, putting his hands gently on Michelle's shoulders. "She's a great girl."

"I know. And don't think you're off the hook for not telling me about her being in that alley."

"Yeah. No kidding."

"What was the other lead you said you were still chasing?"

Mike continued massaging Michelle's neck. "It's the car we traced to a building downtown. We're watching it, hoping to identify somebody we can squeeze. So far, we're coming up snake eyes, but it's about all we have."

"Well, good luck. I hate it when you and Jason get stuck on a case. You both get distracted and insufferable."

"We do not!" Mike protested.

"Sure."

"We don't. At least, I don't."

Michelle patted Mike on the chest. "OK. We'll say you don't. But I still hope you get a break. You're much more fun when you're chasing somebody than when you're waiting for a lead."

"Fine. I'll cop to that."

Chapter 32
Busted

STAR TEXTED RYAN from the subway:

We need to talk. Tonight. Important.

Ryan texted back while she was walking from the 14th Street stop toward her dorm, suggesting they meet in his room. She arrived, set down her doggie bag on Ryan's desk, and started talking before she removed her coat. "You talked to my uncle Mike today and didn't tell me?"

"Wait, what? I did?"

"You did! The cop, Mike Stoneman? That's my uncle Mike!"

"It is? Oh. Wow. Really? That was your uncle? I guess he mentioned it, huh?"

"Yes, he mentioned it!" Star's distress preempted her general reticence to seem like anything but a supportive girlfriend. "I nearly peed my pants. How could you let me go up there without letting me know?"

"I'm sorry, Star. I didn't know that was your uncle. I didn't want to freak you out about me talking to the police. It wasn't a big deal. He and his partner wanted to know if Uncle Lou said anything to us that might help them figure out what the guys who killed him were looking for. I said he didn't. That was it."

"So you withheld information from the police. Great. You lied to them!" Star was becoming more and more agitated. She threw her coat onto Ryan's bed.

"No. That's not true. We don't know the dingus had anything to do with Lou's murder."

"Maybe not, but maybe it does. Maybe it's a lead the police need to have. Ryan, we have to tell him."

Ryan sank to the floor with his knees up, his head hanging between his legs. "I can't do that to Will. I just can't." He lifted his head, eyes pleading.

Star towered over him, still fuming, but she began to thaw at seeing Ryan's pain and impossible dilemma. She knew Will was his closest friend. She also knew that Will would be devastated if he got expelled from NYU. She knew Ryan had feelings for her, but Star came into his life barely two months earlier. He had been Will's wing man since grammar school. She couldn't ask him to make a choice. She would lose.

"What are we going to tell Will?" she said softly.

"Nothing. There's nothing to tell. He knows I talked to the cops and that I didn't give them anything. There's nothing more to say now."

"Wait." Star's sympathy for Ryan instantly morphed into annoyance. "You told Will, but you didn't tell me?"

"Yeah. Well. I figured he needed to know, in case they came around looking to talk to him, too." Ryan looked increasingly pathetic.

Star collapsed to the floor next to Ryan, leaning her head on his shoulder. "This is so messed up."

Ryan rubbed his palm on Star's back. "I agree with that. Hang with me and we'll make it through this. Will is right. Nothing we do is going to bring Lou back. I don't really care if the guy who shot him gets caught. It won't make me feel any less guilty. It's all my fault. I won't be able to live with myself if I'm responsible for both Lou's death and Will getting expelled. Not to mention getting myself expelled. My parents would kill me. I have one chance here to not make things worse. Do you understand?"

Star put her hand on Ryan's. "Yeah. I get it. I'm going to have to keep holding back information from Uncle Mike. I'll do it for you, and for Will. But if it ever means that you're in danger, I'll do what's best for you."

They sat on the floor in silence for several minutes. Ryan's phone played music while he was studying. He didn't turn it off when Star arrived so suddenly. Now, in the quiet, they could hear the soft strains of John Legend singing "All of Me" leaking into the air.

When the song ended, Ryan said, "Do us all a favor. If you hear anything from your uncle about their investigation, let us know. It might be important for us to know what they know. If it looks like they might come looking for us, we can come forward voluntarily. That way it will seem like we're cooperating. Can you do that?"

"Sure," Star said, although her stomach turned a somersault at the thought of being a spy for Ryan and Will when she talked to her uncle.

Ryan hugged her gently. "You should probably get back to your room. I have some work to do for tomorrow's class. Unless you want to stay here."

Star leaned in for a quick kiss. "This isn't the time." She gathered her coat and bag. "I'll see you tomorrow."

Chapter 33
Domestic Disturbance

THAT THURSDAY NIGHT, the ACN news hour included a story on the triple murder that had captured the attention of the city. ACN touted it as a national story, but none of the big broadcast networks included it on their daily national news shows. All the network affiliates in New York mentioned the case, but they had nothing new or exciting to report. ACN, however, had reporter Rachel Robinson.

With all her friends and family watching closely, the four-minute report included a recap of the horrific triple murder and an exclusive interview with the victim's 19-year-old nephew, a computer science student at NYU. Ryan Gelb spoke lovingly and even reverently about his uncle, whom he characterized as a "genius" and "the nicest uncle any kid could have." The interview shone a bright light on the tragedy of the seemingly senseless killing. The report did not mention Lou Palazzo's decade-old ties to organized crime, which were widely reported elsewhere. Instead, the piece focused on a law-abiding shop owner who was gunned down in Manhattan for reasons not yet fully apparent to the police.

The report then made a sharp turn. Rachel said the police were aware that a deputy mayor, Mr. Adam Erickson, visited the pawn shop a few hours before the murders. Mr. Erickson's answer to Rachel's on-screen question on the steps outside the municipal office building left viewers with the impression that he was being evasive. Rachel had advocated for including the man's final statement about why he was refusing to answer the question, but Sandi and Dave decided to cut it for time, and because it "didn't add anything significant" to the report. Rachel thought it would have provided some balance, but it wasn't her call. She was happy to have as much on-air time as she got.

The segment ended with thirty seconds of Rachel speaking directly into the audience's living rooms, expressing her own sadness and outrage at the tragic death of Lou Palazzo. She signed off, "For ACN, this is Rachel Robinson reporting."

In the Robinson home in Brooklyn, the commercial break that followed Rachel's sign-off reignited the argument Jason and Rachel had been having since Jason got home and heard about Rachel's day over dinner.

"Mike and Sully are going to think I leaked the information about Erickson to you," he said, making the point for the fifth time.

"But it was already leaked!" Rachel retorted, also for the fifth time. "You can tell Mike and Sully that *The New York Times* had it on their website at 5:47 p.m. Dexter Peacock broke it before I did. So the leaker was somebody other than you. I just happened to get it second."

"You would not have been there stalking the deputy mayor if I hadn't told you about him being on the camera from the bank across the street."

"I could have obtained the information independently from some other source," Rachel said. "They don't know for sure."

"But I know you didn't!"

"Nobody else does!" Rachel snapped back.

"And what's with the comment about the police investigating the deputy mayor?"

"I didn't say that. There was a comment to that effect in the *Times* article. The surveillance camera footage was reviewed by the police. I did not say there was an investigation. Besides, you can't get in trouble because I knew something that Dexter Peacock already knew. Maybe he told me."

"Why would he tell you? Why would he share his story with a rookie reporter from a cable news network?"

"Because he needed a film crew to get Erickson's comments on video and he thought I was pretty!"

Jason slumped into the easy chair where Rachel's father, Ernie, always sat. Since he died from the COVID-19 virus in 2020, Rachel avoided sitting in his chair, but Jason had no such aversion. "ACN could have scooped Peacock."

"But I told him I wouldn't, and he accepted the deal. I got him the video, and he shared his information with me."

"OK." Jason fought to keep a calm voice. "Let's say all that is true. We still have to explain why you were even there to talk with Peacock. How did you know to bring a cameraman and stake out City Hall?"

Rachel paused to formulate her reply. "You can admit that you told me about Erickson being on the security camera video. But you told me I could not use the information, that it was not considered relevant to the investigation, and that it was confidential. I agreed and I kept my promise. I went there to ask the deputy mayor general questions about the investigation and whether he knew the victim. I wanted to see if he would lie about it, without revealing anything about him being caught on the camera. If he had lied, that would have helped the police in any later interrogation. But when Peacock told me about the security cam video, I was free to ask about it. The NYPD needs to figure out who leaked the information to Peacock, which has nothing to do with you or me." When she finished, Rachel raised one eyebrow, proud of herself.

Jason sighed. "I still have to admit to sharing the information about the security video with you, which I should not have done."

"Oh, fine," Rachel conceded. "But I'm sure all cops share information with their spouses. As long as it didn't do any actual harm, what's the problem?"

"The problem is, Sully was very clear with me that I should not be sharing *anything*. I told you because I love you and because we agreed that you wouldn't use it and it wouldn't blow back on me. Now, here we are."

Rachel sat down on Jason's lap and wrapped her arms around his thick neck. "I know. You didn't want to tell me, but you did because I insisted. I love you for that." She kissed him, happy Olivia was already in bed and didn't see them making out in Ernie's chair. "I'm sorry that I went to City Hall. I was desperate. I needed something. I didn't want to violate the trust you put in me. I fully intended to guard the information I wasn't supposed to have. But it worked out in the end. You won't get into trouble. Just tell them I got the information from Peacock."

"They won't believe me."

"Maybe not, but they won't know for sure. You don't have to lie. I did get the information from Peacock."

Jason lowered his head into Rachel's chest. "OK. It won't be the worst little white lie I ever told Sully, or Mike. Hopefully, we'll get a real lead soon and everyone will forget about this."

"You'll share it with me as soon as anyone in the media gets it, right?" Rachel massaged the back of Jason's neck, scraping her fingernails along his skin in a way he enjoyed.

"Not a moment sooner," Jason said, rising unexpectedly from the chair and sweeping Rachel into his arms. "In a few months, I won't be able to do this."

"I know. Let's not worry about that right now." She leaned in and kissed Jason's neck, twirling her tongue in tiny circles.

Jason moved carefully toward the stairs leading up to their bedroom.

Chapter 34
Clearing the Decks

MIKE AND JASON GOT some good news Friday morning. The surveillance camera installed across the street from the parking garage on 9th Street hit pay dirt. They got a clear shot of a large man in the passenger seat of a black Explorer as it exited the parking lot. They got the driver also, but it was the passenger who mattered. The image was clear enough for facial recognition software to make a positive ID on Lloyd Cannon.

After thanking the tech team, Mike knocked on the jamb of Captain Sullivan's door. "Sully, we have something on the triple murder."

Sully's head snapped up and he motioned the detectives in. Jason closed the door. "Tell me this is good news."

"We think so," Jason replied. "We have a positive ID on Lloyd Cannon, who is a known lieutenant for Fat Albert Gallata. Our surveillance camera caught him riding in an SUV matching the images from Monday morning. It was coming out of the parking lot at the building downtown where we previously tracked the wrecking crew who rolled the pawn shop. He fits the shooter's description we got from the one eyewitness. He also fits the profile we got from the street cams, although those images are not good enough for a positive ID. We're not sure what the Gallata gang is up to inside that building, but it's a connection."

"Oh, great mother of crap," Sully lamented, raising his eyes to the ceiling. "Not a shocker, I guess. We knew this Palazzo guy was connected. Now we got a known Gallata officer involved. Was it a mob hit?"

"Seems likely," Mike said. "Now we have not only a suspicion, but a positive ID. We're going to keep digging at this and now we have a target. It should be enough now to get us a search warrant for the building."

"Alright. Keep going. But you should give a heads-up to the feds so you don't end up stepping into something they're already working on. For all you know, the building is already under surveillance and they got wire taps and shit. If you go charging in there and mess up their operation, there will be hell to pay. You got a Fibbie you can call. Right?"

"Yeah, Cap. We know somebody," Jason said. He nudged his elbow toward the door, signaling to Mike that it was time to get out.

Before they could fully rise from their chairs, however, Sully had one more subject to discuss. "Dickson, did you see the ACN story last night on your triple murder case?"

"Sure, Cap. Of course I saw it. My wife was the reporter."

"That's what concerns me." Sully was not yelling, which made Jason twice as wary as normal. "Tell me she didn't get any inside information from you for that report."

Jason had rehearsed his answer, but it still required careful language. "I heard that Dexter Peacock at *The Times* broke the story yesterday afternoon. Somebody in the department shared information about the deputy mayor being on a security cam going into the pawn shop. I was most certainly not the source of that leak. I can't stand Peacock. So, whatever information Rachel reported was already leaked before her report."

"Hhhmmpf." Sully was not satisfied with the answer, but couldn't immediately contest it. "Dickson, make sure your wife doesn't get any more details about your investigation unless they are included in a formal department press release first. Do you get that?"

"I do, Cap. Absolutely." Before Sully could ask any further questions, Jason exited the office with Mike on his heels.

* * *

AN HOUR LATER, the detectives adjourned to the small conference room in the corner of the bullpen. Mike had sent a message asking FBI Special Agent Everett Forrest for a confidential consultation. Everett was calling back.

"Thanks for calling, Special Agent," Mike said into the cell phone now lying on the pitted conference table.

"It's just me, Stoneman, so you can forget the Special Agent bullshit. What's the urgent matter?"

"Everett, I'm here with Jason Dickson. Nobody else. We're working a triple murder from last Sunday. You may have heard about it. Shopkeeper gunned down in the middle of an intersection. Two Asian goons dead inside the shop – likely at the hands of the dead guy, Louis Palazzo. Are you up to speed on it?"

"Not me, Mike. Not my beat. But I've seen a few bulletins about it. The Chinese muscle were recent arrivals. Makes it look like one of the Chinese organizations – or maybe the government – had a sudden interest. Your text said you were looking into Lloyd Cannon from the Gallata gang. Is that right?"

"Yes. Right. And we recently got a solid connection, placing him in a building, 311 East 9th Street, where a group of four perps went after rolling the dead guy's pawn shop the night after the shooting. They apparently lifted all the computer equipment from the store, then dragged it down to that building. Clearly, the Gallata organization has something going on there, and Cannon – who could be the trigger man – was there. So, we're zeroing in on him, but we want to make sure your boys don't have some other operation running. As you know, we are extremely careful not to interfere with federal cases."

"Yeah, Mike. You would never do that." The sarcasm in Everett's voice was partially offset by his immediate laughter. "Well, at least this time you're asking in advance."

"We didn't know you were running an operation on Justin Heilman, and that was a long time ago," Jason playfully countered.

"OK. OK. No recriminations. Thanks for calling me on this. I'm not sure what we might have at that location, but let me look into it and get back to you. If we're running an operation, you can coordinate with those agents. If we're not, then maybe we should be. Either way, you stand by. Don't charge in there yet. I'll expedite this."

"Thanks, Everett. We owe you one."

"Mike, you owe me a dozen. And say hello to that gorgeous doctor of yours for me."

"Will do. Thanks."

When the call disconnected, Mike and Jason brainstormed about what their next move would be, depending on the information they got back from Everett. "I hate having to coordinate with the FBI," Jason groused, "but I'd rather not make this a problem for the department."

"Yeah. You have political aspirations now, so suddenly you're careful."

Jason laughed. "I've always been careful. You generally don't notice." They shared a chuckle and exited back into the bullpen.

While they waited for clearance from the feds, Mike and Jason were also waiting for a call back from Keith Harris, an assistant district attorney who often worked with them. They asked Keith to prepare a search warrant for the building where they suspected the Gallata boys dumped the pilfered computer equipment. If the Gallata organization had people looking through it, searching for whatever was important enough to kill Lou Palazzo for, Mike wanted to get inside. And that required a warrant.

While they waited. Mike suggested they work on their report on the Joe Aaronson murder.

"Mike, you know how much I love doing paperwork."

Chapter 35
A Little Birdie Told Me

LLOYD CANNON WAS BACK in the boiler room on Friday morning. Four Chinese technicians were working away on the remaining devices lifted from the pawn shop under the watchful eyes of Yung Ji. The four Gallata techs had been relieved of duty. The explanation from their higher-ups was that there were not enough remaining devices to search, so they didn't need eight men. Cannon was not happy that their Corporate Dragon *friends* were now in charge of the whole process. Glaring menacingly at Ji, The Cannon made clear his unhappiness about his counterpart shooting one of his boys.

Cannon strolled over to the surveillance table to talk with Lenny. His knee still hurt when he put weight on it, but it was on the mend. "We're the only bastards talking English in this pit. What's the latest?"

"Well, Ryan and Will still haven't found the dingus."

"Dingus?"

"That's what they're calling it. They mean the data file. They still think they can figure out where it is, but they haven't found it yet. Ryan's pretty sure Uncle Lou cracked the encryption and would have put it in a secure location with a password that they would be able to guess. Something having to do with *The Maltese Falcon*."

"What the fuck?" The Cannon's puzzled mug let Lenny know the boss' patience would expire soon.

"Uncle Lou was a big Humphrey Bogart fan. The message he left for Ryan called the ding – the data file – the *falcon,* as in the statue from the movie. The point is that they think they can find it, and they're pretty sure they'll be able to recognize the file name and guess the password."

Cannon sat down in an empty chair next to the table. "Are they still working on it?"

"Yeah," Lenny replied. "They keep playing *Blades of Karma,* trying to find the clue that will help 'em find the file. It sounds pretty nuts to me, but they seem to believe it. If they do find it, then we can grab it. Maybe they'll spill the password while I'm listening, or maybe we have to squeeze it out of them. I hope we don't have to hurt them, though. They're good kids."

"Don't get attached to them, Lenny. The boss may not want them around. Anything else new?"

Lenny frowned, then picked up two pages of handwritten notes. "Yeah, Ryan gave an interview to a television reporter. Then, he got called to a meeting with university security. Later on, he told Star – his girlfriend – that he didn't tell 'em shit. He told 'em he got hacked and that he didn't think the hackers got the data. He said he gave the thumb drive with the file on it to his uncle, which is true. He says they wiped the laptop's hard drive and that the uncle wiped the thumb drive, which is bullshit because they're still looking for the file." Lenny paused and grinned like a kid on Christmas morning.

Cannon patted Lenny on the shoulder. "Good work. I'm glad we have the info. Without the bug, we would have grabbed the kid and leaned on him to give up the information. We probably would've killed him and we still wouldn't have the file. If these Chinese geeks don't find it on the machines we swiped from the pawn shop, then maybe these kids will lead us to it. You keep listening. If we end up with the data, the boss will be very happy with you. And me. Got it?"

"OK, Boss. I got it."

Cannon walked away to speak with Ji, not that he expected anything honest from him. The more they worked together, the more he got the definite feeling that the Chinese boss thought the Americans were stupid. After Ji shot Little Tony – no matter what the provocation – Cannon didn't trust the Dragoons to play straight. He wondered whether they would even pay Fat Albert if their guys found their precious data file.

Chapter 36
Federal Approval

IKE AND JASON WERE NEGOTIATING with Detectives Steve Berkowitz and George Mason about who would go out into the freezing rain to pick up the pizza from Pietro's on Columbus Avenue. There was brief consideration given to having it delivered, but the combination of the pie getting cold and the extra cost, including a tip for the delivery guy, made the option unappetizing.

"How 'bout we do rock, paper, scissors?" Steve suggested.

"Fine with me," Jason said, holding out a fist.

"What about George and me?" Mike asked. "Are you letting us off the hook?"

"Sure." Steve conceded. "I'm hungry. If I lose, I'll go. Otherwise, Jason can go, which he should do anyway since he's the least senior."

"Only because none of you sorry saps want to retire, ever." Jason smiled, still holding his fist in the air at waist level.

"We'll retire after we've taught you how to properly work a case," George quipped. "Isn't that right, Mike?"

Mike burst out laughing. "Jason works a case better than either of you goof-balls. Or did I forget which one of you figured out that the Righteous Assassin case was a serial killer? Oh, no, that was Jason, after you punted those files over to us because you called them all dead ends."

"Fuck you, Stoneman," Steve shot back. "That was five years ago. Give it a rest." He turned to Jason and held out his own fist. "One, Two, THREE," he counted out before flashing a flat palm. "You suck, Jason." He slapped away Jason's two fingers in the shape of the scissors. "Don't you know that most people choose rock?"

"Yeah, I know. Which is why most smart people choose paper, which beats rock. And since you're a smart guy, I figured you would choose paper."

"Yeah, Steve," Mike yelled so everyone in the bullpen could hear, "Jason thinks you're a smart guy. Say thank you and get going. We're all hungry."

As Steve struggled into his overcoat, Mike's phone rang. After answering, he motioned to Jason to move into the conference room. He placed the phone in its black rubber case on the table and pushed the speaker button. "Special Agent Forrest, it's nice of you to return my call. I'm here with Jason."

"Great," Everett said. "We know about the building you want to search. It's owned by the family through a union pension fund. We figure they use it as a kind of safe house for their business operations, but we don't have any active surveillance going on there. So, you're free to storm in if that makes sense for your case. If you do it, please let me know in advance so I can have a few agents there backing you up. They can help collect any evidence that might be relevant to our open files. But there's something else."

"There's always something with you guys," Mike jabbed. "Anything relevant to our investigation?"

"Maybe. I saw a confidential bulletin today. I can't disclose details, but it was someone asking to be notified about any activity connected to the triple murder. I'm not sure why we're interested – and I couldn't tell you if I knew – but I'll report up the chain about our conversation and let them know you're planning to raid the Gallata building. If they give me back anything that's relevant for you, or anything that would suggest you should hold off, I'll let you know."

"Sounds fair," Jason said. "We'll appreciate any help we can get. We've got two dead Chinese goons and a Gallata lieutenant involved, so it's not a shock that you guys are interested."

"Understood," Forrest responded. "I'll call you if I hear anything. And thanks again for the heads up on your raid."

When the two detectives emerged back into the bullpen, their pizza was sitting on Steve's desk, four slices already gone. Mike and Jason were two sloppy bites into their first slices when they heard their captain's voice.

"Stoneman!" Sully's annoyed shout cut through the bullpen's chatter. There were more cops than usual hanging out in the building at lunchtime since it was freezing outside. "Your warrant came in!"

When Mike grabbed the envelope containing four copies of the search warrant from his captain's hand, he asked, "Am I clear to take Steve and George as back-up?"

"Sure. Get 'em the hell out of here. But make sure they come back when you're done."

"We'll need some uniforms, also. Maybe four?"

"Yeah. Fine. Make 'em drive. You get one car from the pool."

Chapter 37
Hard News

RACHEL STOOD BEHIND the video editor's control board at the ACN offices on Twelfth Avenue. The editor, a thirty-year-old in a Grateful Dead t-shirt with long, unwashed hair, manipulated a large round dial. He kept moving the video forward and backward, then clipping or adjusting the image.

"Don't let them see me adjusting my hair," Rachel barked, then apologized. "Sorry, Dwayne. Please cut that and pick up with my lead-in."

She scolded herself for being impatient with the editor. The story was about a group of high-school students who were raising money to compete in the national cheerleading championships at Disney World. It was good work by the students, who were adorable. Dave had assigned it to Rachel two weeks earlier for airing in a regular spot they called "Friday's Heroes." When she got the assignment, Rachel was happy to have a piece where she could do the stand-up for the camera on location, and also host it in the studio when it aired during the six o'clock news hour. Now, while working on the final editing, she was annoyed that it was taking time away from her reporting on the Lou Palazzo triple murder story.

She was also worried about her studio wardrobe. She had a smart pink and black skirt and jacket combo, but the expanding area around her waist was starting to strain the buttons. She wondered whether chasing witnesses on the streets of New York would be a good idea in a few more months.

Thursday's story generated more than 100,000 clicks on the ACN website. The print media in New York jumped all over the possible connection to Deputy Mayor Erickson. Although the story was most often sourced to Dexter Peacock's article in *The New York Times*, ACN was able to license the video Rachel and Terry shot and her questions to Erickson, which ran on several local broadcasts. Dave was pleased, but as always he wanted more. Rachel pitched the idea of trying to track down the reason why the deputy mayor had visited Lou Palazzo's pawn shop. As juicy as that story might have been, every media outlet in the city was currently chasing it. Since Rachel had no inside access to the mayor's office, the chance of ACN scoring a scoop on that front was not worth the expenditure of resources. So said Dave.

Rachel spent the morning contemplating her options. The kid, Ryan, seemed to be Lou Palazzo's closest relative. Finding more friends or family to talk about how sad the man's death was would be repetitive and likely not as impactful as what she already got. Jason was crystal clear that Rachel could not mention any possible connection between the murders and the Gallata crime family unless she had a source to which it could be attributed other than Jason. But Jason had not given any instructions about the connection to the two unidentified Chinese men.

One source of information Rachel could mine without a hint of impropriety was her best friend, Dr. Michelle McNeill. Michelle said she already submitted her report to the police and that there was nothing particularly important or unusual in it. When Rachel called, Michelle confirmed that the two other victims were Chinese and had been identified from their entry into the US. But she had no other information about them. They seemed to be ghosts. Internet searches of their Chinese names produced far too many matches to be useful. Being "mystery men" was enough for Rachel to pitch a potential story to Dave, who agreed to send her out with Terry. But only after she finished her fluff piece.

"Are we done?" Rachel asked hopefully.

"You want to watch the edited version through once for QC?" Dwayne asked.

"I should, right?"

"Yeah. It's standard procedure."

"Fine." Rachel leaned on the back of Dwayne's chair, peering at the small monitor. "Let's do it quickly."

* * *

AT 2:40 P.M., RACHEL SMOOTHED her hair and pulled on her blouse to even it up so her dangling necklace was properly centered. The interview was mercifully indoors, allowing her to shed her wool overcoat and scarf. She looked into the camera and signaled to Terry that she was ready. When the red light blinked on, Rachel's smile lit up the small room as much as Terry's fill light.

"On Sunday, local businessman Louis Palazzo was murdered in downtown Manhattan. Two men of Chinese descent were found in Mr. Palazzo's shop, dead from shotgun blasts. They were presumably shot by the murdered shopkeeper during a holdup, or some other confrontation. The Chinese men were not immediately identified and are believed to have recently entered the country. Why were they in that shop? What were they looking for? The answers are critical to the ongoing police investigation. I'm here with Kasper Gutman, an expert on international terrorism and counter-intelligence, who has some thoughts. Mr. Gutman, tell us what you're thinking?"

Kasper was a lump of a man with a round face, a drooping chin, and a thin moustache. He spoke with an air of authority. "Well, it seems pretty clear to me that the two dead men were Chinese agents, sent into the country to retrieve something their syndicate bosses consider quite valuable. We know that the Chinese government and certain quasi-governmental criminal organizations there are engaged in various hacking and data-gathering operations designed to destabilize the U.S. economy. Since the dead man was running an electronics store and since he had ties to US organized crime, I'm thinking he was involved in a conspiracy with Chinese mobsters. Probably something to do with mining the personal data of US citizens and the financial information of US companies."

"If Mr. Palazzo was involved, why would the Chinese syndicate kill him?" Rachel looked dramatically at the camera as she asked the question.

"I would say the most likely reason is that he was trying to double-cross them or holding out on turning over information they wanted. Whatever it was, it was worth killing him over it. So, look out if the Chinese get their hands on it, whatever it is."

Rachel pulled back the microphone and made eye contact with Terry behind his HD camera. "Thank you, Mr. Gutman. I share your hope that the Chinese government never gets its hands on that information. Rachel Robinson reporting for ACN. Back to you, Veronica."

When the camera light went out, Rachel thanked her expert witness and helped Terry pack up the portable light stand. Gutman came up behind her. "You know, I'm also an expert in international finance and cryptocurrency. So, if you need someone for any story like that, I'm your guy. Have you seen my website? It's globalconspiracy.com and I've got links there to some amazing videos that your network could run."

"Thanks, Mr. Gutman. I'll keep that in mind."

"Please, it's Kasper." The man leered down at Rachel. He was everything she found most repulsive in men. There was no chance.

Rachel backed away a step. "OK. Well, we have another interview, so we have to run. Right, Terry?" Rachel turned away from Gutman and opened her eyes wide, begging for help.

"Yes. We're already late," Terry said. "Grab that light stand and take it to the van, please."

Rachel hustled to the ACN van carrying the twenty-pound base that supported the fill lights. By the time she emerged, Kasper was gone. Rachel breathed a sigh of relief.

"Where did you find that guy?" Terry asked, his head down while carefully packing up his camera.

"He was the best I could do. The internet is a bizarre place sometimes." Rachel chuckled.

Chapter 38
Serving a Warrant

A T TWO O'CLOCK, Mike and Jason unfurled themselves from the back seat of the black-and-white and strode purposefully through the icy Manhattan wind toward the glass-and-steel doors leading to the lobby of 311 West 9th Street. Each detective had two copies of the search warrant, in case they needed to split up. They were confident they could narrow down their target's location, but it was always possible that the Gallata operation was segmented in more than one location. It was even possible that their assumption about the basement level doors was entirely wrong. Searching the entire building, if they were wrong, would take time.

An attendant in a blue uniform, wearing a night stick but no gun, came out from behind the lobby desk to meet the approaching officers and detectives. His desk partner stayed behind, immediately dialing a clunky phone perched on the counter. Mike and Jason anticipated that the front desk would alert the Gallata bosses if the cops showed up. Mike signaled to Officer James Garofolo, a thick fireplug of a man from Brooklyn, who charged forward, placing himself between Mike and the oncoming security guard.

"Police business, Sir, please step aside. These detectives are here to serve a warrant and conduct a lawful search."

The security guard, not wearing any name badge, stood his ground. "Show me the warrant." He held out a hand, which pressed against James' chest because the officer was so close. The two men's faces were separated by less than six inches, like prize fighters at a weigh-in.

Jason intervened, nudging James out of the way. "I'm Detective Jason Dickson. Here is the search warrant. It's fully in order. Our first stop is the mezzanine level. Please step aside."

"I need to review this and contact building management."

"Contact them all you want," Mike said, turning toward the bank of elevators accompanied by one of the other officers. "We're going down."

"You don't have permission, Sir," the guard shouted, still holding the warrant. "I'm ordering you to stop now and wait at the desk for permission to enter."

"I don't recognize your authority to give me orders," Mike shot back, already halfway to the elevator. He pressed the down button and stepped back, looking up at the number indicator above the nearest door. The light read *7*. Above the two other doors, the yellow numbers flashed *4* and *12*. Mike listened to Jason and the guard continuing to argue about the warrant. He was happy to have his own copies to serve on the occupants of the downstairs offices.

After thirty seconds, Mike furrowed his brow, staring up at the elevator numbers. They had not budged. He turned toward the front desk, where the second attendant still held the telephone receiver against his face. Mike walked to a metal door with a red EXIT light over its head jamb. The horizontal handle did not budge when Mike attempted to push it down. It was likely more of an emergency exit to the lobby for the basement dwellers than an exit to the street for building residents. Mike shrugged and walked calmly to the front desk.

"I'm Detective Mike Stoneman, NYPD. I'm here to conduct a lawful search pursuant to a warrant that your partner there has in his hand." Mike gestured toward the other guard, who was now in Jason's face, pointing and shouting. "I'm going to assume you are responsible for the elevators not working. I'm going to give you one opportunity to use your master key, unlock the door to the stairs, and allow us to enter."

"I'm sorry, Officer, but I can't do that. I have my orders." The guard made no move to gather his keys.

"It's Detective." Mike turned to his accompanying uniform. "Officer Garofolo, please arrest this man for obstruction of justice and cuff him."

The guard made no attempt to resist as James spun him around and applied the cuffs.

"Now, Officer, please search him and see if he has a set of keys."

The officer patted down the guard. "Got a set of keys, Detective," he said, handing over a small ring with a New York Mets logo fob.

Mike walked briskly back to the stairway door. He glanced over his shoulder at the continuing altercation in the middle of the lobby. Officer Maggie Mitchell put the first guard on the ground and slapped a pair of cuffs on him. Upon arriving at the stair door, a smiling Mike deftly went through all the keys on the ring, but none came close to fitting the lock. Mike noticed a small black pad on the wall near the door. He called back to the officer, still at the desk with their detainee, "Garofolo, see if the guy has some kind of key card."

Mike walked back to the desk while James searched the guard again. Unfortunately, the silver ID card he found did not unlock the stairs door. By the time Mike returned to the desk, Jason was there, searching in the cubbies and drawers behind the lobby barrier for something to unlock the door. Jason used one of the second guard's keys to open a locked drawer under the desk phone, where he found a white card on a lanyard without any markings.

"Mike – try this one."

Jason tossed the card to Mike, who walked back to the stairway door. A flash of the white card on the sensor produced a satisfying click. James pulled the door open.

Before Mike could descend to the basement, a screechy voice called out behind him, echoing across the marble floor. "Stop right there!"

Mike turned to see a man in a suit shuffling across the lobby in what appeared to be an attempt at running. He was thin and spindly, a tendril of shoe-polish-black hair dangling between his eyes and beads of sweat dripping from his nose. He panted up to Mike and the two officers on either side of him. "I represent the building management, Officer, and I object to this intrusion." He was barely able to complete the sentence without running out of breath.

"It's Detective, Sir, and I don't give a rat's ass who you represent. You will stay here in the lobby." Mike turned to Maggie. "Officer Mitchell, please detain this man." He turned and hurried down the stairs.

When they pushed through the heavy fire door into the basement corridor, Mike and James made a beeline to the first blue door, which had a black sticker bearing the number "M2" above it. Mike pushed down on a long chrome handle, pushed the door open, took three steps inside, and stopped. He turned in a 180-degree arc, surveying the space. It was expansive, extending a hundred feet to his left, parallel to the exterior hallway, and fifty feet in front of him. And it was deserted.

A long row of ten double tables pushed together side to side lined the center of the room. Black power cords dangled across the tables, snaking underneath where they plugged into outlets inset into the floor, covered with gray industrial carpet. At the far end, a cluster of smaller tables formed a square. At the other end, a counter built into the wall was cluttered with cups, coffee urns, a microwave oven, and wire baskets filled with snack items. A black refrigerator dominated the corner. A five-gallon water cooler stood half-empty next to the fridge. The open space was interrupted at twenty-foot intervals by support pillars. Each one was flanked by a four-foot tall garbage can. Smoke rose from a sink near the fridge and coffee machines.

"Looks like they bugged out in a hurry," Jason, who had just arrived, observed.

Mike pulled rubber crime scene gloves from his jacket pocket. "Let's see what they left behind."

* * *

WHILE MIKE AND JASON WERE TRYING to get through the stairway door, Steve Berkowitz and George Mason sat in an unmarked Lincoln sedan parked half a block from the building. Their assignment was to back up Mike and Jason if they called for it, and to keep watch in case any of the rats tried to abandon the sinking Gallata ship.

"Incoming," Steve said, reaching for the dashboard camera and switching it on as an extra-large white panel van pulled out of the parking garage. It was the size of an Amazon delivery truck, with two men in the front seats. The one in the passenger seat, with Asian features, held a cell phone to his ear. The van paused at the exit. The driver, who wore sunglasses, craned his neck to look at the two NYPD cruisers parked at the curb in front of the building, one of which had its lights flashing. A lone figure sat in the back of one car. After a long pause, the guy with the phone motioned with his arm for the driver to move forward and take a right, away from the cop cars.

After the van passed, Steve started the engine and followed at a reasonable distance. George texted Mike and Jason to let them know that the NYPD backup team was leaving. The van, which was easy to tail, snaked through the Lower Manhattan traffic until it reached the Manhattan Bridge. Steve and George followed it into Brooklyn until it reached a curving street in Dyker Heights. The van stopped and waited while two heavy wrought-iron gates opened. The vehicle disappeared up a winding driveway as the security gates closed behind it. The detectives made a note of the location, took some photos, then turned around and headed back to Manhattan.

Upon returning to the building, George saw Mike's text asking them to come inside when they got back. In the lobby, two uniformed officers were directing pedestrian traffic. Three men, including two wearing the uniforms of security guards and one in a business suit, sat in a corner with their arms behind their backs. An officer keeping watch on the detainees directed Steve and George to the stairway door.

They walked into the boiler room, now a crime scene of sorts. Several uniformed officers were gathering evidence, along with two dark-suited men Steve immediately pegged as FBI. He and George snapped on latex gloves. "Looks like you busted up a Spirit Halloween store on November second," George joked.

"Very funny," Mike said. "The douche bags packed up and fled town as soon as the guard in the lobby gave them a heads-up that we were there. Where the hell have you two been?"

Steve explained their surveillance of the white van and its disappearance into a gated compound in Brooklyn. "We ran the plates on the van and it's a rental."

"I'll bet that property is a Gallata compound," Mike mumbled. "They were ready like a MASH unit."

"We'll check that, Mike, but I can tell you one interesting thing."

"Yeah?" Mike raised an eyebrow.

"You remember the GPS tracker you put on an SUV on Tuesday? Today's van went to the same address."

"You're right," Mike smiled, "that's very interesting, particularly since, according to Jason's research, it's owned by Fat Albert Gallata's sister."

George tapped Jason's arm. "Did you find anything here?"

Jason leaned against one of the sturdy portable tables, its black iron legs supporting his weight easily. "We figure this room was base camp for at least ten people working with computer and AV equipment. They left in such a hurry that they abandoned the power cords. They unplugged their computers, grabbed the rest of their gear, and ran. There's a door down the hall leading into the parking garage. Your van was jammed with goons and gear. They didn't leave much."

"Why ten?" George asked.

"Based on the number of abandoned cords." Jason pointed at the black tails hanging from the table, then gestured toward the square composed of four small tables. "At least one other guy was at the table in the back, over there. We're not sure why that one was separate, but it had at least two computers. He left the monitor. We found a bunch of handwritten notes on papers in the trash cans, mostly in what looks like Chinese. Could be Japanese, for all I know, or Korean. But you get the idea. Since the dead goons from the pawn shop were Chinese, we figure Chinese."

"What's with the smoke?" Steve asked, sniffing the air and making a sour face.

"They started a fire in the sink, probably burning documents. The smoke detectors were disabled. We're packing up all the garbage in case there's something in there they didn't have time to destroy."

George surveyed the open space. "Must have been working hard at something."

"Yeah," Mike said. "We're speculating that this operation was mining the computer equipment lifted from Lou Palazzo's shop. They're looking for something. The fact that they were still here with ten guys means they haven't found it yet."

Steve stated the obvious. "Too bad we don't know what the thing is."

James, who was carefully extracting items from the garbage can nearest to the square, called out, "Detective Stoneman. Come take a look at this."

All four detectives marched to the other end of the room, where bits of garbage in plastic bags lined the floor. James handed Mike a baggie containing a scrap of lined paper. It had obviously been crumpled and then smoothed out before going into the bag. Mike held the plastic up to the light, trying to make out the scribbled writing. There were numbers that Mike couldn't decipher, and a name: *Ryan*. Mike also could make out the words *Still looking*.

Mike looked at Jason. "You think?"

Chapter 39
Making Connections

AT 5:15, MIKE AND JASON WERE in the fifth-floor communications department conference room on a video call. The meeting was titled "Joint Task Force – Project Hack."

When the conference call started, the two detectives were joined by Special Agent Everett Forrest and a new face. Forrest introduced him as Miles Jacoby, a former FBI agent now working for the Department of Homeland Security. "Jacoby is one of the good guys," Forrest said, "and he's a Mets fan. He's now saddled with the title of Homeland Security Investigations Special Agent."

"Call me Investigator, or just Jacoby," he said demurely.

Mike sized up their new potential colleague over the video. Since Everett had vouched for Jacoby, he was going to give the guy the benefit of the doubt. Investigator Jacoby looked like a typical Fibbie. While sitting, it was impossible to judge height, but his bulked-up upper body, broad shoulders, starched white collar, thin black tie, square chin, and buzz cut fit the mold. Mike was certain he was a solid six feet and that his black loafers were well-shined. But his eyes were soft. He didn't have the laser death stare of many FBI agents. In that way, Jacoby and Everett resembled each other.

Once Jacoby started speaking, Mike was impressed with his directness. "Agent Forrest has vouched for you both, and my quick background check supports him. I don't have time to dick around, so I'm going to share. I expect you to do the same." Jacoby paused until he got silent nods from Everett and Mike. "I'm assigned to a task force tracking foreign governments that are trying to destabilize our economy and hack our infrastructure. You won't be shocked that two of the main bad actors are Russia and China. Not the only ones, but our main focus. I have twenty investigators tracking hackers, mainly the Chinese, who are unfortunately very good at it." Jacoby hesitated, waiting for a laugh that didn't come. "Which is why I'm here. A regional director at the FBI put out an inquiry two days ago about a possible hack and data breach in New York. That hack was potentially connected to the murder of two Chinese nationals. I believe you are acquainted with the case."

Mike took the cue from Jacoby's pause this time. "We have two such Chinese nationals in our morgue. Nobody has claimed them. In the interest of mutual sharing, I'll say they may be connected to a local organized crime syndicate, the Gallatas."

Jacoby gave Mike a quick incline of his head, acknowledging the voluntary contribution. "What you don't know, Detective Stoneman, is that those two dead Chinese dudes are known muscle for a gang from Shanghai. I'll spare you the Chinese name, but it translates to The Corporate Dragons. They're on a restricted Interpol list. Someone from the NYPD pinged our system. The Corporate Dragons are practically the ministry of hacking for the central Chinese government. Xi Jinping wants to have plausible deniability if one of his minions gets caught with their hand in the cookie jar, but these guys are effectively government agents. The syndicate has been working mostly on economic hacks and data breaches: financial management companies, major corporations, charitable organizations, and big universities. We think their objective is to harvest personal data from wealthy donors, executives, and depositors and then leak it to undermine confidence in the financial system."

"So, what were these two doing in a crappy pawn shop with a Gallata lieutenant?" Jason asked. "How is that connected to Chinese government hacking?"

"We're still fuzzy about that. They were for sure in New York on behalf of the Corporate Dragons. Those guys don't send their muscle to the US and risk them being detained here unless it's a big deal operation. They're apparently working with your Gallata gang – like a sister city gang – which is provocative. We have some intelligence suggesting the Dragons have a small ongoing operation here in New York. The fact that a high-ranking FBI official was asking about it, off the record, in connection to a possible hack . . .well, that's too much smoke for there not to be some fire."

Jason turned to Mike, who inclined his head. "Investigator Jacoby, our working theory has been that the murdered shopkeeper, Lou Palazzo, was in possession of something the Gallata gang wanted. Something digital. Palazzo had a past connection with the Gallatas. We couldn't figure why the Chinese guys were working with the Gallatas, but if there's some kind of data hack involved, I guess that could explain it. We were a little surprised that Palazzo was able to take them out."

"I can understand," Jacoby agreed. "Maybe they were overconfident, being two against one. Palazzo probably didn't seem like a formidable opponent. But I'm sure you're right about them wanting something. If they wanted to ice the guy, they would have done it. But if they were trying to extract information from him, they would have wanted him alive, at least for a while."

"So," Jason pushed forward, "you think they were looking for something connected to a Chinese hack job? Is it possible Palazzo carried out the hack for them and was holding out on the goods?"

"It's a theory." Jacoby stroked his smooth-shaven face. "But it's not the Corporate Dragons' usual operating model. They generally conduct the hacks from offshore. That's what makes them so hard for us to stop. They clone domestic machines, hack into servers, and steal data. Mostly, they use spear-phishing tactics and con insiders into giving up their passwords, but sometimes other methods. We're thinking that, maybe, Palazzo was their conduit into something."

"What could Palazzo have access to that they would care about?" Mike asked.

"Not sure. Yet. But it seems like it might have had some connection to NYU, according to the FBI inquiry. Now it's your turn, Detective. Have you uncovered anything in your investigation that might be connected?"

Mike hesitated, but had to admit the federal agent was more forthcoming than he and Jason expected. Share and share alike seemed to be the theme of the afternoon. "I wish I had something concrete for you. Somebody ransacked the pawn shop right after the killing and grabbed a laptop computer and some amount of additional equipment. Then, we have video of four Gallata operatives breaking into the shop at two in the morning and doing a more thorough job, taking every computer in the place."

"That tracks with them looking for data." Jacoby leaned forward.

"Yeah. We don't know what, but we have the four guys in a car on street cams driving to a building on 9th Street."

"Agent Forrest filled me in on your raid today. I spoke to the FBI agents who assisted. Seems like you collected some interesting trash."

Mike smiled. "True. We bagged up all their garbage. We found some scrap paper with notes written in what we think is Chinese. We need to get it translated. Maybe your guys can help with that?"

"And there is a connection to NYU," Jason broke in. "Palazzo has a nephew named Ryan Gelb, who is a computer science student there. Gelb visited Palazzo at his shop the day he was killed. And we found a note during our raid with the name Ryan on it."

Jacoby said nothing, taking in this information. "We can certainly help with the Chinese translation," he offered. "And there's definitely something here linked to NYU. When can you get that downtown to Foley Square?"

"What's in Foley Square?"

"Our task force's operations headquarters. We're inside 26 Federal Plaza."

"Makes sense," Mike mumbled. "We'll get you photographs of the Chinese notes."

"Great." Jacoby scribbled something on the desk in front of him. "Let's hope there's a lead in there somewhere."

"What about the student, Gelb?" Jason asked.

"I've got a few ideas," Jacoby said with a level of excitement he had not previously displayed. "But let's not get ahead of ourselves. You say this Gelb kid is Palazzo's nephew? And he's a computer student at NYU? That's exactly the kind of target the Dragons go after. Maybe he had a job that gave him access to passwords. He could have been an entry point for a hack. I'd say we need to talk to him. You boys busy tomorrow?"

"Our schedule is clear," Mike said. "We'll gather a pile of garbage and meet you at your place in the morning."

Jacoby smiled. "I'm going to enjoy working with you."

Chapter 40
Late Night News

RACHEL HAD BEEN NERVOUS about whether Dave would approve running the interview with Kasper Gutman. Her apprehension proved unnecessary.

"I love it!" Dave beamed at Rachel after he screened the tape. "It's a foreign incursion. These Chinese agents came gunning for an American businessman. This Palazzo guy was like a real-life Rambo. He pulls out his shotgun and blows two of them away, but can't escape the third guy, who executes him in the middle of Avenue C. It's a great narrative. We'll air the interview tonight. Then, I want you to work on a studio piece for tomorrow. See if you can get somebody a little more reputable to talk about the Chinese angle. And see if you can get the police to verify the connection between the two dead guys and the Chinese mafia. This is good. Our viewers will eat it up."

Rachel smiled and said she was thrilled.

That evening, she sat with Jason's arm around her shoulder, watching the ACN news hour. Her mother rocked in her chair, sipping an iced tea. When Rachel's piece ran, they all watched in silence. When the news show cut back to Veronica in the studio, wearing a tight-fitting top exposing one creamy shoulder, Olivia clicked off the television.

"You couldn't find a more authoritative source?" Olivia asked with a raised left eyebrow.

"He had a strong opinion," Rachel said. "It's what I needed. Somebody who would say something interesting. My boss loved him."

"Your boss is a moron," Jason said, trying to sound like he was joking.

"He's interested in ratings," Rachel defended. "Besides, it's a reasonable theory. Do you have a better explanation for why those two Chinese guys were there confronting Lou Palazzo?"

Jason shook his head. "I don't, but neither does that idiot. He's just speculating wildly. He's got no evidence that the Chinese government or the Chinese mafia are involved."

Rachel responded more sharply than she intended, "But they could be. I mean, it's a possibility. It makes for good speculation in the comments on our YouTube page. It's what people like to talk about."

"Dear," Olivia cut in, "is that the kind of reporter you want to be? Fanning the flames of conspiracy theories and pushing the wild theories of anyone who has a website?"

"He's a legitimate expert." Rachel tried to defend her choice, but even she could not put much energy into it.

"Sweetheart, I know you were under pressure to find somebody willing to give you content. This schmuck would say anything to get on TV. But you got a piece on air. So good for you. Now, you need to find something legitimate for the next one." Jason stroked Rachel's hair, trying to be supportive rather than critical.

"OK. Fine. I'll do that. I don't suppose you have any information you can share with me to help me get on the right track, do you?"

Jason held up two open palms. "I really can't say."

"Well, let me ask this: Do you have information inconsistent with them being agents of a Chinese criminal organization or the Chinese government?"

Jason sighed. "It's consistent with them being a hundred different things. But I'll tell you one thing. Tomorrow, Mike and I will be working overtime. We're meeting with some feds downtown who are setting up a joint task force with the NYPD to continue investigating this case."

"That sounds like exactly what the feds would do if the Chinese guys *were* government agents. Until proven otherwise, I'll assume they were muscle for the Chinese government, who were working with the Gallata family on an international conspiracy. Unless you would like to give me some official statement from the NYPD contradicting the theory espoused by noted international counter-terrorist expert Kasper Gutman—"

"Oh, please!" Olivia could not help herself.

"—then I'm going to run with this theory. Do you have something better, sweetheart?"

Jason shook his head and chuckled. "Alright. You got me. I'll anxiously await the next installment of your investigative report."

Chapter 41
When the Walls Close In

NYU PRESIDENT SHARRON HENRY PACED across her office's purple carpet wearing khaki slacks and a white polo shirt with an NYU logo. She was never in the office this early on a Saturday morning. Dire circumstances called for unusual hours.

Her head of security was on his way. Yates said he couldn't discuss his concerns on the phone. Never good news, she thought ruefully. For the past three days, she had dreaded bad news about the data breach. But she had also been making contingency plans, because that was what competent leaders did. Her gut said the news was going to be bad. When Yates walked in with a sour face and sat in the guest chair without offering to shake hands first, there was little doubt.

"We have the final analysis of the data breach, Sharron. I'm afraid it's not good. It's now a certainty that the breach included details of donors, including credit card numbers and banking information. We still don't have confirmation that any of the data has been used or transferred by the hackers, but at this point, we cannot keep the breach quiet. We have an obligation to notify the affected donors. And we'll have to advise the FBI formally. I'm sorry, ma'am."

President Henry sat behind her massive mahogany desk with a resolute expression. "I understand. We have plans in place to send out the notices. Do you have a list of those affected?"

"Yes, ma'am. Shall I send it over confidentially to Erika?"

"Sure. She's supposed to be in charge of communications, so let her handle it. Also, send it to Alumni Affairs. Howard will need to formulate a plan for damage control. Can we work through Chester at the FBI, or do we have to file something on their website?"

"That's a bit of a gray area. If we work through Mr. Miller initially and document a contact today for the record, and then file on the FBI website on Monday, we should be OK. Is that what you want me to do?"

"Yes. I'll reach out to Chester. Maybe the authorities can track down the data before Monday. It's at least worth trying."

"And, Sharron," Yates said hesitantly, "there's one more thing."

"The Aswani investigation files?"

"I'm afraid so." Yates stood. It was a subconscious move to force the other person to look up at him, giving him a superior position. "The files were definitely downloaded. But, as we've discussed, the documents themselves were password-protected. If the hackers were after financial information, which is how it looks, they may not bother with text files. And even if they were curious, they would not be able to open the documents. There is no need for us to specify that those files were part of the hack. Only personal information of third parties needs to be reported."

The two disappointed executives exchanged mournful stares. Yates left the office without any farewells. Henry punched buttons on her land line.

"Chester, it's Sharron. We got bad news on the data breach. I'll fill you in, then you do what you have to do."

Chapter 42
Puzzle Pieces

MIKE AND JASON SAT IMPATIENTLY in the visitor lobby inside the Department of Homeland Security's New York field office Saturday morning, waiting for Investigator Miles Jacoby. He escorted the detectives to a windowless conference room. Four other agents, three men and a woman, were seated around a document-strewn table. The assembled group collectively looked up when Jacoby entered with his guests. They all set down their pens and coffee cups, removed thumbs from cell phones, and sat back in thickly cushioned boardroom chairs. Mike and Jason remained standing.

"I'm Detective Mike Stoneman, NYPD. This is Detective Jason Dickson. I'm sure Investigator Jacoby has briefed you on our murder case, which we think is connected to both the Gallata organization here in New York and your bunch of Chinese creeps. We're here to share information."

"We checked you out," the lone woman at the table said. "I called FBI Special Agent Angela Manning. She vouches for you both. That's high praise, since Angela doesn't like men much."

Mike let out a belly laugh. "Well, we picked up on that in the time we worked together. It's nice to hear that she didn't give us a failing grade."

"Alright, let's get this party started." Jacoby clapped his hands, removing his jacket and placing it on the back of his chair. Mike and Jason took adjoining seats as Jacoby addressed the room. "Stoneman, Dickson, you don't know this morning's news, so I'll fill you in. Remember I told you about a possible hack involving NYU? Well, today we got specific confirmation. The FBI Regional Director who put out the confidential alert earlier this week told me that the university had a data breach twelve days ago. Their cybersecurity team says the hack came in through a student account. They talked to the student, a kid you have met named Ryan Gelb, who confirmed that his laptop computer was compromised."

"Lou Palazzo's nephew," Jason cut in.

Jacoby nodded. "That's the connection. The kid's a computer science major and he told university security he recognized the hack and shut down his machine. He found a file on his hard drive, which was probably the data downloaded from the NYU server. The student says he tried to open the file, which was a stupid idea, but it was encrypted. So, he copied the file to a flash drive and gave it to his uncle, who was apparently a computer expert, to see if he could get it open. As we know, Palazzo was murdered two days later."

Mike and Jason exchanged a glance. Ryan had not informed them about the flash drive he gave his uncle.

Jacoby continued his briefing. "The NYU crew is hoping the data was not actually received by the hackers, which is why they didn't immediately report the breach. Today, they acknowledged that the downloaded data includes sensitive financial information about university donors and alumni, including credit card numbers and bank account data. Now, we need to work together to unscramble this egg."

Mike said, "We suspected the kid was holding out on us. I guess now we know why. I doubt Ryan Gelb is an agent of this

Corporate Dragons gang. You think these Chinese mob guys were looking to retrieve the hacked file?"

Jacoby moved to a whiteboard mounted at the far end of the room. Mike noticed it when they walked in, but had not carefully scrutinized the writing. Jacoby rolled up his shirt sleeves and pointed to a rough square at the top of the board. Inside was the word *Dragons*. Snaking down from the top box, five lines led to other boxes labeled *ABC*, *BoA*, *UM*, *ML*, and *GS*. Under those boxes were lists of names. Under the GS box, Mike recognized the word *Gallata*.

Before Mike could digest more information, Jacoby started talking. "We've been tracking hacks linked to The Corporate Dragons. What we would love is some insight into a hack in progress."

"You mean, like that data file Ryan had," Jason said. "If you had that downloaded file, it might help you."

"Damned right," Jacoby agreed. "These hackers have been able to breach high-security firewalls and encryptions. We'd love to get our hands on whatever algorithm they're using. So, what can you two tell us about your investigation that will help us find a hacked file?"

"How did the Chinese know the kid gave the file to his uncle?" Mike mused.

"We're not clear about that, either," Jacoby admitted. "We think the Chinese hackers used this Gelb kid's university log-in credentials in order to get into the system. So, they would know the name of their stooge. They might have simply followed him."

Jason asked the obvious question. "Why didn't they grab the flash drive from him if they were tailing him?"

"The hackers generally conduct their incursions by secretly taking over their target's computer," Jacoby explained. "The target generally doesn't know what's happening. The hackers probably figured the kid didn't know the data file was on his computer."

Mike jumped into the speculation. "So, what they wanted was the computer. I'm surprised they didn't break into his dorm room and steal it while he was away."

"Maybe they did," Jacoby mused. "But we know from the reports from NYU that the kid was aware of the hack. He knew there was a file and he downloaded it to a flash drive and gave the drive to Palazzo."

"So," Mike said, "the kid might have been walking around with the file in his pocket, and the Chinese Dragons might have been following him and not realized it."

"But if that's true," Jason picked up the thread, "how did they figure out Palazzo had the file?"

"Maybe he didn't," Jacoby said despondently. "Maybe the kid took it back. Maybe he still has it. Whatever the explanation, the Chinese operatives decided that Palazzo might have it and they showed up to retrieve it or force him to tell them where it was."

"But they didn't get it," Jason observed. "Even as of yesterday, after several days of sifting through all the computers they lifted from the shop, they didn't have it."

"How can you know that?" a curly-haired man with rolled-up sleeves asked.

Jacoby responded before Mike could. "I told you all earlier that these detectives raided a Gallata building yesterday. There was a large operation there that included multiple computers. But they scrambled when the police arrived. These detectives found some scraps of paper in the garbage written in Chinese. They scanned a few of them over yesterday and they include notes about not finding the file they were looking for." Jacoby gestured toward Mike and Jason. "If they had found it, they wouldn't still have been working at it when you arrived."

"Exactly." Mike walked to the whiteboard, studying the notations. "I'm thinking we need to have another talk with Ryan Gelb. You want to come along?"

Chapter 43
It's in the Game

RYAN THREW HIS GAME CONTROLLER on the bed in disgust. He and Will had once again failed to clear what they called the falcon level. They had lost count of the number of times they tried, but it was certainly more than twenty. With no classes on Saturday, they vowed to play all day if necessary.

"Why would Lou put the information about the falcon someplace so hard for us to get to?" Ryan lamented.

"We're still assuming the information is there. I'm starting to wonder." Will flopped into Ryan's desk chair and stared at his phone.

A knock on the door broke the sour mood. Will welcomed Star and Sarrie. Star settled into a cross-legged posture on the floor, leaning against Ryan's bed. Sarrie flopped onto the bed next to Will.

"Any luck with the falcon?" Star asked.

"No," Ryan mumbled, moving over to drape his legs on either side of Star and gently massage her neck. "We're still stuck."

Star leaned back into the pressure from Ryan's thumbs. "Mmmm. That's nice. So, when are you going to let me help you?"

"Like *that's* our problem?" Will responded skeptically.

Ryan attempted to maneuver the thin line between his best friend and his girlfriend. "Will, you remember I told you that maybe it would make sense for us to find a third player?"

Star jumped in to back up Ryan. "It makes sense. When the three of you played together, you had three fighters working together, right?"

"Of course," Will said, "but developing three-man teamwork takes time."

"You'll never know for sure unless you try, right?" Star put a hand on Ryan's knee and squeezed. "It's not like you're getting it done by yourselves."

Will did not try to hide his opposition. "You can't possibly play as well as Lou. We're better off working together without adding somebody new." He made eye contact with Ryan, wanting to make sure he didn't say anything that would mess up his best friend's relationship with his hot girlfriend.

"I'm fully serious, Will." Star crossed her arms across her chest. "I'm pretty good. What would it hurt to try?"

"It would waste our valuable time," Will responded quickly. "We're having enough trouble without having to get you up to speed on the gameplay. It's—" Will stopped talking when he noticed Ryan's pained expression.

"Maybe it's worth a try," Ryan said. "I mean, maybe it would give us some new perspectives on the level and the boss if we let Star join us for a few runs. Even if we don't beat him, it might help us find some new attacks. I'm willing to try."

"Give Star a chance," Sarrie said, looking at Will.

Will was now caught in a pincer from which he could not escape. He could push back against Star's wishes as much as he wanted and knew that Ryan would ultimately give in, but did not want to piss off Sarrie. After a moment, he relented, clearly more as a favor to Sarrie than because he thought it was a good idea.

"I promise not to pout or complain if we don't beat the boss," Star began. "But first, we need to talk about what you're going to do if you find that data file. You have to turn it over to the police or to the university. I don't want you getting killed over it."

Will looked at Ryan rather than Star. "If Lou decrypted the file, then we'll be able to see what's in it, assuming we can guess the password. We should be able to tell whether it was ever accessed by the hackers. If not, then we can give it to the university and say that we prevented a data breach."

"What if the hackers did get it?" Star said.

"How about this," Ryan put a hand up with his index finger extended, "we'll reserve judgment about what we'll do with the file until after we find it. If it's true that the guys who killed Uncle Lou were looking for the dingus, then it means they didn't get it from the hack. If we can prove that, then the university would want to know it. But we can't do anything until we have the file. OK?"

"OK," Star agreed. "Now, how about you boys show me around that falcon level?"

Ryan dragged out his laptop and set up Star as a player using a free trial *Blades of Karma* account. They spent half an hour running Star and her newly created avatar (a warrior princess) through the game's early levels. Will played on his own laptop, while Ryan plugged in through his PS4 console. The three combatants embarked on the journey through the stages together. Gaining experience and coordination along the way, they finally reached the falcon boss. Will remarked that Star was pretty good, especially when deployed as a decoy to draw attention away from the heroes, which was what Lou usually did as part of their team. Ryan always thought Lou did that to be nice, so Ryan and Will could get the kill shots. But as they approached the difficult boss' hideaway, he wondered whether Uncle Lou was intentionally employing a winning strategy that was essential to success.

The threesome's first foray against the falcon boss was unsuccessful, but Will admitted they inflicted more damage on the boss with Star's assistance than they had in any of their prior efforts as a duo. On the second try, Star disabled the bird and attacked the boss' feet. It was a strategy the boys had not considered. Ryan and Will took up flanking positions and launched a barrage at the suddenly stationary enemy. When Ryan's attack caused the boss to topple to the rocky ground at the foot of the cliff, all three players let out whoops of excitement.

"You did it!" Star cried out, sharing a high-five with each of her two companions. She squeezed Ryan's thigh.

It was nearing noon, but nobody was hungry. They waited to see if there was a message at the end of the level, or if the giant bird flew somewhere that would point them toward their prize. But they got nothing from the game except the reveal of a gateway leading to the next level.

They explored every corner of the next virtual world, looking for a clue or a message from Lou. There was nothing. They fought new enemies for another hour, reaching the level's boss, and failed miserably in their first attack.

Star announced that it was time for lunch. They took a break from playing *Blades of Karma* while Will called in a pizza order.

"Thanks for helping," Ryan said to Star. "I really thought we'd find something there."

"I had fun," Star said, planting a soft kiss on Ryan's lips. "Thanks for trusting me. If there's something in there, we'll find it. Together." She kissed him again, then bounced up from the bed. "We'll keep going later."

Propped on one elbow on Ryan's bed, Sarrie said, "It makes sense that you needed three players to beat the boss man."

"Just boss," Will said. "It was lucky that Star stumbled into the secret passage. That was the key to getting behind the boss. It's too bad it was all for nothing."

"It's not nothing," Star said, offended. "There has to be something there. I thought maybe that secret passage was the path your uncle was talking about. Maybe it's in the next level. Ryan, your uncle's note to you said it would be there, didn't it?"

Ryan leaned against the single window in the dorm room. "The message said, *Find the secret path. The falcon is uncaged and it's in the game.*"

Sarrie offered, "So, you're working on the assumption that there is some clue in the game that will tell you where the program is."

"It's a file, not a program," Will corrected, drawing an angry look from Sarrie.

Will opened the mini-fridge and grabbed a Red Bull. "I still don't get it. Star found the secret path – the secret passage in the falcon level – and we beat the boss. There should be a message or a clue that will lead to the dingus."

"Maybe it's on the path," Star suggested. "Maybe somewhere inside that secret passage is where the clue is."

"But you went through and didn't see anything," Ryan said. "Besides, it's not like Lou could have reprogrammed the entire game to put a message inside that corridor. He doesn't have source code access. It has to be something else."

"Will, honey," Sarrie said, sitting up on the bed. "When I save a file on the university server for one of my projects, I have to put it in a folder and give it a name. That file location is called the *path*, right?"

"Yeah. Sure. Every file on a drive has a file path."

"Well, maybe the clue in that message from Ryan's uncle was about the secret *file* path. You have to find the secret file path and get the falcon. Maybe the file's name is 'falcon.'"

"That makes sense," Will agreed, "but it doesn't help us. We don't know what computer it's on."

Star shot to her feet and excitedly said, "Wait! Wait! Lou's message said that it's *in the game*. Isn't the whole game just a bunch of data files? I mean, programs are files, aren't they?"

"Yeah ..." Ryan said in a faraway voice. "The game files are stored on a DVD disk that you load into the console. But there are also some files that get downloaded onto the machine's hard drive. Or, for a game like *Blades of Karma*, they get uploaded to the cloud so players can access their player data from any computer. That's things like personal information about the players and game history, like what level we're on."

"But on other games on the PS4, all the data is stored inside the console," Will said, his excitement level building.

"You think?" Ryan held up his game controller. Will took a swig from his Red Bull, then emitted a loud burp.

"Gross!" Sarrie said.

"But you might be right." Will smiled at his girlfriend. "Ryan, if your uncle wanted to put the file somewhere nobody would look for it, could he have uploaded it onto the PS4's hard drive?"

Ryan scratched his chin. "I suppose, sure. That drive is big enough. I could see how the guys who stole all the computers and storage drives from the shop would have missed it. The console doesn't look like a computer. If the secret path means the file path, then Lou was telling me the data file is hidden *inside* the game – meaning inside the PS4. It's not inside *Blades of Karma*, it's inside the console. All we have to do is find the file path."

"How will you know the name of the file?" Sarrie asked.

"If Lou was trying to make it hard to find, he would've either given it a coded name that we would recognize, or embedded a word clue in the name, like 'falcon' or 'Bogart.' If the dingus is on the PS4 drive, I'm sure we'll find it."

"You think the PS4 is still there in your uncle's shop?" Star asked.

"Yes!" Ryan's excitement level was growing. "We were there and played the game from Lou's account."

"You went back to the pawn shop since the murder?" Star was incredulous. "When? Why?"

Ryan exchanged a glance with Will, who said, "It was my idea. I thought maybe if we were in Lou's account, we might be able to find something in his sent messages, or have more luck with the game. I talked Ryan into it. We went on Wednesday."

"And you didn't tell us?" Sarrie jumped to her feet. "What else aren't you telling us?"

"Nothing!"

Ryan raised his voice to get everyone's attention. "It's no big deal. We didn't find anything inside Lou's account. We were in and out in about an hour. But we're looking for something different this time."

"We have to go get the console," Will said. "You still have the key to the back door into the shop, right?"

"I sure do."

"Let's go right now." Will looked around the room, silently asking if everyone agreed. "Screw the pizza. We grab the console and bring it back here. We can eat while we search its files."

"Um, I'm not sure that's a good idea," Star said. "That shop is still a crime scene. And you don't know whether the guys who killed your uncle are still watching the store, waiting for somebody to go there to get the data file, if it's even still there. It's great that you have a new theory, but you've been wrong before. You may be wrong again. I think you should tell the cops, or university security, and let them handle it. It's too dangerous for you to go by yourselves."

Will responded confidently, "Star, it's fine. We were already there once and nothing happened. The bad guys are long gone. You don't have to come, but Ryan and I are going. Ryan, you're in, right?"

"Hell yeah," Ryan said. "Star, don't worry. It'll be fine. You want to come, too, Sarrie?"

"Sure. I'm not afraid."

"Ryan, I can call my Uncle Mike. It's his investigation. He can keep it confidential."

"You can't guarantee that," Will shot back. "Can you?"

"I'm not sure," Star admitted. "But I can call him and find out. I don't have to tell him everything."

"No way!" Will shouted. "We've finally got a chance here. I'm not going to blow it. It's my scholarship at stake. You need to keep this to yourself, Star. Right, Ryan?"

Ryan looked like a puppy that had been smacked with a rolled-up newspaper. He didn't want to disagree with Star, but also didn't want to go against Will. "Star, I know you're trying to be careful. But, like Will said, we were there once and it was fine. Please don't tell your uncle. You can't do that to Will – or me. Once we find the dingus, we'll figure out what to do. OK?"

Star reluctantly agreed. As she watched her friends gather their coats and boots, she was certain of one thing: She had no good options.

* * *

IN A CLUTTERED GARAGE CONNECTED to a Queens row house, Lenny dialed The Cannon. After being displaced from the Lower Manhattan boiler room, the Chinese tech team had relocated to a Gallata property in the Bronx. Lenny had successfully lobbied his boss for permission to work from home rather than commute an hour and a half each way just to be surrounded by a bunch of guys speaking Chinese.

"Boss, Will and Ryan think they figured out where the data file is."

Cannon was silent, prompting Lenny to ask whether he was still on the line. "Yeah, I'm here. I had to move to get some privacy. You say they found it?"

"They don't have it yet, but they think it's back at the pawn shop. They're going there now to retrieve it."

"How the fuck can it be in that shop? We cleaned it out."

"They think Uncle Lou stashed the file inside his video game console."

"No shit? I didn't know you could do that. So, the Chinese know about it, too, right?"

Lenny sighed. "Yeah, pretty likely. We gave them the frequency and the encryption code for the signal booster, so they're probably listening. They don't trust us to share the info. Do you believe that shit?"

"Yeah. I don't trust them, either."

"Well, if they're listening like me, then they heard what I heard. If they have someone who can understand English." Lenny paused, gauging The Cannon's mood. "What happens now, Boss? Are you going to let 'em get the file and walk away with it?"

Cannon grunted. "No. If the Chinese were listening, they're for sure gonna ambush the kids as soon as they have your dingus."

"You gonna send any of our guys?"

"Yeah, but I gotta talk to the boss first. You wanna come along? You're in love with them, right?"

Lenny fumed. "I'm not *in love* with them. I want to find the dingus, that's all. And sure, I'm in for coming along. It'll get me out of these headphones."

The Cannon immediately called his boss. "If I thought the Chinese fuckers didn't know what's happening, I'd say we let the kids find the file, then grab them when they come out of the shop. But the Chinese are impatient. They'll probably kill them before they find the stupid file."

"That stupid file is worth two million. Remember that."

Cannon held the phone away from his ear, swearing at himself under his breath for making Fat Albert angry – at him. "Boss, I'm worried that Ji will get the file, waste the kids, and skip town without paying you."

"That's the smartest thing you've said," the boss responded. "I want you to get a few of your boys together and get over there. Make sure our Chinese friends don't double-cross me. And don't fuck it up!"

Chapter 44
Final Level

A T THE CORNER OF 12TH AND AVENUE B, Ryan grabbed Will's shoulder and pulled him to a stop on the slick sidewalk.

"Hey, you know, let's be a little careful here. Like Star said, the guys who murdered Uncle Lou over that data file could still be watching the shop."

"They already had their shot at the shop. They're long gone." Will dismissed Ryan's concern and resumed his forward motion.

"Wait!" Sarrie called, causing Will to skid. He could blow off Ryan, but his girlfriend was an entirely different matter. "Ryan's right. Let's at least take a look around and make sure it's safe. We're not in a rush, right?"

Will was compelled to agree, for Sarrie. The group walked past the front of the shop, looking in the windows. Everything looked quiet. The metal grill covered the front windows. Yellow crime scene tape was still strung across the threshold.

"What if the guys who killed Lou have a camera set up so they can watch the shop remotely?" Ryan said.

"You're being paranoid," Will responded tersely. "We were here on Wednesday and there was no problem."

"I'm just trying to consider all possibilities," Ryan shot back.

Sarrie sided with Ryan. "He's right. Keep your eyes open."

Will sulked, but swiveled his head to check the light poles and other places where a camera might be mounted. "I don't see anything."

"OK." Ryan licked his lips and blew out a breath, producing a plume of steam in the icy air. "We're going in the rear door. Let me go first and wait for you in the alley. That way, if there is anybody watching, they won't see three of us all go in together."

"You've got the key, man," Will shrugged. "If you want to go back in there by yourself, I'm not going to stop you."

Ryan's face flashed a shot of fear at the thought of being alone in the narrow air shaft behind the shop. "OK. But you position yourself where you can see me. If there's anybody back there, you can call 9-1-1."

"Fine. Let's go. I'm cold."

Moments later, Ryan crept past the shop's main entrance and around the corner, then ducked into the rear alley, disappearing from the view of anyone on the adjacent street. Will and Sarrie watched from across Avenue B until Ryan reached the rear door. He waited there, as planned. When nobody accosted Ryan, Will and Sarrie crossed the street and dashed into the narrow lane.

"Looks like the coast was clear all along." Will's defiant voice couldn't hide a hint of apprehension as he looked around for any wall-mounted cameras while Ryan opened the door.

Once inside, they made their way quickly to Lou's office, guided by the flashlight functions on their phones and holding their breath against the stench of death. Will snapped on the light once inside the office, which had no windows. Ryan climbed over the rubble still strewn around the cramped space and went directly to the left middle desk drawer. Placing his left hand on the cold steel handle, he hesitated. "What if it's not still here?"

"Open the damned drawer!" Will shouted. Sarrie yelped at the sudden loud noise.

"Fine." Ryan pulled the squeaky metal and shined his light inside. A black plastic rectangle sat silently in the shadows. "Bingo!"

Will and Sarrie both blew out the breaths they didn't realize they were holding. "Grab it and let's get out of here," Will said.

"I gotta disconnect it first," Ryan said. He picked up the PS4 and worked on unplugging the HDMI cable that snaked through a small hole drilled in the side of the desk and up to the cracked computer monitor on Lou's desk. Then he pulled out the power cable.

"Keep the power cord," Will said. "We'll need that back at the dorm."

"Right," Ryan said, reaching into the crack behind the desk. "Hey, gimme a hand here and slide the desk away from the wall."

Will pushed the desk. Its metal legs caught on the thin carpeting, making a ripping noise.

"That's good," Ryan called, yanking the plug from the wall. He pulled the back of the cord through the hole in the drawer, then held out the console so Sarrie could put it in her backpack for the walk back. Before she could grab it, she froze.

An unfamiliar voice with a Chinese accent said, "I will take that."

Chapter 45
Surprise Players

THREE YOUNG HEADS TURNED IN UNISON to see the source of the voice, an Asian man with short-cropped black hair and black-rimmed glasses, wearing a tan London Fog overcoat. Two more men, taller and wearing long black coats, stood directly behind him. Both had Asian features. Both held dark pistols pointed at the students.

"Oh, shit," Will said, dropping onto his butt and instinctively holding up his arms. Ryan dropped the PS4, which clattered onto the carpeted floor. Sarrie gasped and put one hand over her mouth, as if allowing the gunmen to hear her scream would be embarrassing.

The closest gunman said something in Chinese, without moving his eyes from Ryan. He couldn't translate the meaning, but knew it was Chinese because he had a classmate from Beijing who kept trying to teach him phrases.

Ryan had never seen Yung Ji, but it was immediately clear that he was in charge. In English, Ji said, "Do not kill them yet. We need the boys to identify the file and the password if the old man encrypted it."

Sarrie sucked in a sharp breath and reached out her hand to clench Will's.

The first tall man replied in Chinese. Ji replied in English, so Ryan and his friends would understand. "Take the girl outside. If the boys do not cooperate, we remove her fingers to motivate them."

Sarrie screamed and clutched at Will.

The second tall man, who had not spoken, grabbed Sarrie's arm with a painfully strong grip and lifted her off the floor.

"Ow! Will!" Sarrie yelped out of a combination of pain and fear.

"Hey, leave her – Ugh!" Will's attempt at chivalry was cut off by the Chinese man's shoe making contact with his kidney. He doubled over, hands on the dirty carpet, unable to speak.

Ryan had been in a crouching position when the guns first appeared and remained frozen in place. Now, he fell backward onto the floor. His vision fixed on the gun pointed at Will.

The tall man dragged a squirming and screaming Sarrie from the room. "Will!" She cried out. She went quiet when a slapping sound filled the otherwise silent air. Ryan could hear Sarrie whimpering down the hallway leading to the retail space in the front of the shop.

The boss stood over Ryan. "Which one knows where the data file is?"

Ryan's mind raced. Where did these Chinese guys come from? How did they know that the boys knew about the data file? Would they really hurt Sarrie? If they cooperated, would the Chinese men kill them anyway? Could they possibly find a way to escape? All these questions raced through his mind in a nanosecond, but he uttered no sound in response to the boss' question.

"Hey! Ryan!" Ji shouted and clapped his gloved hands in front of Ryan's face, making him blink and suck in a breath. "Come on. Time to get to work. Or you want a bullet in your foot first?"

"How? H-how do you know my name?" a confused Ryan stammered.

"I know everything. I know where you live. I know about the falcon. I know about your girlfriend, Star. Maybe she'll help us find the file if you don't. I might like that. But I'll make you a good deal, Ryan. You get me the file and I will not kill you and your friends. How about that? Good deal, yes?"

Ryan struggled to overcome his terror. Having a gun pointed at him made his sphincter clench. "W-why should I t-trust you?"

"You have no choice." The man grinned. "If you do not help, my man will hurt the girl. Then we hurt your friend." He gestured at Will, who had scrambled backward and now sat with his back against the cinder block wall, his eyes the size of golf balls. "Then, I will kill you and take the game drive and my techs will find the file for me. But that could take time, and I do not enjoy waiting. So, you do it quick and you live. Your choice, huh?"

Will found his voice and said, "We can't get the file without a computer and a peripheral drive to load it onto. There's no computer here. So, how do you expect us to—"

The butt of the remaining guard's pistol smashed into Will's temple. His head snapped back, leaving a scarlet blotch on the white wall.

"Hey!" Ryan moved a few inches in Will's direction, but the boss kicked into his gut. Ryan gasped for air. Will leaned against the metal desk, one hand pressed against his head.

"You understand?" the boss snapped. "You do it, or you all die."

He spoke in Chinese to the tall man with the gun, who pulled several long, gray zip ties from the pocket of his coat. After hoisting a woozy Will into one of Uncle Lou's guest chairs, the man tied Will's hands behind his back and secured them to the chair. He bound Will's ankles as well, then left the room.

"He will bring a laptop," Yung Ji said to Ryan. "You sit." Ji picked up the PS4 console and placed it on the desk. In Ryan's face, he saw only fear. The boss smiled. Fear was an effective motivator. Fear and pain.

* * *

THE CANNON AND HIS TEAM ARRIVED at 12th Street and Avenue B moments before the gray Escalade with Yung Ji and his two helpers pulled up in front of the pawn shop. The four Gallata men watched as the three Chinese piled out of the SUV and stealthily approached the front door. One tall helper pulled up the mesh security screen. The other tall man bent down to work on the door lock.

"Ryan and Will must be inside already," Lenny observed.

"Yeah," Cannon agreed, "they wouldn't be so obvious if they were still waiting for the dumb kids to arrive. They've probably been here waiting."

"Should we go with them?" Lenny asked.

"No!" Cannon barked. "Let 'em go in first. We'll make sure the cops aren't watching the store. Dog!" He turned to the solidly built man behind the wheel with a thick scar on his right cheek above a black Fu Manchu beard. "Back us off a bit."

The Dog complied, backing down the street and parking next to a fire hydrant. Pedestrians padded down the sidewalk in both directions, taking no notice of the dark Explorer.

When there was no sign of squad cars around the storefront, Cannon made his next move. He instructed his men to insert Bluetooth earbuds and join a conference call on their cell phones. It wasn't secure, but unless the police were monitoring burner cell signals, it was nearly as good as high-tech communications.

"OK, Dog. Take Oscar and go give some back-up to our Chinese friends."

"What if they don't want back-up?" The Dog asked with a sly smile.

"Don't take no for an answer," was The Cannon's response. "And if those bastards want to kill the dumb kids, let the Chinese do the shooting."

The Dog and Oscar crossed the intersection with a gaggle of Saturday strollers and shoppers. Oscar was not as tall or muscular as The Dog, but was known to be lethal in a fight.

Back in the Explorer, Lenny asked, "What should I do?"

Cannon replied without turning his head, which was fixed on his other two associates. "Sit tight and be ready."

As Cannon and Lenny watched, The Dog and Oscar casually approached the shop's door. Before they could enter, the door opened and one of the tall Chinese men emerged. The Dog, who was in front, froze, then held up a hand. "It's cool," he said. "The Cannon sent us to give you boys some back-up."

The Chinese man said nothing. He pushed past The Dog and went to the gray Escalade. After unlocking the vehicle and lifting the rear door, he retrieved a black computer case, closed the door, and marched back toward the shop. He motioned with his head for the two Gallata men to follow.

Inside, The Dog immediately saw one of the other Chinese men, bending down next to a chair in which a young girl sat with a cloth gag in her mouth. The man stood abruptly, raising a pistol and eyeing the new arrivals suspiciously. He exchanged some rapid-fire Chinese with the man holding the computer case.

The man next to the chair called out, "Aye!" and rattled off another sentence in Chinese.

The Dog heard a muffled Chinese response. He and Oscar spread out, not offering their Chinese colleagues a clean shot at both of them, just in case.

The man with the case motioned toward the hallway. "You come. Talk to Yung Ji."

The Dog and Oscar cautiously followed. They both glanced down at Sarrie, her eyes showing abject terror, as the other Chinese man resumed securing zip ties around her ankles.

Halfway down the hallway, Ji stepped into their view. "You Fat Albert's men?"

"Yeah," The Dog replied. "We're here to help."

Ji's face was expressionless. He pointed to Oscar. "You, go help Li-Wei. Watch the girl." He waited, staring, until Oscar turned and retreated down the corridor. Ji then turned to The Dog. "You come in with me. Help with the boys."

Chapter 46
Treasure Hunt

IN LOU PALAZZO'S OFFICE, Will slumped in the guest chair where he and Ryan had spent many hours. His head still throbbed as he tested the strength of the zip ties binding his wrists and ankles. They flexed slightly, but held fast against his struggles. One Chinese guard, holding a pistol, eyed both boys menacingly.

Ryan made an assumption that the Chinese boss understood basic English, but might have trouble with complex words and sentences. When the boss ducked into the hallway and they heard some muffled conversation, he risked communicating with his friend, playing their vocabulary game.

"Will. Remain silently concentrating upon melodious verbiage beyond yonder sentry's comprehension."

Will nodded and flashed a tiny smile, understanding Ryan's intention. Ryan stole a glance at the doorway.

"Cooperation and capitulation likely will engender a statistically significant marginal likelihood of discovering camouflaged avenues of egress and succor in our immediate future. Elongating timelines and obfuscating intentions are indicated. Affirmative confirmation?"

"Absolutamente," Will responded.

"What you say?" Yung Ji reappeared in the doorway, accompanied by a man Ryan had never seen, who was clearly not Chinese.

"I told him to stay cool and follow instructions," Ryan replied, his nervous voice cracking.

Ji scowled, then put a black case on the metal desk. The tall Chinese guard had returned with him, but Ryan's attention was fixed on the new man, who reminded him of Samuel L. Jackson's character from *Pulp Fiction*. When Ji asked the new man's name, he replied, "Just call me Dog."

Ji pointed at the laptop case. "Open," he grunted toward Ryan, who was still gawking at The Dog, trying to figure how this new man was connected to the Chinese. "You find the file, you live."

Recovering his focus while glancing at Will, Ryan unzipped the computer case and extracted a laptop and a power cord. His pulse was racing. He could hear animated voices from the hallway, but could not make out the words. He reached into the gap between the desk and the wall to plug in the cord. Ryan connected the PS4 console to the boss' laptop with a USB cable. Yung Ji unlocked the machine with a four-digit code, then twirled the unit so the screen faced Ryan and motioned for him to get to work. Ryan spent the next five minutes accessing the PS4's file drive and running searches for file names. He carefully inserted misspellings or extra characters in the search terms so they all produced no results.

"I'm going to have to search each folder on the drive to find the file. Uncle Lou could have put it anywhere and I don't see any folders with obvious names."

"Go fast!" Ji barked.

The progress was slow. Ji was tech literate enough to follow along while looking over Ryan's shoulder, but made no comments as Ryan opened every folder in the master file tree on the PS4's drive. There were more than fifty folders, each of which contained dozens of subfolders, many of which had their own subfolders. Ryan's search pattern figured to take many hours.

After ten minutes of tense silence, Ji grew impatient. "What are you doing? Go faster!"

"I'm going as fast as I can. If Uncle Lou buried this file here, he would have put it somewhere nobody would look. I have to check every place it could be. It takes time," Ryan responded. "It would be faster if Will could help me." He gestured toward his bound friend.

The boss pondered the prospect of untying Will. "OK. But do anything funny, and he gets shot." Ji motioned to their gun-toting guard to release Will from his bindings. The man pulled out a Swiss Army knife and easily sliced the plastic zip ties. Will stiffly rose, massaging his wrists, and positioned himself next to Ryan where he could see the laptop screen. The Dog leaned against the door jamb, seemingly bored.

The boys had not seen the third Chinese man since he left the office with Sarrie in tow. They both presumed he was guarding her somewhere in the front of the store. They had not heard any shots or screams from Sarrie, so they hoped she was still alive and unharmed. There was no way for them to know for sure whether the three men they had seen constituted the entire Chinese posse, and whether there were any colleagues of The Dog in the shop. Will spoke to Ryan in their high-vocab code, hoping that the boss and The Dog would not fully grasp their meaning.

"Spelunking amidst gargantuan receptacles would be most efficacious. A contrarian strategy is affirmatively indicated, don't you think?"

"That's an amazing idea, Will," Ryan replied, allowing the boss and The Dog to catch some simple English and hopefully cut them some slack during the next phase of their conversation.

"Agreed." Will flashed a tiny smirk. "It is imperative that we orchestrate a strategically convoluted circumlocutory intervention to efficaciously reallocate perceptual attention and engender a sufficiently obfuscatory situation."

"A strategic donnybrook would facilitate sufficient temporal opportunity," Ryan replied in a hushed voice, as if in deep concentration on the laptop in front of him.

"I can help with that," Will replied.

"Apply extraordinary discretion, mi compadre."

Will pointed at the screen and yelled, "You idiot! You've been rooting around in the sub-files. You need to be in the main file tree."

"Don't tell me how to search, you moron!" Ryan shouted back, slapping away his friend's hand in a solid approximation of actual anger.

"Ow! Don't touch me!" Will shoved Ryan's shoulder, knocking him off-balance in his chair.

Ryan swung his right arm, putting his fist into Will's stomach, but pulled the punch at the last second. Will, however, reacted as if he had been slugged by George Foreman. He groaned and doubled over, falling onto Ryan's shoulder and collapsing to the floor.

The boss motioned to their tall sentry, who grabbed Will by the upper arm. The Dog jumped in to help. Will squirmed and struggled, while Ji, now holding his own gun, stepped backward in order to maintain some distance from the combatants.

Will struggled against the restraint of the two men. "Lay off me!"

The Dog slashed his right hand through the air, making contact with Will's face. Will's head snapped back against the cinder block wall with a dull crunch. He grunted in pain and slumped forward as the Chinese guard dragged him back toward the chair. Will, groggy from the blows to his head, kicked out a leg at The Dog, catching him in the knee.

The Dog yelped and let go of Will, who fell to the thin carpet. The Dog pulled out his gun and fired. The report of the shot filled the small room and echoed off the walls. Will screamed in pain as the bullet bisected his kneecap. In response to the gunfire, the other Chinese guard appeared at the office door. Ji spoke to him quietly in Chinese, then sent him back outside.

For the next few minutes, the Chinese guard and The Dog were busy hauling Will back to his chair. Blood flowed from the wound and Will continued to cry out in fear and pain. Ji produced a white handkerchief, which he tied around Will's knee. It plumed scarlet while Will screamed.

While the boss, the guard, and The Dog focused their attention on Will, Ryan quickly ran the search Will had suggested during the thesaurus conversation. He sorted all the files on the drive by size, with the largest at the top. The PS4 contained plenty of huge files in its operating system, and the downloaded NYU data file was not likely to be the largest, but Ryan and Will both remembered from when they were trying to open it after the hack that it contained more than one hundred megabytes of data.

He spotted a file near the bottom of the first screen of search results. It was the right size. Its title, 100110000101101HB, confirmed that it was their prize. Only a coder would understand, and only a coder who knew Uncle Lou would recognize it. The binary code, read in five-digit clusters, was 10011 (S) – 00001 (A) – 01101 (M). To Ryan, knowing the reference, the file was titled SAM for Sam Spade, the character played by Humphry Bogart (HB) in *The Maltese Falcon*.

Will had created an effective distraction at great personal sacrifice. While the guards were wrestling Will back into his chair and the boss was covering Will with his gun, Ryan moved the falcon file off the PS4 drive and into a sub-file within the operating system files on the laptop. He would be able to find it there, but anyone else would think it was a system file.

With the distraction still in progress, Ryan clicked on the laptop's Wi-Fi icon and logged into Uncle Lou's Wi-Fi. The password was *Casablanca42*. Once connected to the internet, the question for Ryan was how to send a distress signal. Logging into his own email account would take a minute and would require him to log out again to cover his tracks. He didn't have that kind of time. He scanned the desktop screen and saw the icon for Google Messaging. He clicked and the app popped up, showing a connection to a cell phone. Probably the boss' phone, he thought. Clicking on it, he typed in Star's cell number and then the message, "911 Ryan." After sending the message, he exited the app and returned to the file manager screen showing the PS4's files.

When Ji moved back toward the desk, Ryan clicked on a random file, exposing the underlying code. The boss grabbed his arm and ripped it away from the laptop. He spun the machine. Examining the screen, he fixed a menacing stare into Ryan's eyes. "What are you doing?" he bellowed.

"Trying to save my freaking life," Ryan replied as calmly as he could manage.

"You find the file?"

"No. Not yet. I'm still looking."

The boss turned away, twisting the laptop back toward Ryan. "Go faster!" The boss smacked his palm against the back of Ryan's head.

"OK. I'm working on it." Ryan returned to his search, now without any chance of discovering the file on the PS4 drive. The dingus was safely hidden on Yung Ji's laptop.

The Dog massaged his knee where Will had kicked him. Ji leaned into the corridor and called out something in Chinese. A moment later, a gunshot from the hallway caused Ryan to jump in his chair. He heard what sounded like someone saying, "Shot."

The Dog ran into the hallway and froze when he looked down the dim corridor, seeing Oscar on the ground and one of the Chinese men holding a gun. The Dog fell into a crouch, pulling his own gun as another shot exploded through the cramped space, but missed its mark. The Dog fired three times at his assailant, who spun backward and fell. Sarrie turned her gagged face away from the gunfire.

The Dog turned toward Ji in time to see the muzzle flash three feet away. Ji's bullet split the big man's eyes. The Dog's gun rattled to the tile floor as a pool of fresh blood formed around his lifeless head.

Ryan's hands still covered his ears, where they had flown after the first gunshot. When the last reverberation subsided, he stared at Will and mouthed, "Holy shit!"

Chapter 47
S-O-S

STAR COULD NOT CONCENTRATE on her literature reading. Ryan, Will, and Sarrie had been gone forty-five minutes. She sent Ryan a text after a half-hour, asking for an update, but got no response. The plan was to go into the shop, get the PS4 console, and immediately come back to Sarrie's dorm room, where the boys would try to find the dingus file. They should have been back already, or at least on their way back. Why wasn't Ryan responding to her messages? Looking out her frosty window toward the arch in Washington Square Park, she was getting more and more worried. What if the hackers were watching the shop and intercepted Ryan? With each tick of the clock, her worry increased.

When Star's phone pinged, signaling an incoming text, she grabbed for it, knocking it from her desk onto the floor. She scrambled after it and stared at an unfamiliar number. She moved her finger to delete the spam message. Then she saw the preview text: *911 Ryan*. She gasped. It had to be real. Sending this cry for help from a strange phone meant that Ryan and her other friends were in serious trouble for sure. She opened the text, but it contained no further message. She stared at the screen. *911 Ryan*.

With her anxiety level now through the roof, Star dialed her Aunt Michelle.

Chapter 48
Where's Ryan?

THE UNMARKED FEDERAL SEDAN pulled into the no-parking zone adjacent to Washington Square Park. Investigator Jacoby emerged, followed by Mike and Jason. They crossed the street and entered the lobby of a dormitory building, where a uniformed NYU security guard greeted them. She escorted the entourage past the dumfounded student attendant who normally checked the IDs of entering residents and guests. Another NYU security officer stood by the elevator, sent by Jan Yates after he got the call from Jacoby. They were not certain Ryan Gelb was in his dorm room, but they were sure he had not left the building in the past ten minutes.

In the elevator en route to the 6th floor, Mike's cell buzzed. It was Michelle, so he answered. "What's up?"

"Mike, it's Star. She called me just now and she's semi-hysterical about her boyfriend."

"Why?"

"I'm not sure. She said she needs to talk to you about Ryan, but she didn't have your number. I told her I'd call you. She said it was urgent."

"Her boyfriend's name is Ryan?" Mike asked.

"Ryan?" Investigator Jacoby said. "You have something?"

"Maybe," Mike said, holding the phone away from his face.

"Can you please call her back?" Michelle said, now audible to everyone in the elevator.

"Fine." Mike made eye contact with Jason, who extracted his notepad from a jacket pocket. "Tell me the number."

Jason recorded the number as Michelle recited it and Mike repeated it aloud. The elevator bell dinged and the group of cops exited into the shabby corridor. Several students in the hallway stopped and stared as the men in overcoats marched down the narrow space. Mike dialed Star's number, but delayed pushing the button to activate the call.

Jacoby pounded a fist on the door to Ryan's room. "Ryan Gelb. Open the door. Federal agents!" After hearing no response for ten seconds, Jacoby pounded and called out again, but still the door silently blocked their advance.

Mike pressed his call button. Star picked up on the first ring. "Hello?"

"Star, it's Uncle Mike. Michelle said—"

"Uncle Mike!" came a breathless reply. "It's Ryan. He and Will, and Sarrie went to his uncle's pawn shop. I told them they should tell you first, but they wouldn't listen. Now they're in trouble!"

Mike processed the information. Star had lied to him, or at least withheld a significant piece of information about her boyfriend. His anger with Star, however, was overridden by the more important issue – the location of the young man they very much wanted to talk to. "Why did he go to the pawn shop?"

"They think the data file is there," Star responded.

"The data file?" Mike looked around at Jason and Jacoby, getting their full attention. "What data file?"

"It's a file that got hacked through Ryan's laptop."

"What makes Ryan think the data file is at the pawn shop?" Mike chose his words so the rest of the team would pick up on what was happening.

"They think it's in the game machine."

"Who is *they*? What game machine?"

"Ryan and Will and Sarrie."

"Who?" Mike was trying to remain calm as Star became more hysterical.

"Ryan's best friend and his girlfriend. Oh, Uncle Mike. I told them they shouldn't try to get it alone, but they wouldn't listen. And now Ryan sent me a text from somebody else's phone. It says 911. He's in trouble! You need to go there. I'm so worried."

"OK, Star. Thanks for letting me know. We'll get there as soon as we can."

"Thank you, Uncle Mike. I'm sorry I didn't tell you about Ryan."

"It's OK, honey. We'll worry about that later." Mike pressed the END button and motioned for the group of agents to follow him back to the elevator. "Our boy Ryan and his friends have gone to the pawn shop. According to Star, they think the data file is there, inside a game machine."

"What?" Jacoby blurted as the group waited for the elevator. "What does that mean?"

"No idea," Mike said, "but Ryan sent a 911 text to Star. We need to get over there and see what's going on."

The down arrow lit up and a loud ding emitted from the elevator. Mike and Jason dashed across the lobby and out the door. Jacoby followed, calling out, "Who's Star?"

Chapter 49
A Cry for Help

AT ONE O'CLOCK ON SATURDAY, Rachel and Terry were parked outside the ACN offices on Twelfth Avenue. Waiting. Rachel had wheedled out of Jason where he would be working on a Saturday. He and Mike were going to a meeting with some federal agents in Foley Square. He wouldn't say exactly where or with whom, but it obviously was related to the triple murder case. Based on this inside information, Rachel convinced Dave to give her Terry for the day. He warned her that it was her last shot at the story unless Rachel got something big and scoopy by day's end.

As they waited, munching toasted corn muffins from a nearby food cart and sipping tepid coffee, Rachel got a call from Michelle.

"Rachel. Star called me. Her boyfriend, Ryan, and two of their friends went to Lou Palazzo's pawn shop. Star didn't go with them, but Ryan sent her a 911 text message. She called Mike and Jason and they're on their way. But now Star says she's going there herself and I'm worried. Mike and Jason will be there soon, but they don't know about Star and I don't want to call Mike again just because I'm worried about her. Are you somewhere you can get to her?"

"Whoa, Michelle, slow down. Why is Star's boyfriend going to the scene of that crime?"

"Because he's Lou Palazzo's nephew."

"What? Star is dating Ryan Gelb? And he's involved in the murder, somehow?"

"I don't know," Michelle said. "I'm not sure what's happening, but Star is scared. That's why she didn't go with the others. She said it was dangerous."

"OK, OK." Rachel waved to Terry with her left hand while trying to comfort her friend. Michelle sounded as calm as ever, but Rachel knew her well enough to hear the veneer of control over her fear. "OK. If Star thought it was too dangerous, and she didn't go with her friends, why would she go now?"

"Because she said she changed her mind!"

"Alright. I'll call Star. I'm not far away. I'll tell her to wait for me before she does anything dangerous."

"Thank you, Rachel," Michelle said. "Call me when you find her. I'm so worried. Especially after the last time."

"What last time?"

"Never mind. I'll tell you later. Just go."

"OK, honey. Bye." Rachel hung up, threw the remainder of her muffin into a trash can, and headed toward their news van. "C'mon, Terry. Something big may be happening."

While they were stuck in Manhattan traffic en route to Avenue B, Rachel dialed Star's phone. After ringing five times, it flipped to voicemail. Rachel hung up and tried again. On the second try, Star answered.

"Star! It's Rachel. Michelle called me. Where are you?"

"Don't try to stop me. I'm going to Lou's store. Ryan is there and he's in trouble."

"I'm not going to stop you. I want to help. I'm on my way there, too. Meet me in front of the Citibank across the intersection from the store."

The line was quiet except for the sound of the wind blowing into Star's phone. After a long pause, Star said, "OK. But I'm not waiting for you."

Chapter 50
Taking Sides

THE CANNON AND LENNY HURRIED across the Avenue B intersection, weaving between meandering pedestrians. The winter sun had inflated the temperature to the low 30s. It seemed like every resident of New York was out on the streets. Cannon assumed that somebody walking by Lou's shop had noticed the gunfire, which was so loud in his earbud. It was certainly possible that someone had already called 9-1-1. He listened carefully for approaching sirens, but for the moment, the only sounds were the rumble of traffic and an occasional honking horn.

The mobile conference call was still active, but there had been no conversation from The Dog. Oscar had not made a sound since saying he was shot. The Cannon feared the worst. He slipped on the ice outside the pawn shop momentarily, then took up a position next to the large shop windows, where he could see inside. His Colt .44 dangled from his gloved hand, pressed between his leg and the window to avoid being obvious to the passing walkers. He motioned to Lenny to position himself around the corner of the building, where he could see anyone exiting out the rear. If the Chinese had executed his men, The Cannon was going to make sure they paid the price. He no longer cared about the data file or about the college students, who may or may not be alive inside the store.

* * *

WHEN TERRY PARKED THE ACN VAN in front of the Citibank at the Corner of 12th Street and Avenue B, a gray Escalade was parked directly in front of the pawn shop. The metal security grid was in the up position and crime scene tape fluttered near the sidewalk. Somebody was inside. In the chilly sunshine of a Saturday afternoon, the sidewalks bustled with New Yorkers. After two days of snow and slush, the sidewalks were mostly cleared and people had delayed errands and shopping to do. In front of Lou's Pawn and Electronics, the sidewalk was still encrusted with ice, prompting the pedestrians to slow down and tread carefully.

Before Rachel could ask Terry his opinion about what they should do next, a flash of red coming from the west caught her eye. "There she is!" Rachel yelled, leaping from the van onto the sidewalk. She dashed toward Star, bumping into an elderly couple, who gave her the stink-eye when she failed to apologize.

"Rachel!" Star called out. "I think there are people inside the shop besides Ryan, Will, and Sarrie."

Rachel pulled Star into the doorway of the closed Citibank building. "We need to get you away from here." She reached out for Star's elbow.

"No!" Star said, pulling her arm away from Rachel's grasp. "Ryan is in there. And he's in trouble. I heard a gunshot. Have you seen Uncle Mike?"

Rachel saw two men walking briskly across 12TH Street on the east side, moving in the direction of the pawn shop. One wore a black knit cap on his head, with no hair showing underneath. The other was shorter and thinner. But what caught Rachel's attention the most was the silver muzzle of a pistol held in the taller man's gloved hand.

The two men pushed past a mother with a huge blue baby carriage and made a beeline to the door of Lou's shop. The man in the knit hat took up a position to the left of the front door, his back pressed against the window. The shorter man reached inside his coat and withdrew his own handgun as he moved in the opposite direction, stopping where the corner of the store building turned south.

"You think those guys are cops?" Star asked.

"No," Rachel said with a quaver. "They are definitely not police."

* * *

INSIDE THE ONCE-AGAIN BLOOD-SPATTERED STORE, Yung Ji pointed his gun at Ryan. He spoke in agitated Chinese to his remaining accomplice, berating the man for not properly gunning down The Dog and allowing the Gallata man to kill Li-Wei. He instructed the man, whom he called Jun, to check Oscar, make sure he was dead, and take his gun so they could use it to kill the students. Neither Will nor Ryan understood the conversation.

Ji stepped toward Ryan, who cowered and put his hands in front of his face, expecting another slap or worse. Ji instead reached past Ryan, grabbed the PS4 console, and ripped the USB cable and power cord from the machine. He hurriedly stuffed the unit into the black laptop case, zipped it, and slung the bag over his shoulder by its long strap. Then, he turned to Ryan, grabbing him above his right elbow. "You come!" The wiry Chinese man was stronger than Ryan expected. He struggled, but was pulled from the desk chair while he made eye contact with Will – still bound to the guest chair and grimacing in pain from his mangled knee.

"You have the file, man. You don't need me," Ryan pleaded his case.

"Need you. Go!" Ji put his gun into the small of Ryan's back, grabbed the collar of his t-shirt with the other hand, and pushed him forward into the hallway. Jun stood by the rear door, a pistol raised in his right hand. On a command in Chinese, Jun pushed the rear door open and carefully moved through, lowering his pistol into a forward-facing posture. Ji shoved Ryan ahead of him, using his hostage as a human shield and following his companion.

A layer of frost and ice covered the asphalt ground in the air shaft, where sunlight reached the surface only a few minutes per day. A gray rat scurried into a crack in the bricks of the adjoining building. Ryan shivered, being forced into the December chill without a coat. Jun moved into the mouth of the urban tunnel as his boss moved along more slowly, owing to Ryan's reluctance to hurry the process of being forced forward.

As Ryan watched, their advance scout suddenly slipped his pistol into the pocket of his overcoat, then raised his left arm, palm out, and waved his hand back and forth. Despite Ryan's abject fear at his predicament, he thought the man's wave resembled Queen Elizabeth during a parade. Ji pulled backward on Ryan's shirt collar, choking him momentarily as they skidded to a stop.

A back-lit shadow appeared at the head of the alley. Ji could not make out a face against the bright sunlight behind the man – at least, the silhouette looked more male than female.

Jun called out, "Hello, Mr. Lenny. You come help us." He stepped back two more steps. Then, Ryan saw that Lenny held a gun in his hand.

Lenny fired two shots into Jun's chest. A woman screamed out on the sidewalk. A dog emitted a high-pitched yip.

As the last member of the boss' support team crumpled to the icy pavement, Ryan felt the barrel of Ji's gun pull away from his back. An explosion louder than anything he had ever experienced cracked into Ryan's right ear. Acrid smoke stung his nostrils. The reverb from the gunshot pulsed against his head as a pinpoint of pain seared into Ryan's brain and radiated outward into his eyes and forehead. A low-frequency humming filled his aural spectrum as Ji pulled him backward.

Lenny dropped to the ground a moment before Ji fired. He scrambled on his hands and knees back around the corner at the mouth of the air shaft. Then, he heard the sound of approaching sirens and sprinted back across the street, dodging traffic.

"I'm heading back to the car!" he shouted, hoping The Cannon could still hear him through their mobile connection. He reached the Explorer and jumped inside, slumping down in the front passenger seat.

* * *

YUNG JI PULLED RYAN BACK through the metal door, pushing him forward down the dim corridor. For a moment, Ryan was not within the boss' grip. The ringing in his right ear pulsated with each heartbeat, but he realized he could still hear some through his left, although sounds were muted. He lurched forward, trying to get some separation from his captor without seeming to be running away. As he passed the doorway to Lou's office, he glanced inside and saw Will, his chin hanging against his chest. Ryan yearned for some eye contact with his friend, but Will's limp head did not move.

Ryan stepped over The Dog's body, then paused in front of Sarrie, who was also bound to a chair but obviously awake. Her eyes opened as wide as porcelain tea cups. Her gagged mouth prevented any communication, but it didn't take a psychic to see she was terrified and wanted Ryan to help her. Ryan held a clenched fist at his side and waved it in her direction as he passed by. He hoped it would signal for her to be strong.

Ji shoved his pistol into Ryan's back again and pushed him forward with an open palm. Ryan stumbled ahead. It dawned on him that, having been ambushed at the back door, Ji was hoping to exit through the front. Ryan immediately recognized the futility of the plan. If the guy named Lenny was waiting for the Chinese hackers at the rear exit, it was a certainty that someone was similarly covering the front door. Whoever these men with guns were, he doubted they would worry about his safety. To avoid walking into an ambush, he desperately tried to think of a way to avoid leaving the store.

* * *

A DARK SEDAN WITH A RED SIREN BALL stuck to its roof rolled into the intersection of Avenue B and 12th Street. It stopped in the middle, blocking traffic in both directions. The Cannon's attention shifted from the figures inside the store to the commotion in the street. He saw three men wearing neckties under their overcoats emerge from the sedan and wave their arms at the angry obstructed drivers. One man directed eastbound traffic down Avenue B and blocked traffic along 12th Street. The two other men motioned to pedestrians to move away from the corner in front of the pawn shop.

The Cannon knew his time to avoid capture was running out. A moment later, a black-and-white police cruiser joined the sedan in the intersection.

"Get out of there, Boss!" Lenny called into Cannon's earbud.

"No shit," Cannon mumbled. Getting across the intersection to the Explorer where Lenny hid was not likely with the cops there and more on the way. It was a matter of minutes before the officers would have the scene secured and would approach the shop. Looking east, pedestrians stood gawking at the activity. The flashing lights of another newly arrived patrol car at the Avenue C intersection cut off escape in that direction. He dashed to the curb, ducking down behind the gray Escalade, which he knew belonged to the Chinese. Keeping the vehicle between himself and the cops, he tried the rear door handle. It opened and no alarm blared. The Cannon exhaled, carefully squeezed himself inside, and closed the door with as little noise as possible.

"Where are you?" Lenny called out.

"I'm in the Chinese truck," Cannon replied softly. "As soon as the cops get distracted by something, get your ass over here and pull up next to me so I can transfer over and we can get the fuck out of here."

Chapter 51
Back Again

MIKE, JASON, AND DHS INVESTIGATOR JACOBY STOPPED their unmarked sedan in the middle of the intersection at 12th and Avenue B. A removable red flashing light perched on the roof above Jason's head, but with no siren. They had heard a report over their radio about possible shots fired in the area. That, along with the 911 text, caused them to approach the situation as potentially dangerous – to them and to the public. As it turned out, they were on the scene before the first black-and-white unit.

Their first priority was to clear the traffic and pedestrians from the potential danger zone. If there was gunfire, bystander injuries were unacceptable. Jacoby sprinted toward the west side of 12th Street, diverting the unhappy eastbound drivers north on Avenue B. Mike waved at the pedestrians who were moving south across the intersection, pushing them back to the north side of the street. Since New Yorkers are not easily herded in a direction they don't want to go, the process was slow. Jason went to the south side of the intersection, encouraging pedestrians moving east to turn around and meeting similar resistance. A small crowd of stopped walkers on the sidewalk east of the pawn shop gathered to gawk and speculate about what was happening.

Within a minute, two squad cars arrived. Their vehicles and the uniformed officers expedited the process of securing the intersection.

Mike, Jason, and Jacoby regrouped next to their car, still mid-intersection. Cold wind whipped across their faces. Looking at the pawn shop, there was no obvious activity, but the security screen was rolled up. If they didn't know Lou Palazzo was dead, they might have thought the shop was open for business. A gray SUV was parked directly in front in a no-parking zone, partially blocking their view of the front door.

"Who do you suppose came in that?" Mike asked, gesturing toward the Escalade. "Maybe some Gallata boys?"

"Why would they be here now?" Jason retorted.

"Who knows. Maybe they're tailing Palazzo's nephew. We need to be careful."

"It could be the Chinese," Jacoby pointed out.

"I'm not betting against it," Mike replied.

They held position, watching for any sign of movement inside the store.

"We have to assume those kids are in there," Mike said. "If that's the Chinese goons' car, or the Gallatas', and they were waiting for them to get here, it's not likely they would park so obviously in front. They'd be giving themselves away. If it were me, I'd have waited across the street until they went inside. Then I'd move my car up to the front so it would be there for a quick getaway. My guess is that both the kids and whoever came in that car are inside now."

"I agree," Jason said, glancing at the blocked-off intersection, where another squad car had arrived. "We need some back-up."

As two fresh officers exited their car, Mike waved them over to the detectives' group. One was a thick Black man, the other a shorter female officer with a red ponytail. "Delgado,

Rogers, this is Investigator Jacoby from Homeland Security. He's with us. As of now, you're our backup." Both officers nodded without speaking.

Jason said, "Let's go in slowly. Jacoby, you and Rogers circle around the back. There's a rear door to the shop off an air shaft. Don't be obvious."

"Not my first rodeo," Jacoby responded with a wink.

Mike and Jason watched the DHS investigator and Officer Rogers stomp through the slush toward the shop. Mike could see their steamy breath. Jacoby reached inside his wool overcoat and extracted a black pistol.

Before Jacoby and Rogers disappeared around the side of the building, Mike led Jason and Officer Delgado to the front of the shop, circling around the parked SUV until they reached the brick wall to the east of the tall front windows. Jason and Delgado wore black leather gloves. Mike, who had not been expecting an outdoor operation, managed with bare hands.

"Do we risk going in without knowing the situation?" Jason asked in a hushed voice.

Mike breathed in, feeling his heart pound faster. "I don't think we have a choice."

On a nod from Mike, Jason moved toward the door. Mike followed, peeking in the shop window. The scene was almost too much to take in. He saw Sarrie bound to a chair with a gag in her mouth. On the floor at Sarrie's feet, a Chinese man lay face up on the floor, which was again drenched in fresh blood. Next to the Chinese corpse, another male lay face down, his black hair stained by a crimson puddle. Who were these guys? And who killed them? The situation was fraught with unanswerable questions and warranted extreme caution, but patience was off the table. The tinkle of bells signaled that someone was coming through the front door.

Mike clutched his Glock 17 against his chest with both hands, wondering how he was going to get out of the situation without firing it.

Chapter 52
Emergency Exit

RYAN STUMBLED ON PURPOSE and fell to the floor in front of the door. His hand slid on a smear of frozen blood.

"Get up!" Ji kicked Ryan in the thigh. Ryan heard only dimly, but got the message.

"Ow! Come on. Gimme a break." Even his own voice sounded like it was filtered through a wet sock.

"Up!" came the unsympathetic response.

Ryan knew the falcon file was no longer on the PS4 console inside the black case slung over Ji's shoulder. As long as the boss thought it was, though, Ryan figured his captor would want to keep him alive so he could find and unlock it. But he worried that Ji's temper might negate his safety net. He needed to avoid pissing the guy off too much – Ji could always go back and get Will to be his dingus finder and human shield.

"I'm trying," Ryan grunted while struggling to his feet.

Ji grabbed Ryan's arm before he was fully upright and pulled him sideways. The gun barrel was back in its familiar place in Ryan's lower back. With his attention focused on Ryan, Ji did not notice the flashing lights in the street outside the shop's windows. "Open the door!" he grunted at Ryan.

Ryan reached for the knob, leaning forward against the force of Ji's arm around his chest, creeping toward his throat. A cold breeze rushed into the already frigid interior. The hinges creaked and a bell above the door chimed out happy sounds announcing the arrival of a customer. Ji pushed Ryan forward, pressing his body against the back of his human shield.

* * *

MIKE FROZE AND CROUCHED onto a knee, bringing his Glock 17 into firing position. A cloud of breath-steam billowed briefly in his vision. He ignored the wet, cold stain spreading through his slacks on the slushy sidewalk.

Ryan's leg came through the exterior door first. Mike flinched, but did not fire. A moment later, he recognized the boy's frightened face, followed immediately by the black hair of a Chinese man whose left arm was wrapped around Ryan's neck.

"Police! Freeze right there!" Jason called out.

Ji turned abruptly, wrenching Ryan in that direction.

Ryan saw Mike, recognizing him as the detective who had questioned him a few days before. He mouthed the words, "He has a gun!"

Mike nodded, already assuming the gun's existence. He had no shot at Ji that didn't have to pass through Ryan first.

"You drop!" Ji yelled, moving his gun to the side of Ryan's head. "Or boy is dead!"

A dark spot formed under the crotch of Ryan's blue jeans. He made eye contact with Mike, terror etched across his young face.

Mike was fairly certain the Chinese man was not going to shoot his human shield. It would leave him wide open to three cops who would easily take him down. But protocol required the police to prioritize the hostage's safety. "Calm down," Mike said with a steady voice, slowly lowering his gun. He laid his Glock on the icy pavement and held out his hands, palms up. "There's no reason to hurt the kid."

Jason and Officer Delgado both lowered their weapons and allowed them to drop to the ground with a slushy clatter.

Mike's eyes shifted from Ryan to his captor, then to the area over the man's shoulder. Investigator Jacoby crept along the wall, his service weapon in ready position. Like Mike, he had no shot at his target that wouldn't also put Ryan at risk. Plus, Mike, Jason, and Officer Delgado were in the line of potential fire.

Mike averted his eyes, not wanting to alert their Chinese adversary. He wondered how the Chinese man thought he was going to escape the situation alive. Mike wondered the same thing about Ryan.

* * *

ACROSS THE STREET, Rachel and Star huddled together, watching the scene unfold. When the shop door opened, Star gasped. "That's Ryan!" A man with black-rimmed glasses had Ryan in a neck-lock from behind. As they watched, the man raised a dark pistol against Ryan's head.

Rachel gripped Star's hand, knowing that Jason was in the middle of a perilous situation.

Star's other hand reflexively snapped to her own neck, tracing the outline of the scar where a killer's hot pistol barrel had pressed against her flesh a few months earlier. Her breath came in short gasps.

Rachel said, "He's gonna be OK, Star. The cops have the guy penned in. He'll have to surrender."

"But what if . . ." Star's tears flowed with each blink. She brushed the back of her hand under her frozen nose.

Rachel had no effective words of comfort left. She gripped Star's hand harder as they both watched the unfolding events.

* * *

JI SAW MIKE'S EYES SHIFT. He spun to his right, dragging Ryan's limp body along. Now he had his back to the SUV parked at the curb. He saw Jacoby and shouted, "Drop it!"

Jacoby glanced at Mike, who nodded. Stalling, without getting Ryan shot, was definitely the strategy.

Jacoby tossed his gun up against the side of the building and held out both arms. The pistol bounced and came to rest only a foot away from Jacoby's foot.

Then, a woman screamed, "He's got a gun!" She was among the pedestrian gawkers who were gathered a safe distance down the sidewalk on the south side of 12th Street. A small, reddish dog with long fur pulled at a leash in her hand. The dog began barking in a shrill yip. Ryan was barely aware of the noise.

Ji yanked Ryan backward toward the curb and the gray SUV. He maneuvered sideways, keeping Ryan between himself and Mike, then yelled at Ryan, "Open the door!"

Ryan froze, not sure what to do. The boss had shouted into his right ear, which was still ringing. The voice sounded as if at the end of a long tunnel. He looked at Mike, who held up an open palm, signaling to be calm.

"Open! Now!" Ji shouted again.

Ryan reached out a hand awkwardly, with the boss' arm still wrapped around his neck. He grasped the handle and pulled, hearing the familiar ker-chunk of an opening car door. Ji spun back toward the door and pushed it with his shoulder, his gun now pressed against Ryan's neck. The small man was surprisingly strong and agile. He stepped backward into the SUV and hopped onto the passenger seat, dragging Ryan with him. Swinging his legs like a gymnast on a pommel horse, he levered himself and Ryan inside, then reached to close the door.

Mike lunged for his Glock and crouched in ready position, but could not see through the smoked glass windows. Ryan was still in the line of any random fire, taking away the option of peppering the vehicle with bullets. Jacoby scooped up his pistol a moment before Jason did the same. The two detectives dropped to a knee, making themselves lower targets for the man inside the car in case he was inclined to fire at them. They heard a scream of pain come from inside the SUV.

As soon as the door closed, Ji shifted his gun, holding it by the barrel. He slammed the butt down on Ryan's knee, prompting a shriek. He didn't want Ryan going anywhere, but still needed him alive. Ji scooted over the center console into the driver's seat, pushed a button to lock the doors, then swung his pistol again toward Ryan, who turned away. The blow caught Ryan above the ear with a crack. His head snapped sideways into the window. A trickle of blood slid down his neck as he lolled like a punch-drunk prize fighter.

Ji depressed the brake pedal and pressed the button on the dash to start the engine.

* * *

WHEN MIKE AND JASON HEARD the SUV's starter grind, followed by a vroom from the engine, three things happened simultaneously. First, both detectives fired their guns into the SUV's tires. It wouldn't prevent the vehicle from moving, but would slow down any escape.

Second, another SUV, this one a black Explorer, motored into the intersection at a recklessly high speed. It caught the officers by surprise because the street had been secured and blocked. The Explorer weaved around a squad car and skidded to a stop next to the Escalade. With the gray vehicle obscuring their vision, Mike and Jason could not see who was driving the new arrival or what was happening on the other side of their barrier.

Third, a shot rang out from inside the Escalade, causing everyone to freeze. A bullet slammed through the windshield in front of the driver, followed immediately by a spray of red stain covering the inside of the glass. The horn blared from the SUV, its engine still running. The loud whine startled Mike and Jason more than the gunshot, which they were conditioned to expect.

In the confusion, Mike and Jason did not notice the rear passenger door of the Escalade open. The Cannon tumbled out, his Colt's muzzle still smoking. He fell into the open passenger door of the just-arrived Explorer, which sped away with a screech of tires. Cannon pulled his leg inside and closed the door, slumping down to avoid any incoming gunfire.

"Follow that—" Mike started to shout in the direction of the nearest uniform, but he cut himself off when the Escalade's passenger door swung open and Ryan spilled down onto the sidewalk. His head hit hard as his body crumpled, apparently unconscious. Mike saw a stain of blood next to his left ear. "Jason! Secure that car!"

Mike leapt forward to help Ryan. Jason circled around behind the Escalade, coming up on the driver's door carefully. Jason slammed his service weapon into the glass, shattering it. He expected exactly what he saw, but knew better than to take anything for granted. Yung Ji's lifeless head was slumped against the steering wheel. A hole above the hairline on the back of his skull oozed dark blood. Jason reached in and pulled out the man's body. It dropped to the pavement with a squishy thud, terminating the blaring horn. After confirming the obvious, Jason told a uniformed officer to search the rest of the SUV.

Jason called out to another nearby officer who was talking into his radio. "Call in a BOLO on that car. Did anybody get a plate?"

None of the nearby officers responded. Jason scowled and hustled around the front of the Escalade to assist Mike. As he rounded the fender, he stopped cold. "Rachel?"

* * *

"I TOLD THEM IT WAS DANGEROUS," Star lamented, gripping Rachel's hand as tightly as if she were hanging over a ledge. They watched as Yung Ji dragged Ryan toward the street, then into the gray SUV.

When the engine started and gunfire broke out, Star screamed. Rachel released Star's hand and threw both arms around the younger woman's body, as if that would protect them both. When another SUV drove up, a large bald man exited the back door of the gray car and climbed into the new one. When the black Explorer sped away, Rachel and Star could see through the open rear door of the gray Escalade into the front passenger seat.

"Ryan!" Star yelled, leaping to her feet and pressing forward while Rachel held her back. They saw Ryan fall out of the car door and disappear from their sight.

"There's an active shooter there!" Rachel scolded. "I'm not letting you charge in and get yourself hurt."

Then, they saw Jason carefully inch around the back of the vehicle, his gun drawn. People were screaming all around them after the shooting. Several dogs barked. The uniformed officers shouted instructions. Amid the cacophony, Star and Rachel heard nothing from across the street. As soon as Jason smashed the window, opened the front door, and pulled out the bloody body of the man who held Ryan hostage, both Star and Rachel ran into the street. An officer called out, "You there! Stop!" but neither woman paid any heed.

Rachel went around the back of the SUV while Jason gave instructions to an officer. She knew better than to interrupt him at an active crime scene. She rounded the rear bumper and saw Ryan on the pavement, with Mike hunched over him. She heard one of the officers call into his radio for an ambulance.

Holding Star back with an extended arm, Rachel said, "Let me." She charged forward, pushing Mike's shoulder to clear some room around her new patient.

"Rachel?" Mike exclaimed. "Where—?"

"Step back so I can work on him." Rachel's voice was suddenly calm and authoritative. She was in her element as a trained EMT. Even without a medical kit, she knew how to stabilize an injury victim until the ambulance could arrive. Mike didn't protest. When he looked up and saw Star, he escorted her back a safe distance, putting an arm around her shoulder.

"He'll be alright," Mike said sincerely. "Rachel knows what she's doing."

Star wrung her hands, watching Rachel prop up Ryan's head and check that he was breathing. Ryan's eyelids fluttered. Mike looked around at the increasing number of uniforms.

He called out, "Delgado! Rogers! Grab a few officers and clear this building. There could be more hostages inside and there might be more hostiles. Be careful and follow protocol."

"Yes, Detective," Rogers replied, moving swiftly toward her patrol partner.

Mike turned back and noticed Jason standing over his wife as she worked her first aid magic on Ryan.

Nobody paid any attention to Terry, who moved into a position where he had a clear view of the storefront and put his high-definition camera to good use.

Chapter 53
Clean-up

RYAN LOOKED UP AND SAW MIKE. "You need to go help Will. He's hurt pretty bad!"

"Where is he?" Mike asked urgently as an ambulance's siren wailed in the distance.

"In the office in the back. He was tied to a chair. That other dude shot him. And Sarrie's in there, too. Help her." Ryan tried to sit up, but Rachel's firm hand pushed him back down until his head hit the rolled-up coat donated by one of the nearby officers. His head throbbed and his knee ached, but he was regaining his faculties minute by minute.

"OK, son. You relax and let us handle this. I'll want to talk to you in a few minutes." Mike turned to one of the officers standing nearby. "We need another ambulance – make that two."

A female officer stepped out of the shop, her arm around Sarrie's shoulder, which was draped in a blue Mylar blanket. By then, Ryan was standing, groaning at the pain in his knee. He lurched forward. Sarrie embraced her friend, tears running down her cheeks.

"Where's Will?" she sobbed.

"The cops will take care of him," Ryan soothed, patting Sarrie's back. "There's an ambulance coming."

The officer who had been helping Sarrie stepped in, guiding the shivering, traumatized girl toward a squad car where the heat was running.

Two minutes later, Delgado and Rogers, along with two other officers, emerged from the shop and announced that the building was clear. "There's a male, approximately twenty, in the back office. He was tied to a chair and appears to have a gunshot wound in his leg. He's semi-conscious. We left an officer with him and need a medical team."

"The ambulances are on their way," Mike said.

Ryan looked at Rachel. "Can you help Will?"

Rachel didn't hesitate. She rushed in through the front door, accompanied by Officer Delgado, ignoring the gory scene inside. She found Will lying on his side on the thin carpeting in Lou's office. Another officer she didn't recognize knelt next to him. Remnants of gray plastic zip ties hung off a tipped-over chair. Will was semi-conscious and exhibited signs of having a concussion as well as a nasty wound on his leg.

Rachel and Delgado carefully rolled Will onto his back, placing a blue down jacket under his head. He was able to talk and the bleeding from the side of his head and from his knee was mostly clotted. Rachel took a field first-aid kit from the officer and went to work putting pressure on the gunshot wound and getting the blood flow fully stopped. She was again in her EMT element and continued to minister to Will until the actual ambulance crew arrived with a full kit and took over. By that time, Ryan and Sarrie had arrived with Mike and Jason. They stood back, as instructed. Sarrie, still recovering from her own trauma, fretted over Will, who kept telling her he was fine.

The EMT crew moved Will onto a backboard and whisked him out the front door into a waiting ambulance. Sarrie rode with him, apologizing repeatedly.

"It's not your fault, Sarrie," Will mumbled.

"Did you ever find the file?" she asked as the EMT closed the rear door and the ambulance moved forward.

"Shit!" Will's voice was barely audible. "I don't know."

* * *

WHEN WILL AND THE AMBULANCE CREW LEFT the office, Ryan sat back in the chair behind Uncle Lou's desk. Ji's laptop was lying on its side, the screen half-open, looking like a discarded textbook. The USB cord that had connected the laptop to the PS4 lay in a clump on the floor like a dead black snake. Star sat on the floor at Ryan's feet, holding his hand.

"Ryan," Mike said in his best fatherly, concerned tone, "It's time for you to tell us the whole story."

Ryan said, "OK, but first, let me do one thing."

Without waiting for permission, he flipped the laptop back to a functioning posture and was happy to see that it had not locked itself. He quickly navigated to the folder where he had stashed the dingus and found it still waiting for attention.

Reaching into his pants pocket, Ryan extracted a small black flash drive, which he inserted into the laptop. After confirming a copy of the file had successfully transferred, he moved the file on the boss' computer to the desktop and renamed it "falcon." He knew a police forensics expert would have been able to restore the file if he deleted it, and he figured the police would insist on having a copy. He closed the laptop and pushed it toward Mike.

"OK." Ryan took a deep breath. "Here's what happened."

* * *

LATER THAT AFTERNOON, the crime scene team packed up their gear and once again left puddles of semi-frozen blood on the floor of Lou's Electronics & Pawn. Inside the gray Escalade, the crew found one spent .44 shell casing. The bullet had exited Yung Ji's skull and then crashed through the windshield, disappearing into the Lower East Side. There were a few unidentified fingerprints, but in the cold, most of the passengers had worn gloves.

The two dead non-Chinese men inside the pawn shop turned out to be known Gallata operatives. Investigator Jacoby's contacts identified the two dead Chinese men as muscle for the Corporate Dragons and Yung Ji as a mid-level lieutenant. After matching the slugs in each dead man with the guns lying on the shop floor, the forensics team pieced together which man shot which other man. Andre "The Dog" Kaleem was shot by two different guns, including one bullet from Ji's, recovered from the Escalade. Clearly, the New York mob and the Chinese mob were not playing nice with each other.

After canvassing the security cameras in the area and the video shot by an ACN cameraman, the police still hadn't been able to get a clear image of the bald man who exited the Escalade and sped off in the black Explorer. They pieced together a license plate number, which came up as a stolen 2017 Subaru Outback.

In the aftermath, Mike and Jason concluded that the chances of solving Lou Palazzo's murder were near zero. Lloyd Cannon was likely the bald man who shot Palazzo, and also likely the man inside the Escalade who snuffed Ji and saved Ryan's life. But they had no evidence and no leads likely to produce any. Similarly, they could not connect a Gallata operative or contractor to the execution of poor Joe Aaronson. The cases remained open and unsolved on Mike and Jason's reports.

* * *

WHEN THE POLICE ACTIVITY calmed down, but was still visible, Terry set up his camera so that Rachel could do a stand-up with the active crime scene behind her. Blue and red lights flashed in a syncopated rhythm. Yellow crime scene tape cordoned off the storefront. Rachel's report was captivating, but the accompanying video Terry shot during the active hostage situation was pure gold.

"This small shop was the scene of a triple murder last Sunday. Today, associates of a Chinese organized crime group believed to be responsible for last week's slaying of store owner Lou Palazzo returned to the same location, where they took three NYU students hostage. The Chinese gangsters may have been involved in an international data hacking ring. They reportedly attempted to infiltrate the university's financial records, but their efforts were thwarted by these same students, along with the FBI, the Department of Homeland Security, and the NYPD. All the Chinese agents, along with two other men believed to be connected to the infamous New York Gallata crime family, were killed during a shootout here today.

"In this video, you can see a man believed to be the leader of the Chinese gang holding one of the students, Ryan Gelb, hostage as he attempted to escape from the police. I must warn you that portions of the video may be disturbing."

As the video rolled, with the spray of blood from Ji's head blurred out, enraptured viewers heard Rachel's voice-over say, "Two NYPD detectives, Mike Stoneman and Jason Dickson, along with an agent from the Department of Homeland Security, took down the perpetrator. You can see an unidentified man exiting the gray SUV and speeding away amid police gunfire. Mr. Gelb and one other hostage suffered non-life-threatening injuries during the confrontation."

Rachel signed off, "For ACN, this is Rachel Robinson reporting."

Chapter 54
Post-Game

NEW YORK UNIVERSITY NEVER SENT out letters to students, parents, and alumni disclosing the data breach. It admitted that Chinese hackers had breached the university's security system, but never obtained any sensitive data. After Ryan turned over his copy of the Falcon file to NYU, Jan Yates thoroughly reviewed it and certified that the file's contents were not accessed after the original download until Lou Palazzo opened it the day he was murdered. This meant that the data was never obtained by the hackers. Yates destroyed Ryan's copy, but knew the FBI and Homeland Security still had their own. The university officials did not mention the confidential Aswani investigation files.

Will and Ryan did not get expelled. Partly because of all the media coverage of the boys' heroism, and partly because they successfully recovered the data file and turned it over to the university, President Henry decided against disciplinary action. She concluded that the media blowback from punishing the students would not play well. She also was keen to avoid any discussion about the Aswani investigation.

Jan Yates met with all four involved students and gave them a stern lecture about their obligations under the school's code of ethics. He also dressed down Ryan for not being completely honest during the university's investigation. He left them all with the firm impression that if they stepped out of line again, they would face the most severe of consequences. None of the students doubted the admonition.

A team from the FBI did a surveillance detection sweep of Will's and Ryan's dorm rooms and found the Gallata listening device inside a light fixture on Ryan's wall. That information helped them piece together how the Chinese agents knew what the boys were doing. Investigator Jacoby told Ryan and Will that, ironically, the bug probably saved their lives. If the Chinese thugs thought Ryan or Will knew the location of the data file, they would have grabbed them and tortured them to get the information. Because they knew the boys were searching for the file, they waited for them to succeed. Ryan explained to Mike and Jason how the Chinese men had turned on the Gallata men inside the shop. The detectives and Investigator Jacoby agreed that, if the boys had turned over the dingus file, Ji would not have left any of them alive.

Ryan and Will both made it a habit to search their rooms periodically to ensure there were no new bugs in play.

* * *

WILL SUFFERED A FRACTURED KNEECAP, torn ligaments, a severed artery, and a mild concussion at the hands of Yung Ji. He was thankful to have emerged from the pawn shop alive. If he had been an athlete, the injuries would have been catastrophic. As a computer nerd and video game player, it was not as awful. He spent the next six weeks in a leg cast and then twenty weeks in physical therapy to recover full motion in his leg. He missed his fall semester finals, but was awarded passing grades, considering the special circumstances.

Ryan's injuries were less severe and did not require hospitalization. He may have had a concussion, but let Star minister to him, which she did happily. They were bonded by their mutual trauma and grew closer. They leaned on each other when they felt the emotional weight of their near-death experiences. Ryan took his finals and completed all his classes for the semester, except for cybersecurity, in which he had not completed his final project. During Ryan's period of convalescence, he and Star watched a ton of old movies.

Michelle insisted on making meals for Star and Ryan on the theory that Ryan needed home cooking to nurse him properly back to health. Whenever he was at Mike and Michelle's apartment, Topsy immediately jumped into Ryan's lap and alternated between Star and Ryan until the kids left for the night. Mike and Michelle decided that chastising Star for not being honest with them was pointless. But Mike pulled Ryan aside one time to impress upon him the need for full disclosure when talking to the police. Ryan did not need to be reminded.

Will and Ryan convinced their cybersecurity professor to let them complete a project after the new year and retroactively earn their fall semester credits. They chose a practical demonstration of an encryption-breaking algorithm, which was based on the program Uncle Lou developed and used to decrypt the Chinese data file. Ryan discovered the program while helping his parents clean out a storage unit where Lou kept old records and a few old computers. Both Ryan and Will added new code to the program as part of their project. The professor advised them to register a copyright on the code in case they could sell it to a cybersecurity firm.

Will and Sarrie continued dating, but Will's long convalescence put a strain on the relationship. Sarrie's recurring nightmares about being kidnapped by Chinese mobsters also made it increasingly difficult for her to hang out with Will and Ryan without having flashbacks. The university provided her with free counseling, but by the end of their Sophomore year, Sarrie found a new boyfriend who lacked the severe emotional baggage. Will took it in stride and found that he and Ryan were minor folk heroes among the girls on campus who played video games. Since Ryan was exclusively dating Star, Will had many options.

Sony sent both Will and Ryan new PlayStation 5 systems and a basket of premium software after learning that the company's console had been such an integral part of recovering the hacked file and capturing the Chinese criminals responsible for the murder of Lou Palazzo. Will and Ryan spent plenty of time playing *Blades of Karma* and eventually completed all the levels. Star frequently joined them as a third player.

They never found a falcon.

* * *

OLIVIA ROBINSON WAS SPITTING MAD when she found out that her pregnant daughter voluntarily put herself within ricochet range of a shootout. The fact that Rachel ran toward the danger zone to protect Star somewhat placated Olivia. But she began calling out, "Stay away from gunfights!" every time Rachel left the house for work.

Dave loved Rachel's daring incursion into an active crime scene. He loved even more the revenue and positive publicity for ACN. Terry's video was exclusive and was immediately licensed to every other news outlet in the city, along with the AP, CNN, and the BBC. It got the most web hits of any ACN video in December. Terry was quick to give credit to Rachel for charging into the dangerous crime scene and said he would never have been able to get the same video with a more conventional reporter.

Within a few days, however, Dave discovered that Rachel had shared information about her reporting with the police – specifically her husband – without permission. He was livid. He called Rachel into a disciplinary meeting with her union rep and ACN's head of human resources. Dave announced that she was fired, despite the good ratings.

The HR head, however, had other ideas. Rachel was one of only two Black on-air reporters, and she was currently pregnant. Dave claimed not to know about the pregnancy, but it was clear that firing her would be a public relations disaster and could expose the company to liability. Dave relented, but told Rachel she would be assigned exclusively to studio pieces and weather. She would never handle a serious news story again as long as he was managing editor.

Rachel's banishment to journalistic purgatory removed any chance of additional conflicts of interest with Jason, at least in the short term. In the days after the shootout, the couple took many walks around their Brooklyn neighborhood to avoid Olivia butting in and to prevent JJ from seeing his parents argue. In one sense, things worked out in the end – Jason was not brought up on internal departmental charges. This, however, did not satisfy Jason's concerns about Rachel's future reporting. She had leaned too heavily on him as her source for information. She used the confidential information he gave her, even after promising not to. Rachel's after-the-fact rationalizations for why she used Jason's tips did not give him confidence about future stories.

While fiercely defending her actions, Rachel admitted that she felt out of her comfort zone working a hard news story. She conceded that she relied on Jason's information because she didn't have anywhere else to turn. She assumed that as she gained experience and developed her own sources, she would be less reliant. Rachel yearned for a more important job after giving up her EMT career. Jason said he understood. He was struggling with his own thoughts about giving up his policing career in favor of something more stable and less dangerous after he got his master's degree in May.

In the end, they agreed to table the discussion. Rachel acknowledged that the duration of her pregnancy would be a bad time to go dashing into dangerous situations, or even trudging across the wintery streets of New York in search of the next story. Even if her boss would let her. Olivia was relieved by the resolution. No confidential investigation information was likely to come up while Rachel was interviewing Spelling Bee winners. The tension level in the Robinson house returned to normal, which meant Rachel and Olivia worried only about Jason's dangerous occupation. And, since Dave now knew about the pregnancy, Rachel did not need to worry about her wardrobe of obfuscation wear.

* * *

TWO WEEKS AFTER THE PAWN SHOP SHOOTOUT, Dexter Peacock broke a new story on Deputy Mayor Adam Erickson. With some help from a team of forensic accountants from *The New York Times,* Peacock uncovered payments to Lou Palazzo originating from a city accounts payable bank account. The city comptroller investigated and concluded that Erickson had funneled payments through Lou's electronics shop for repairs to non-existent computer equipment. A review of the security camera images from the Citibank ATM near Lou's Electronics & Pawn, spanning six months, revealed a total of sixteen instances of the deputy mayor making brief visits to the shop. His own banking records showed sixteen corresponding cash deposits in the days following his visits to see Lou.

Adam Erickson resigned, telling the assembled media that he wanted to spend more time with his family and denying any wrongdoing.

* * *

COMMISSIONER EARL WARD was grudgingly happy that his detectives got so much positive publicity. The Department of Homeland Security was similarly happy with the media's positive depiction of their agent. The FBI was pleased to expose the Chinese hacking ring, even if they could not tie the activity directly to the Chinese government. The situation was a win for all the government agencies involved.

Sully spent half an hour questioning Mike and Jason about whether Jason improperly leaked information to his wife. Mike was able to establish that Michelle got the information about the boys heading for the pawn shop from Star and passed it along to Rachel. The NYPD was not the source of any information provided to Rachel that Saturday. Rachel had relayed word of Ryan's 911 message to Jason, so, if anything, the police got information from her. Several other news crews heard the police radio dispatches about the hostage situation and arrived after Yung Ji was dead and the mysterious bald man was gone. They were not as close to the action as Rachel and Terry, but the event would have been fully covered by the New York media regardless of Rachel's involvement.

Sully nevertheless gave Jason a dressing down over the issue and put him on what the captain called "double secret probation" regarding any future confidential information disclosures.

* * *

THE DEPARTMENT OF HOMELAND SECURITY searched the records on Yung Ji's laptop computer and the three burner phones recovered from him and the two dead Corporate Dragons. Most importantly, they had the data file from the hack. There were enough remnants of the root algorithm still in the download for the FBI and DHS labs to isolate the method used to bypass what were supposed to be rock-solid firewalls. After a month of intense study, the FBI issued an alert to Amazon Cloud Services and to all its users about a bug in their security software and how to patch it to avoid a breach by "foreign actors."

Investigator Miles Jacoby received an internal award from DHS for his part in uncovering the Amazon vulnerability. Jacoby, in turn, credited the quick-thinking college students who managed to preserve the file before it could be uploaded by the Chinese hackers. That praise was never publicly reported, but Jacoby made sure that word trickled down through back channels to the cybersecurity faculty at NYU and to a few IT managers in large multi-national companies, who would be hiring new techs in the coming years.

* * *

FAT ALBERT GALLATA DID NOT GET the two million dollars he was promised by the head of the Corporate Dragons, since the data file was not delivered. He did negotiate a small fee from his Chinese counterpart to cover expenses, lost equipment, and funeral arrangements. He did not disclose to the Corporate Dragon bosses that he knew the truth – that Yung Ji gave the order to kill Oscar and The Dog. Assassinating your colleagues was not the best way to demonstrate a cooperative business relationship. The Gallata organization did not continue working with the Corporate Dragons.

The Cannon was able to blame Ji and the Corporate Dragons for the failure of the Palazzo operation. He convinced Fat Albert that he made a decision to take out Ji after the Chinese ambushed their men and that he hid inside the gray Escalade intentionally as part of his plan. Lenny had enough good sense not to contradict the story. Since all the Dragons involved were dead, there was nobody left for Fat Albert to kill as revenge.

Lenny got credit for handling the surveillance operation and giving The Cannon correct intel. The Cannon overlooked how Lenny had developed an attachment to Ryan and his friends that could have compromised their operation. Lenny also received good marks for gunning down the Corporate Dragon who killed Oscar and for having the backs of the tech team during the boiler room fight. As a result, The Cannon assigned Lenny to his personal team, handling eavesdropping and electronic security. He was still near the bottom of the pecking order in the Gallata organization, but he now had a regular job.

The NYPD did not have sufficient evidence to arrest The Cannon for the Palazzo murder or for conspiracy to murder Joe Aaronson. But the FBI put surveillance on the building at 311 East 9th Street, diminishing its usefulness for Gallata operations. They also made it a priority to collect better photos and DNA samples from The Cannon to assist in future investigations. They figured it was only a matter of time before his bald head popped up again.

* * *

MICHELLE AND STAR HAD a long telephone conversation with Star's mother, Rosie. They jointly provided a somewhat sanitized version of the harrowing events at the pawn shop. They emphasized that Star was never in danger and never near any gunfire. Rosie was still distraught at her daughter's close proximity to violence in New York City twice in four months, but Michelle and Star assured her that Star was flourishing in the big city.

Star began her internship on Broadway, working under the supervision of acclaimed director Nathan Matthews. This helped quell Rosie's anxiety, since she was a huge fan. She also knew that Star would be heartbroken if she was unable to work on Broadway.

In the end, Rosie did not try to force Star back to Georgia. She did extract a pledge from her daughter to be entirely truthful about any future incidents involving criminal activity or dangerous situations. Star swore that she would never withhold important information from her mother again. She and Michelle exchanged shrugs when the call was over, then hugged for several minutes.

* * *

THREE WEEKS AFTER the murder of the Chinese boss, Mike and Michelle sat down for dinner. Winter had settled in hard, but the window above the dining alcove radiator was still open a crack. Christmas was behind them. Mike marked the baseball equinox – the date when the beginning of the next Mets season was closer than the end of the last one. The exact date and time were announced by Mike's favorite blog, *Faith and Fear in Flushing*. That put Mike in a good mood on this particular January Saturday.

Michelle prepared a stir-fry of Chinese vegetables, shrimp, scallops, and squid. Mike thanked her for including extra tentacles, which were his favorite part. Mike brought home a bottle of Spanish bubbly so they could have a toast with the seafood. They clinked glasses and enjoyed a calm moment.

"I haven't discharged my service weapon in more than two weeks." Mike sat back, stretching his arms above his head. "And I haven't missed any of my gym workouts. Maybe we'll have some normal months for a change, huh?"

"What's normal?" Michelle placed her empty champagne glass on the table.

"Normal is when I don't have to apologize for anything, you don't have to be mad at me for anything, and we get to enjoy each other's company without any distractions."

"Oh." Michelle smiled mischievously. "I don't ever recall that happening."

Mike chuckled. "Well, perhaps not *normal* so much as *happy*."

"I'm always happy when we're together," Michelle said softly.

"Me, too. I feel like I'm usually the one throwing monkey wrenches into our calm, happy moments. I apologize for that."

"Don't apologize for things you can't control. I knew what I was getting into when I moved in with you. And when I married you. It's like Billy Joel said, I love you just the way you are."

"Thanks. But I still want to try harder to take care of you and give you more calm moments."

"Calm is boring, darling. I'm happy to have excitement – as long as you're not on the edge of getting killed."

They shared a laugh, but knew there was truth in Michelle's comment.

"I can think of a few things we could do to generate a little excitement." Mike raised and lowered his eyebrows suggestively.

"But we haven't cleaned up the dishes."

Mike abruptly stood and walked around the small table. He reached down, scooping Michelle from her chair. She wrapped her arms around Mike's neck as he carried her toward the bedroom.

"You promise to be honest with me?" she whispered into Mike's ear.

"Yes. Right now, I honestly want to get you out of those clothes."

"See how easy that was?"

Mike used his foot to close the bedroom door behind him. He had learned that letting Topsy on the bed was distracting at critical times.

Topsy deftly leapt onto the dining table and licked the shrimp remnants from Mike's plate.

THE END

Thank you for reading *Treacherous Hack*. I truly enjoy hearing from readers about their reactions to my characters and stories. I welcome critical comments and suggestions that can help me improve my writing and urge every reader to **please leave a review**. Even a few words will go a long way and I will be grateful. Post on Goodreads, Amazon and/or BookBub to let other readers know what you think. I want honest reviews – tell other readers exactly what you really think! And feel free to send me an email directly via my website at www.kevingchapman.com to tell me your thoughts about this book.

And please tell your friends (and book club leaders) about this book. As an independent author, I need all the word-of-mouth plugs I can get. Keep reading books by indie authors; there are a lot of great writers out there just waiting for you.

Kevin G. Chapman
December, 2025

ABOUT THE AUTHOR

Kevin G. Chapman is, by profession, an attorney specializing in labor and employment law. He is a past Chair of the Labor & Employment Law Network of the Association of Corporate Counsel, leading a group of 6800 in-house employment lawyers. Kevin is a frequent speaker at Continuing Legal Education seminars and enjoys teaching management training courses.

Kevin's Mike Stoneman Thriller series, seven full-length novels (so far), includes *Lethal Voyage*, winner of the 2021 Kindle Book Award, and *Fatal Infraction*, winner of the CLUE Award Blue Ribbon as the #1 police procedural of the year. You can preview the series by reading the award-winning short story, *Fool Me Twice*, available free on most ebook retailer websites or you can get it directly from Kevin's website.

Kevin has also written two stand-alone mysteries. *Dead Winner*, published in 2022, was the Blue-Ribbon winner of the CLUE Award for the best suspense/thriller of 2022. And *The Other Murder*, was the **Grand Prize winner** of the 2023 CLUE Award as the best overall suspense/mystery/thriller in all sub-genres.

Kevin has also written a serious work of literary fiction, *A Legacy of One*, originally published in 2016, which was a finalist for the Chanticleer Book Review's Somerset Award for Literary Fiction.

Find Kevin on Facebook (Kevin G. Chapman - Author) and at his website: KevinGChapman.com.

Book Club discussion questions for
Treacherous Hack

1.   Do you think there's a hero in this story? If not, did that detract from your enjoyment, or did you like that?
2.   Ryan and Will made some bad choices. What would you have done differently and why?
3.   Keeping secrets and maintaining confidentiality are recurring themes. Which characters do you think made good or bad choices about whether to tell the truth or whether to keep a secret?
4.   What did you think about the conflict between Rachel and Jason and how they handled it?
5.   How do you feel about how Star handled her decisions?
6.   How did you feel about the conflict between the New York and Chinese gang members?
7.   Did you like Lenny? Do you think he was trying to protect the students?
8.   Did you figure out where the data file was before the students solved it? If not, where did you think it was?
9.   Were you satisfied by the ending? How would you have written it differently?
10.   Do you think The Cannon will come back in a future book?

If your book club would like to read *Righteous Assassin*, book #1 in the Mike Stoneman Thriller series, please contact me for information about how your group can get discounted or free copies of the ebook and/or audiobook to get you started. Send me a note via my website at www.kevingchapman.com or by email at Kevin@KevinGChapman.com.

AUTHOR'S NOTE & ACKNOWLEDGEMENTS

As always, I must give credit to my wife, Sharon, for supporting me throughout my writing process. I also owe a debt of gratitude to my son, Connor, who is a video game expert and who helped me ensure that the video game references in this book were accurate and realistic.

I also thank my brilliant editor-daughter, Samantha (Samanthachapmanediting.com) whose willingness to tell me when I was being stupid focused the story and helped me avoid stepping off an unintended cliff . She's the editor that every author wants. And kudos again to my cover designer, Peter from bespokebookcovers.com. Peter did a wonderful job creating this eye-catching cover. Also kudos to Jiawie "Peter" Hsu from Fotolux in Princeton Junction, NJ for making me beautiful prints for my publicity posters.

Also thanks go out to several of my newsletter subscribers who volunteered the use of their names as characters in this book. These include Cheryl Ridgeway, Jan Yates, Kevin Cannon, Lloyd, Maggie Mitchell, Roxanne Dupuis, Sarrie Devore, Sandi Risbey, and Sharron Henry.

My beta readers provided me with invaluable perspectives and ideas as the book was in development. Thanks so much to Fred Casiello, Gayle Wilson, Jerilyn Schad, Joanna Joseph, Kay Hagen-Haller, Robert Williscroft, Roxx T, and Judith Dickinson for scrutinizing the early draft and guiding me toward the numerous revisions that made the book what it came to be. Everyone contributed something to the final product that would not have been there otherwise.

I also thank my intrepid band of Typokillers, who combed over the finished manuscript and rooted out the last few errors, large and small, to make the final text as clean as it can be. (But, if you find a flaw, please let me know so I can fix it.) All authors should use the typokillers. Thanks to Jerilyn Schad and Roxx T (who did both a Beta and a typokiller read) along with Kay Hagen-Haller, Matt McKeown, and Sue Martin. Also special thanks to Mimi Bailey who was my beta-listener and proof-listened to the audiobook to root out errors.

Other novels and stories by Kevin G. Chapman

<u>The Mike Stoneman Thriller Series</u>

Righteous Assassin (Mike Stoneman #1)
Deadly Enterprise (Mike Stoneman #2)
Lethal Voyage (Mike Stoneman #3)
Fatal Infraction (Mike Stoneman #4)
Perilous Gambit (Mike Stoneman #5)
Double Takedown (Mike Stoneman #6)
Fool Me Twice (A Mike Stoneman Short Story)

<u>Stand-alone Novels</u>

Dead Winner
The Other Murder
A Legacy of One
Identity Crisis: A Rick LaBlonde Mystery

<u>Short Stories & Novellas</u>

The Car, the Dog & the Girl
Ghost Creek (a romantic mystery novella)

Visit me at www.KevinGChapman.com